VISIONS OF SKYFIRE

An Awakening Novel

Also by Regan Hastings

Visions of Magic

VISIONS OF SKYFIRE

AN AWAKENING NOVEL

REGAN HASTINGS

A SIGNET ECLIPSE BOOK

SIGNET ECLIPSE
Published by New American Library, a division of
Penguin Group (USA) Inc., 375 Hudson Street,
New York, New York 10014, USA
Penguin Group (Canada), 90 Eglinton Avenue East, Suite 700, Toronto,
Ontario M4P 2Y3, Canada (a division of Pearson Penguin Canada Inc.)
Penguin Books Ltd., 80 Strand, London WC2R 0RL, England
Penguin Ireland, 25 St. Stephen's Green, Dublin 2,
Ireland (a division of Penguin Books Ltd.)
Penguin Group (Australia), 250 Camberwell Road, Camberwell, Victoria 3124,
Australia (a division of Pearson Australia Group Pty. Ltd.)
Penguin Books India Pvt. Ltd., 11 Community Centre, Panchsheel Park,
New Delhi - 110 017, India
Penguin Group (NZ), 67 Apollo Drive, Rosedale, Auckland 0632,
New Zealand (a division of Pearson New Zealand Ltd.)
Penguin Books (South Africa) (Pty.) Ltd., 24 Sturdee Avenue,
Rosebank, Johannesburg 2196, South Africa

Penguin Books Ltd., Registered Offices:
80 Strand, London WC2R 0RL, England

First published by Signet Eclipse, an imprint of New American Library,
a division of Penguin Group (USA) Inc.

First Printing, October 2011
10 9 8 7 6 5 4 3 2 1

Copyright © Maureen Child, 2011
All rights reserved

To my father, who taught me a love of history.

To my kids, who taught me that imagination is the nation we all belong to.

To my readers, who make it possible for me to write the books I love.

ACKNOWLEDGMENTS

Once again, there are too many people to thank and not nearly enough room to accomplish the task. So I'll keep it short and sweet—

A big thank-you to my friends, the best plot group in the world: Susan Mallery, Kate Carlisle, Christine Rimmer, and Teresa Southwick. Thanks for always bringing me back on track when I start taking those interesting detours. I love you guys. And to Jennifer Lyon, amazing writer and wonderful friend, another thank-you for some truly brilliant suggestions.

To agent extraordinaire, Donna Bagdasarian, thanks for your belief in me and my books and for working every bit as hard as I do.

To my editor, Kerry Donovan, a big thank-you for your hard work, your confidence in this series, and for some really great brainstorming phone calls! Another thank you goes to Claire Zion and everyone at Signet for their support of this series—and to the art department for the most amazing covers I've ever seen.

Thanks again to the Wiccans I keep going to with my questions and concerns. You guys are great and I really appreciate the support and, again, the understanding that my book is fiction and that sometimes "facts" are just a jumping-off point.

And as always, thanks to my family for their patience, their love, and their understanding when I'm on deadline and I forget all about the "real world."

VISIONS OF SKYFIRE

AN AWAKENING NOVEL

Chapter 1

Teresa Santiago opened her arms to the sky as if welcoming a lover. The storm raged overhead and its energy and power filled her like long-dammed water rushing onto a floodplain. She felt it all and gloried in it. The sweep of sensation, the pulse of strength.

Lightning flashed and its charge slammed into the ground at the feet of the woman who stood amid the white-hot bolts like a pagan goddess.

Her long black hair flew out around her in the charged atmosphere, snaking across her eyes, whipping around her throat. Her fingertips practically vibrated with power as lightning danced to her whims.

Electrified white bolts cracked across the black sky, then forked into the desert floor. Sand geysers erupted all around her as energy sizzled and burned. Thunder roared. Clouds roiled. Juniper and manzanita dipped and swayed with the wind. The skeletal arms of the ocotillo behind her waved, scraping at her back like a demon demanding attention.

But she ignored every distraction—including her own apprehension. Exhilarating as it was to command nature in such a way, a part of Teresa cringed, horrified at what she was now able to do. The lightning danced, plowing into the earth at her feet again and again, and every cell in her body sizzled from the near contact. She felt as if she, too, were electrified and that tiny, horrified part of her wanted to run and hide from all of this.

She didn't, though. Couldn't. Couldn't turn her back on the very legacy she had been training for most of her life. Now that it was here, magic opening up inside her, she would simply have to find a way to master it.

Four days ago she had had the first dream. A terror-filled nightmare with flames chewing at her skin while demons howled and crowds cheered. She'd jolted from sleep in a sharp panic, her own hair wrapped around her throat like a noose as she gasped for air that wouldn't come. She had known then that her *abuela*'s prophecies were coming true.

Then the magic appeared. Small things at first. Sparking a match without striking it against anything. Touching the television and it coming to life. Lightbulbs shattering when she touched them. Streetlights blinking out when she brushed against the pole.

And today . . . She had followed her instincts, somehow *knowing* that the lightning was calling to her. At first sight of the storm on the horizon, a deep well of power had opened up inside Teresa, as if it had been waiting for nature's fury to completely awaken. She had driven into the desert outside Sedona, Arizona, to meet that storm head-on. To walk into the maelstrom and somehow master it.

For more than an hour now, she had worked, pulling down the lightning, trying to direct it to specific targets—because what was the point of having the power if she couldn't control it? And in this time, when witches and even those *suspected* of witchcraft were being locked away, or worse, she needed that control. Her new power would make her a magnet for disaster. She had to be able to draw on her own strengths to protect herself and those she loved.

"Come *on*," she whispered. "Focus, Teresa. Make it work."

Red sandstone rock formations surrounded her. With sunlight slanting across them, the rocks seemed to glow a brilliant orange and red. Under a forbidding gray sky, they were filled with shadows, their wind-carved surfaces taking on the shapes of faces that seemed to watch her.

She was just outside Red Rock State Park and hoping that both the weather and the harsh terrain would keep tourists at bay.

October in Arizona meant cooler temperatures and an influx of visitors who came to Sedona not only for the natural beauty but also to gather at the many vortexes in and around the city. The vortexes were sites of spiritual ceremonies and drew the mystical and the curious every year. Teresa had gone to a few ceremonies herself over the years, knowing as she did that there was far more to the spiritual plane than most people suspected.

Now, though, she drew on the spirituality of this place to open the heart of her magic. She waved one hand, directing the lightning toward a tower of red sandstone rocks. The jagged bolt of pure power slammed into the ground twenty feet away from the target and she knew that wasn't nearly good enough. If she were attacked, "close" wouldn't save her life.

Teresa fought to hone her magic. To perfect the power that had begun to quicken inside her only days ago. She had known what was coming all her life. What she was destined for. But the mystery had been *when* her magic would appear. The world wasn't a good place for witches these days, but magic ran in her blood, stretching back through her family's maternal line for generations. She should have been able to draw on that legacy, but in the face of this new and overwhelming power, she was lost.

She stood tall, her cowboy boots planted far apart to give her a sense of stability that she was sorely lacking. Gritting her teeth, she concentrated, and swung her hand out again to direct another whip of lightning across the desert. Instantly a jagged bolt flew—in the wrong direction.

"No!"

Teresa shrieked as her black truck exploded into a fireball. Flames leaped into the air, plumes of smoke twisted in the wind and flaming tires shot off the body of the truck like Frisbees from hell. As thunder still rattled the sky and wind howled, Teresa stared at the smoking hulk of her truck.

"Son of a bitch." She kicked the sand and thought not only about the incredibly long walk back home she had to look forward to but also about her now-burned-to-a-crisp cell phone. She couldn't even call someone to help her. She was stuck—no water, no food, no way home.

She'd grown up here, so she wasn't a stranger to the desert. But the thought of a long walk back to town through the rain with the storm chasing her sent her stomach to her knees. Added to that was the fact that she couldn't quite shake the feeling that she was being watched ...

Steeling her spine, she pushed thoughts of unseen watchers to the back of her mind. If they were out there, somewhere, there was nothing she could do about it. The important thing now, she told herself as she stared at the fire and the billowing black smoke, was control. Just how in the hell was she supposed to protect herself from the coming dangers if she couldn't manage her own powers?

What good is it to be a witch, she demanded silently, *to be able to pull down the lightning from the sky, if you can't freaking control the magic?* Disgusted, she muttered, "Could this day get any worse?"

As if the gods were answering, Teresa heard a distant, pulsing beat, like the heartbeat of a giant. The thrumming sound seemed to jolt up from the desert floor to her feet and into her chest, where it pounded along with her own suddenly galloping heart. Stunned, she just stood there, trying to assimilate it, and then she realized something else.

The sound was getting closer.

She whirled around, gaze searching, straining to see past her surroundings to whatever was coming. Her own heartbeat was pounding in time to that otherworldly sound. She scanned the dark skies in all directions. The shadows of the craggy mountains jutted up from the desert, scratching at a sky still churning with ragged bolts of lightning.

Thunder boomed, but just beneath that awesome noise and power there was something else. Something low-pitched and dangerous, like the deep-throated growl of a predator. Fear tightened into a hard knot in her belly. She trembled, swallowed hard and felt her breath catch in her lungs as she found the source of that growl. Against the lowering gray clouds, there was a darker spot.

A blot of black that was headed right for her. An instant later, Teresa identified the heavy beating sound— the *whup-whup-whup* of helicopter blades churning through the air. Mouth dry, fear racing through her, she looked at the emptiness surrounding her and knew she was in deep shit.

She'd come into the desert to be alone with her burgeoning magic. But being alone also meant that there was no one to help her. Though if that helicopter was what she thought it was, no one could have helped her anyway.

As the chopper closed in on her, she saw the bright yellow slash across its belly. Black and yellow. The MPs' colors. The Magic Police. They'd found her. Somehow they'd found her and she knew that if they got their hands on her, she might as well be dead.

A captured witch had little hope of escape and every expectation of execution. Though not until after torture and imprisonment, of course. Fear nearly choked her. She wasn't ready for this confrontation. She'd had no time to prepare. To conquer her magic and make it work for her.

The power she had been relishing only moments ago now felt like an anvil tied around her neck. She was about to be captured and there wasn't a damn thing she could do about it. She couldn't even hop into her truck and make a run for it.

She had no weapon and the helicopter was even closer now.

Weapon.

"God!"

She didn't *need* a weapon—she *was* a weapon.

"Now's the time, Teresa," she muttered, instantly lifting both hands high over her head. All around her, lightning danced, pulsed, the air scorched from thousands of volts. Her hair lifted in the wind; her eyes narrowed on the helicopter. She stabbed one hand toward it and a lightning bolt sizzled past the black beast, barely missing it. The chopper dodged, dropping several feet in an instant and turning slightly to allow someone to stand in the open doorway.

Someone with a gun.

"Damn it!" Teresa dove for the ground as the first crack of bullets chattering from the automatic weapon enveloped her. *Still too far away*, she thought wildly, *but not for long.* She ran toward an outcropping of rocks. *Yes, there might be snakes in there*, she thought, *but out here there are bigger dangers.* She crouched behind a sand-encrusted boulder and jabbed her hand at the chopper again. Once more, lightning split the sky, racing to do her bidding but still missing the damn target.

"Teresa Santiago!" a voice shouted over a bullhorn. "Surrender now or we will kill you."

The thunder crashed and the helicopter blades sounded like the heartbeat of a hungry beast. Closer now, those same blades were churning up the sand, throwing it at her, stinging her skin and her eyes. She couldn't even risk turning her back to the flying sand, since that would mean turning her back on her enemies. Each second that passed brought them ever nearer and Teresa knew she was out of time. There was no escape. She glanced around at the wild emptiness surrounding her and saw no options.

"Die here," she murmured frantically, "or die in prison. Not much of a choice."

So she did the only thing she could do. She stood her ground and threw yet more lightning at the men who had somehow followed her into the desert. Bolt after bolt shot toward the helicopter heading directly toward her, yet none of them hit. Desperation fueled her movements and she knew that her aim was only getting more erratic, but she couldn't do anything about that now.

How had they found her? How did they even *know* about her?

Fury laced her fear and somehow tangled in the threads of her power. She felt something new . . . something *old* pulse within her, strengthen. As if her power was centering itself. Staring hard at the incoming helicopter, she sent one more bolt of lightning at her enemies and this time she scored a hit. A small, jagged bolt slapped the tail rotor of the chopper, sending the machine into an uncontrolled spin. Torn between elation and fear, Teresa watched as the pilot struggled for control. She didn't *want* to kill anyone, but damned if she'd stand still and be shot, either.

The pilot recovered, the chopper continued on and the gunman took up position again. Teresa braced herself for the inevitable.

She looked up into the face of death—the incoming chopper—and lived.

A wall of fire appeared in front of her and the bullets flying at her embedded themselves in the flames instead. Teresa staggered back in surprise, looked up and met the pale gray eyes of a warrior. Fire surrounded his body, enveloping him in a living wall of flame. His features were drawn tight in concentration and his muscled body swayed with the impact of more bullets, but still he stood between her and danger.

"Hold on to me," the stranger ordered.

Teresa didn't even think about it. She jumped into the fire that covered the man, hooked her arms around his neck and shouted, "Go, go, go!"

And in another bright flash of flames they were gone.

Chapter 2

Rune felt an immediate drain on his strength reserves, but fought past it. The fools in the helicopter had known enough to use white-gold bullets in their guns and the man-made metal alloy was affecting his magic.

Pain was nothing new to him. Centuries of existence had inured him to it. And despite the agony of white-gold bullets tearing up his back, as an immortal he would survive. If those bullets had hit Teresa instead, his witch would be dead.

And the world would not have survived his fury.

Flashing his woman to a small house on the edge of Sedona, Rune held her a moment longer than necessary. He'd waited years for this. Had hungered for the feel of her pressed along his body. Through the pain dragging at him, Rune braced himself for his witch's panic. Her questions. Her fear.

"What took you so long?" she demanded. Pushing out of his arms, she glanced at her surroundings, then glared up at him. "Those guys nearly *killed* me."

Despite the pain of his bullet wounds, astonishment rose up. He hadn't counted on this. Hadn't expected it. He was prepared to deal with her panic. Her confusion over what was happening to her. Grimly, he acknowledged that he hadn't been looking forward to a hysterical female. He remembered all too well how only last month his fellow Eternal Torin had been driven to distraction by his mate, Shea. Torin had had his hands full trying to protect her from both her enemies and her own refusal to accept her new reality.

His own mate, it seemed, was not only aware of the situation but felt free to condemn him for a perceived slight. Annoyance chewed at him even as he scowled at her accusation.

"You know who I am?"

"Yeah." She took a breath and blew it out in an indignant rush. Then she pushed her tangled black hair out of her eyes and brushed at the sand nearly covering all of her. "You're my Eternal, right? Supposed to be my bodyguard for the big 'quest'?"

More than annoyance ran through Rune now as he tried to make sense of her reaction. The pain in his back was a distraction, but it was not enough to stop the hundreds of questions racing through his mind.

"I am Rune and yes, I am your Eternal," he said, his frown deepening. "How can you know about this? Your powers have only just awakened."

"And were nearly snuffed out," she added, taking the time to have a thorough look around her. "If you had taken any longer to show up—"

"I had to wait until your true power erupted."

"That was three days ago," she snapped.

"No." Rune reached out, cupped her chin. The tingle of her skin on his almost deadened the pain ratcheting up from the white-gold bullets that were slowly draining his magic. He fought past the pain, the slow drag on his power, and said, "Your magic quickened three days ago. Your awakened power happened only today—when you gathered your strength and managed to hit the helicopter. Now, tell me, how do you know of Eternals?"

"My *abuela*," she said, then shrugged and translated. "My grandmother."

"I know the word," he assured her. Suddenly he understood a lot more about his witch. Of course Teresa's grandmother would have known. Witches throughout the centuries had handed down the knowledge of the last great coven. Teresa's ancestors would have passed along the legends of atonement and of the Awakening— when the reincarnated witches would reclaim their magic and try to set right what had once gone so wrong.

He knew that Teresa's grandmother was a powerful witch herself. Of course she would have prepared her granddaughter for her destiny.

This meeting wasn't going at all as he'd expected it to. For years, he'd kept watch over her. He had done so for centuries, through every one of her incarnations. In this life, she was—as always—obstinate and independent.

He looked at her now, his gaze moving up her lush body until it finally locked onto her steady gaze. He saw pride there, and self-confidence. But beneath those traits he recognized in her, there was also a touch of vulnerability that called to him. Brought out every protective instinct he possessed.

With the time of the Awakening upon them, Rune had felt the pull of her soul to his more strongly than he ever had before. In all the past centuries, he had been torn between his undeniable need for her and the long-simmering rage at her coven for what they had brought upon them all.

If she and her sisters had not hungered for power . . .

none of this would have happened. They had thirsted for knowledge that came at too high a price. He and Teresa would have mated centuries ago and this time of Awakening would never have been necessary.

What, he wondered, would the world have been like if only his witch and her sisters had chosen wisely? And how could he get beyond his old anger to accomplish what they now must?

"My grandmother told me you'd be coming," Teresa said, and Rune's wandering thoughts arrowed in on her again. "She didn't mention the fire, though. For a minute when I saw you, I thought I'd stumbled into a vortex."

Teresa pulled away from his touch and Rune let her go. For now. Though his fingertips itched for the feel of her. Despite her bravado, Teresa's fear was so thick he could sense it, graying her aura, fraying the edges of her control and patience. But her strength was more than a match for that fear, he told himself, pleased at the set of her squared shoulders and the defiant tilt of her chin.

She would need that strength and more in the coming days.

"You really took your time riding to the rescue," she said softly, scraping her hands up and down her arms as if looking for warmth.

"You were never in real danger," he told her, stung by her accusation. Hadn't he been watching over her for centuries? From one incarnation to the next, she had never been out of his reach. "I was nearby."

"Right." She dropped her hands to her sides and frowned down at the sand that still clung to her clothing. Nodding to herself, she took another deep breath and asked, "So where are we?"

He winced at the pain in his back. "In a house near the edge of Sedona."

"Whose is it?" she asked, instantly wary.

As she should be, he thought. Her magic was alive and already the federal agencies were aware of it. Suspicion would be her closest friend now.

"It's mine," he said and watched her tension relax the slightest fraction. She was still taut with residual uneasiness and the remnants of her own power rushing through her. He felt a quick flare of admiration at her strength of will.

But it wasn't only her character that caught his attention. Rune looked at his witch and felt his body stir in appreciation, despite the agony of the white-gold shards still trapped beneath his skin. She was tall, though since he stood six feet five inches himself, her height was negligible to him. She wore faded blue jeans, dark brown cowboy boots and a forest green T-shirt that clung to her lush curves. Her eyes were the color of dark chocolate and her skin the shade of rich coffee with cream. Her wildly tangled black hair hung past her shoulders. It was all Rune could do to keep his hands off her.

He had already waited several lifetimes for her—another few days while she accustomed herself to the fact that they were mates wouldn't kill him.

He walked to the closest window, peeled back the edge of the curtains and looked out on to a rainy scene. No one was about, which was all to the good.

"You own a house in Sedona?" she asked. "How long have you been here?"

"I bought this house when you were a child. To be close by if you had need," he said, not bothering to tell her that he hadn't *stayed* here all that time. He was an

Eternal, after all, and besides his duty to his witch, there
was also a duty to all of those with power. He and the
others like him were the strongest barrier standing
between witches and the enemies who would destroy
them.

"Where were you, then, when Miguel came into my
life?" she murmured.

Rune stiffened at the mention of the abusive man
who had made Teresa's life a misery for several months
before she freed herself of him. The moment she became involved with the male, Rune had left Sedona. He
couldn't force himself to stay near her and watch her
with someone else.

"I didn't realize what he was until after you left him,"
he said softly.

She threw him a quick, haunted look that disappeared
in a flash. "Doesn't matter. I took care of myself. I always
do."

Her bravado didn't hide the pain in her eyes and Rune
felt another sharp stab of regret slice at him. Miguel had
left town after Teresa showed him the door and Rune
hadn't wanted to leave her to find him. But one day, he
assured himself, there would be reparations made with
Miguel.

He watched her gaze sweep the room and knew what
she was thinking. Spartan, the house held only the bare
necessities. He had no need for luxury. And drawing attention to himself or this house hadn't seemed wise. So
he had stocked the place with only what he needed.
There were couches, chairs and tables. In the kitchen,
there was food, though he rarely required sustenance.
There was a bed, extra clothing and the emptiness that
always filled a place where nothing was shared.

Where nothing mattered.

Until now.

"If this is your house," she asked quietly, "won't the feds know to come here?"

"They know nothing of me. It's you they're following," he reminded her and asked himself how the agents had known about her so soon after her power had awakened. "They have no way to connect you to this place, so you will be safe here."

"For how long?"

He shrugged and winced at the pull of his muscles slicing against the white-gold bullets invading his body. He had to get them out. *Soon.* The drain on his powers was steadily increasing and he couldn't afford any amount of weakness should their enemies find them. "We won't be staying here. But the house is in a dark zone, so we're safe enough for the moment."

"Dark zone?" she repeated, frowning. "What is that?"

He almost smiled. "You live in Sedona and know of the vortexes but nothing of the dark zones? I have much to tell you, Teresa, but now is not the time." He walked toward the bathroom, tugging his black T-shirt off over his head as he went. The simple action of stretching his arms above his head sent new shards of pain through him.

"Oh, my God." Teresa was on him in an instant, grabbing hold of his arm to stop him, then sliding one hand across his torn-up back.

A flash of heat swamped him at her touch, but still he whirled away fast enough to keep her from coming into contact with the white gold.

"Don't touch them," he warned.

Her face paled and her eyes glinted with fury as understanding dawned on her. "White-gold bullets. They were using white-gold bullets and you took them all to save me."

He nodded, then turned again for the bathroom. "The feds learned fast how to stop us. Or at least how to slow us down."

Teresa followed, her footsteps quick. "I know. Silver is an earth element. It focuses our powers, makes us stronger. But white gold . . ."

He glanced at her. "Yes. It does the opposite. Gold can't hurt us. But white gold is a man-made alloy. The chemical makeup of the alloy is poisonous to us. It drains magical ability."

"So it's working on you right now," she said softly. "Which is why we have to get those bullets out of you. Fast."

"I will," he told her, not bothering to look back at her.

"How? How can you dig around in your own back?"

Rune looked at her then, hearing the dismay in her voice. He wasn't yet sure how he would get the bullets out, but he would find a way. His own magic wasn't as strong as that of the witch he was destined to protect and defend. But it might be enough to allow him to *push* the bullets free of his body. "It will be fine."

She hurried to a window and took a look outside. The storm over the desert had rolled into the city. Rain pelted the windows and wind tore at trees, sending a crumpled newspaper hurtling down the familiar street. She smiled to herself and nodded. The hideous three-story house on the corner had made all the newspapers when the owners built it. The neighborhood had been up in arms over the modern monstrosity ruining the Spanish feel of the town.

Turning back to him, she said, "I know where we are

now. My friend's a doctor. Her office isn't far. I can get there and be back in ten minutes."

"No," he said flatly, his tone brooking no argument. He allowed the flames that made up the very heart of him to flicker in the depths of his eyes.

Teresa paid no attention. "You're in no shape to protect me, Eternal, so you're in no shape to stop me, either."

"You think a few pieces of white gold are enough to contain me?" he countered, insulted at the idea. Yes, they caused him pain. And drained his magic. But he was still more than the human mind could contemplate. His inborn strength had been hewn from the center of the sun and molded by his god, Belen. Rune and his brethren were unlike anything else on this earth. And it was best if his witch learned that now.

"Humans don't worry me," he told her. "But they should worry you. I'm immortal. You're not."

"Yeah, but I am a witch," she countered. "And you got shot saving me. So I'm going to get the help we need so you can save me *again*, okay?"

He stalked across the room, ignoring the jabs of pain in his back. Those small pieces of white gold were as nothing to him in the face of his witch's rebellion. As his gaze caught hers, he grabbed her shoulders and held on. "You're not to go into the streets. The feds are out there somewhere, looking for you."

"And the longer we stand here arguing, the closer to town they get."

"You're not foolish enough to believe they are the only ones on your trail, are you?" he argued. "There are more. Already in the city. Looking for you." The men in the desert were no doubt still in the air, headed for the city—but their compatriots could be anywhere. "Here, in the dark zone, it will be nearly impossible for them to track you. Magic is muted here, so whatever they're using to locate you won't work in the zone."

"How big is this zone?" she countered quickly.

"Several blocks."

"Then we're still good. My friend's clinic is two blocks from this house."

Irritated almost to the breaking point, Rune demanded, "Who is this doctor?"

Teresa gave him a fast, brilliant smile as if she knew she had won this round. "Elena Vargas. She's two blocks over. She'll help. I know she will."

Rune still didn't like it, but he liked even less the idea of his power draining further. There was a question he must ask, though. "How do you know this friend isn't the one who turned you in to the Magic Police?"

She laughed and the sound was so unexpected, it jolted through Rune like a hot, luscious summer wind.

"Not a chance. Elena's known I'm a witch since we were kids."

He didn't like it, but she was right that the longer they waited, the more dangerous it was. And if he were to go with her, they would only attract more attention. Even in a city the size of Sedona, a man like Rune wouldn't go unnoticed. His size alone would attract attention.

The idea of her venturing out alone went against every one of his instincts, yet the sooner he was rid of the white gold, the sooner his witch would be safe again. "Fine, then. Go. But hurry—and speak to no one but your friend."

"I'm not an idiot, Eternal," she told him, already headed for the door. "And if we're going to be together through this quest of ours, then you'd better get used to the idea that I don't take orders well."

She opened the door, slipped out and was gone an instant later. So she didn't hear Rune mutter, "But take them you will."

Chapter 3

He hated letting her go alone, but if he refused, he risked her safety anyway. When a choice is not a choice, all that is left is fate.

Trusting in fate was not something that came easily to Rune. Through the centuries he had chafed at the years of atonement that had followed the coven's disastrous actions. His witch and her coven had sentenced themselves to centuries of separation from their magic. The Eternals had been condemned to remain on the fringes of the lives of the women they had been created to protect—and to love.

Now that the long wait was over and their time was finally here, he trusted only himself to keep Teresa safe.

He looked out the window, scowling at the driving rain, and experienced for the first time a sense of helplessness that nearly crushed him. He wasn't accustomed to encountering any situation he couldn't muscle his way through. Now, his woman was out on the streets while he was forced to wait.

But as he waited, nothing was keeping him from attempting to heal himself. Dropping to his knees, he leaned forward, bracing his arms on the floor as he concentrated on the shards of metal embedded in his back.

The poisonous sensation of the white gold felt as though it was moving, tracing through the veins of his body like acid. He hissed in a breath, closed his eyes and gathered his waning strength, focusing it on just one of those shards.

His mind arrowed in on the bullet, which had flattened upon impact with his body. The magic pooled inside him and narrowed into a thin ribbon that pushed against that invading shard.

With his eyes closed against the dragging pain and the pull on his magic, Rune groaned as the bullet slowly inched free of his flesh. Every movement was agony. Every twist of the metal tore at him. The drain on his powers was staggering, making him feel no better than a useless mortal.

Rune dragged in a ragged breath as the first of the white-gold shards fell from him to clatter onto the floor. His gaze dropped to the tiny piece of metal and a fierce fury rose up inside him. If he hadn't been there to prevent it, those bullets would have cut Teresa down. The human world would have succeeded in ending its only hope for survival. *Fools*, he thought as he braced himself for another try at ridding his body of the damaging bullets.

Without the Awakened witches to undo what they had begun so long ago, this earth the mortals fought so viciously to defend against witchcraft would end as no more than a burned cinder floating in space.

Fools. All of them.

Suddenly Rune felt a rush of protective instincts jangle through him and he lifted his head, listening. The sibilant sound of the rain muffled the barely discernible footsteps slogging relentlessly through the downpour. Gritting his teeth, he staggered to his feet and crossed to the nearest window.

Outside, two MPs, their black uniforms sodden, walked slowly down the middle of the street. It was clear they were searching for someone. *Teresa.*

Though the dark zone muted the trace of magic, it didn't make him or his witch invisible. If the feds were to begin a house-to-house search, he and Teresa would be discovered. Unless Rune regained his strength in time to prevent it.

Dropping to his knees again, he shook his head and fought past the pain whispering through him. He wouldn't be stopped. Not by white gold. Not by humans with guns. Not by *anything.* Gathering his waning strength, using what little of his dampened magic was available to him, he focused on another of the bullets lodged in his body.

With one last mighty surge of effort, he pushed one more bullet free of his skin before collapsing onto the floor of the empty house.

And in the silence, his huge body lay still as death.

Chapter 4

The rain had kept most people inside and for that Teresa was grateful. As it was, she kept her head down as she half ran through the neighborhood toward Elena's clinic. Now that she knew for certain the feds were after her, she realized that any number of others could be hunting her, too.

The Magic Police seldom worked alone. If they were here, then agents from BOW, the Bureau of Witchcraft, couldn't be far behind. For all she knew, members of both agencies were already scattered throughout Sedona, looking for her. Even weakened by the white gold attacking his system, her Eternal had realized that the men in the desert probably weren't the *only* ones here searching for her.

He was right.

She could feel it. There were others. Here in town. Looking for her.

Since the moment the world had been alerted to the existence of witchcraft, ten years before, no witch had been safe. Throughout history, but for a few instances, women of power had kept themselves hidden, letting the world believe that magic was no more than a legend.

Until the day that one woman accidentally set loose a power she wasn't even aware of and burned her former husband to death in front of hundreds of witnesses. That woman, Mairi Jameson, had in turn been burned at the stake a few months later.

Fear and panic had erupted all across the planet. In the last ten years, no woman suspected of witchcraft lasted very long. There were internment camps scattered across this country and every other nation. Women were jailed, without trial, without being able to face their accusers. And most of them were never heard from again.

Ironic, Teresa thought with a grim smile, that fear of a common enemy had united the planet in a way it never had been before. Religious wars had gone the way of the dinosaur as nations that had once considered themselves enemies joined forces to track down women of power. The only war today was the war against witches.

Teresa shivered again, dismissing her dark thoughts as she bolted through the cold, driving rain that drenched her. She sprinted across the street and hurried down an empty sidewalk. Stores on either side of the street were open, their interior lights splashing puddles of gold into the encroaching night.

Too many shadows, she told herself, sending uneasy glances left and right as she quickened her steps, her bootheels splashing in the wet.

She slammed into someone and jolted back, fear rising up, then sliding back down as she looked at the woman who had stepped out of a dress shop.

"Excuse me," she muttered.

The woman looked at her as if she was crazy, then scurried away. These days, it didn't pay for a woman to draw attention—even for something as seemingly innocent as a conversation with a stranger. You never knew who might be watching.

At that thought, Teresa sent a quick look around the rain-drenched street. She couldn't see a soul except the woman she had just bumped into. That should have made her feel better. Instead, she felt a cold crawl along her spine, as if there were unseen watchers keeping tabs on her every movement.

She started walking again, flicking another quick look over her shoulder as a half block farther along, she ducked into the doorway of Elena's clinic. The CLOSED sign was on the door, but there was a light on in the back of the building.

Teresa knocked, rapping her knuckles wildly against the glass. "Come on, Elena. Be there."

As if she'd been conjured, Teresa's friend stepped into view, irritation stamped on her features until she recognized Teresa at the door. Then she hurried over, unlocked it and pulled her inside.

"Teresa, what are you doing? Are you crazy or didn't you notice it's raining?" She took a step back, relocked the door and shook her head. "You're soaked."

"Yeah, I noticed." As warmth seeped into her, Teresa looked out the window at the pouring rain and the deserted street beyond. Shadows loomed all around, but they were empty—nothing seemed to be hiding, biding its time. So far. She didn't see anyone out there, but the tingle at the back of her neck that told her danger was close was only getting stronger. Yes, it was just a feeling. But it was one she couldn't afford to ignore.

Turning back to her friend, she blurted, "Elena, I need your help."

"What is it?"

"MPs."

"Oh, my God." Elena's face paled and her dark brown eyes went wide in alarm. She threw a quick look at the street, then grabbed Teresa and pulled her deeper into the clinic, away from the windows and any prying eyes. She hustled her past the narrow coffee table scattered with magazines, past the waiting room chairs and down the hall into her own office. The scent of burned coffee stained the air along with the scent of fear and, of all things, Teresa thought with an unexpected smile, bubblegum. But then, Elena did treat a lot of kids at her clinic.

"Where are they?"

Teresa looked at her best friend and felt Elena's fear as starkly as she did her own. Not surprising, since they'd grown up together, the two of them sharing every major and minor milestone along the way. They'd met in first grade and had bonded over their mutual disgust of boys.

As the years passed, they'd seen each other through misery and laughter, triumph and pain, and each of them had grown into her own gifts. Teresa's was a legacy of power, while Elena had the gift of healing. They were true sisters. Not of blood, but by choice.

They were family.

Elena was short, a little too curvy for modern fashion and far too smart for her own good. If she asked all the questions Teresa knew she wanted to, it would only make things more difficult for her. Her wide brown eyes were worried and her short black hair looked as if she'd already shoved her hands through it a hundred times that day.

"I lost the guys chasing me in the desert," Teresa finally said in answer to Elena's question. Though she wouldn't tell her friend just *how* she'd left those feds behind. Even knowing about the existence of witchcraft didn't negate the fact that a man made of fire was pretty hard to believe. "But there's no reason to think those guys were alone in this. There are probably more of them here in town."

Her friend sent a wary glance toward the front of the clinic, then said, "You've got to get out of here, Teresa. Don't even go back to your place. I've got some money here. It's not a lot, but—"

"No." Teresa pulled in a breath and said, "Money's not what I need." If she needed it later, she'd find an ATM somewhere far, far away from here and make a withdrawal there. "What I *do* need is some medical stuff. The . . . man who saved me was shot. He's still got the bullets in him and I have to get them out."

"Bullets? As in more than one?" Elena shifted into practicality in the blink of an eye. "How bad is it? Major organs?"

She moved to get her black bag that she kept fully stocked at all times. All her neighbors knew that if they had a problem, even in the middle of the night, they could go to Elena and she would help. With her credentials, she could have practiced medicine anywhere. But she'd chosen to come home. To be a permanent part of the neighborhood where they'd grown up.

"I'll be ready in a minute and—"

"No." Teresa stopped her with one quiet word. When Elena looked at her in question, she continued. "You can't come with me. It's too dangerous. Too risky. If they know about me, then they've done their homework and they know you're my best friend. Elena, they'll be watching you."

"I hadn't thought of that," Elena admitted grimly, then narrowed her eyes. "Which means they could be watching the clinic right now."

"Possibly," Teresa said, feeling that odd prickle of danger at the back of her neck again. "But I had to risk coming here. You *don't* have to risk your life."

"It's my life."

"I won't let you," Teresa told her.

After several long, tense seconds, Elena muttered a curse and said, "Fine. I'll give you what you need."

"Thanks. I owe you."

"No, you don't." She walked to the clinic supply cupboard and started rummaging around. "You said he'd been shot. How badly?"

"Bad."

Elena looked at her. "Is he dying?"

"No." Teresa was sure about that at least. Her Eternal was immortal. Shot to hell, in pain and losing his magic to the cloying pull of white gold, but he wouldn't die. "I just need something to dig the bullets out with and—"

"Right." Elena continued to riffle through the contents of the cabinet, tucking surgical implements, gauze bandages, alcohol, antibiotics and pain pills into her bag. Then she handed it over. "Take this and get moving."

"Thanks, Elena. Knew I could count on you." She started for the door, then stopped, turned and came back. Throwing her arms around the other woman, Teresa gave her a hard, fast hug. "You should disappear for a week or two, Elena. You don't want to be around here when they don't find me."

"Don't worry about me. Just make sure they *don't* find you."

Teresa hugged the bag to her chest. She had to leave, but there was more to say before she did. "Have you seen any strangers in the neighborhood today?"

Elena rolled her eyes. "You mean besides the dozens

of tourists hoping to step into a vortex and find the answers to the universe? No."

"Right." Teresa frowned, glanced warily down the hall at the front windows and at the rain-drenched street beyond the glass. No one was out there now, but that didn't necessarily mean a damn thing.

"Elena . . ."

"Save it. I'm not going to run out on my patients, Teresa." She folded her arms across her chest and shook her head for emphasis. "You have responsibilities—well, so do I."

She had known even as she suggested it that Elena wouldn't run. "I don't want you getting hurt because of me."

"If I'm hurt, it's not on you, Terry," Elena said, reaching out to take her friend's hand. "It's on the freaks who are chasing you."

"Small consolation if you're dumped in a prison," Teresa told her. Just the thought of her friend becoming one of the disappeared women terrified her. She could take fear on her own behalf. That was the legacy of witchcraft. But Elena's only crime was knowing a witch. Sadly, these days that was all it took.

"God, you're stubborn."

Elena managed a weak smile. "There's a news flash. Look, I know you'll be leaving. But once you're safe, find a way to let me know, will you? You don't have to tell me where you are." She paused and admitted, "In fact, it would be better for both of us if you don't. But at least let me know you're alive."

"I will," she promised, hugging her best friend as if it were the last time. And maybe it would be. When she stepped back, she said softly, "Elena, don't tell anyone you saw me tonight."

"Who would I tell? Not like I've got a social life." She tried to smile again, but nerves, sorrow and fear chewed at the edges. "Where will you go?"

Good question. Teresa didn't have a clue where she and her mystical bodyguard would end up. Her grandmother's visions had predicted the rise of her magic. The coming of a tall man who would protect her. And a dangerous task whose ending was unclear.

Thinking about the Eternal waiting for her sent a ribbon of heat winding through her system and she really didn't want to so much as acknowledge it. She hadn't expected to feel such an immediate draw to the immortal meant to be her mate. And it worried her.

Right now Teresa would have given a lot to talk with her *abuela*. To get some advice. Maybe another peek at one of her visions. But her grandmother was home in a tiny village in Mexico. Another bright flash of fear shot through Teresa at the thought of her grandmother alone and unprotected. What if the feds went after *her*? Sure, her visions would probably alert her to incoming danger, but she would still be alone.

Alone.

"Oh, God," she said suddenly as something else occurred to her. "Chico. He's alone at my house."

Elena stared at her, clearly stunned. "You're being chased by armed nutcases who have already tried to kill you and you're worried about your *bird*?"

Yes, she was. Okay, sure, he was given to her by Miguel, her abusive bastard of an ex-boyfriend. But that didn't change the fact that she loved that little rainbow lorikeet. Chico was family, too. Besides her grandmother and Elena, Teresa was pretty much on her own. Her parents had died five years ago in a car accident and being an only child meant she had no close relatives. The multitude of relatives she had in Mexico and Spain didn't count with her, since she didn't know them well and never saw them. She couldn't leave town and let her lorikeet starve to death inside her empty house.

"I could go and get him," Elena began to offer.

"No. No, you stay away from my place," Teresa told her quickly. "I mean it, Elena. In fact, I want you to act like you hate my guts. Spit on the street if someone says my name."

"I will not," her friend huffed angrily.

"You will, too," Teresa told her, reaching out to grab her hand in a hard squeeze. "You'll tell anyone who will listen that you found out what I am and tried to report me but you didn't because I threatened you or something. Do whatever you have to do to stay safe. Do you understand me?"

"You expect me to—"

"To stay alive," Teresa finished for her.

"Damn it, Terry . . ."

"Please, Elena," she said softly. "If you love me, then do this for me. And don't worry about Chico. I'll get him before we leave."

"You can't go home—"

No, she thought, but Rune, her immortal Eternal, could go there for her. And she planned on making him do just that.

"Don't worry." Teresa headed for the front of the clinic, but before opening the door, she peered through the window and shivered at the thought of stepping out into that cold rain again. Added to that misery was the very real possibility that someone was watching Elena's clinic right now, hoping to spot her.

"At least go out the back door," Elena said as if reading her mind.

"Good idea." She should have thought of that. Would have, she assured herself, if there weren't so many wild and frantic thoughts racing through her mind. After all, why tempt the fates any more than she had already?

She followed her friend through the clinic, their footsteps echoing on the floor tiles. Rain drummed on the roof and at the windows, pounding a beat so quick and steady, it urged Teresa to move faster.

At the door, which led into a short alley, Elena reached out for another hug. "Be careful," she warned unnecessarily.

"I will," Teresa promised, still clutching the black medical bag to her chest. "You watch your back, okay?"

Nodding, Elena opened the door as quietly as possible; then Teresa slipped through without a sound and lost herself in the drenched shadows.

Chapter 5

"Fucking rain." Landry Harper hunched deeper into his jacket and wished he were chasing a witch in Hawaii. Instead, he was cooling his heels outside a dump of a house in Sedona, Arizona, where it should, he told himself, at least be *hot*.

But no, he was freezing his ass off and getting soaked to boot. He was posted outside Teresa Santiago's house, and trying to stay as inconspicuous as possible. Not easy when even a moron had the sense to get in out of the rain.

Still, he wore a black jacket over his MP uniform, disguising it enough that no casual passerby would notice him for what he was: a man on a mission.

A man determined to capture or kill as many witches as he could find.

Now there was a thought to warm a man's soul despite the fucking cold rain. He smiled to himself and kept his gaze locked on the narrow white house with the red Spanish tile roof. It was empty. He'd already checked that out, despite knowing that the witch was in the desert being hunted by his friends in a helicopter. Landry liked to keep his t's crossed and his i's dotted. And that meant checking everything out for himself. The minute he allowed others to step in, that's when things went to hell.

Just look at what had happened last month. He'd caught a damn witch, turned her over to the internment camp on Terminal Island in California and then left, satisfied that she was at least off the streets. Locked up where she couldn't harm innocents. But no, those idiots in charge had allowed her to escape.

"I should have killed that bitch when I had the chance," Landry muttered. "Just like I should have been the one taking the shot in the desert instead of standing here freezing my nuts off."

"Stop your bitching. Christ, what kind of agent are you, anyway?"

Landry sneered as the voice came sharp through his earpiece. His partner was stationed in a nice, dry room in a B&B, focusing a telescopic lens on the street and the back of the witch's house.

"Yeah," Landry muttered, flashing a furious scowl at a passing man who looked at him as if he were a lunatic, talking to himself. "Easy for you to say," he continued when the man was gone. "You're not standing here drowning, waiting for a damn witch. The others should have killed her back in the desert."

"They missed her. It's our chance at her now," the voice reminded him. "And if you blow this stakeout by pissing and moaning I swear to God I'll kill you instead."

He'd like to see the little pissant try. Fury pumped through him at the criticism. Landry had been on these stakeouts for years. That damn kid in the room with his high-tech equipment thought he was hot shit. But Landry had caught more witches than that know-it-all little bastard could even dream about.

But he wouldn't make waves. One way to get yourself taken off a hunting team was to shoot your mouth off one too many times. And Landry would never give up the hunt. He would find every damn witch he could and he'd kill them dead, given half a chance. And it still wouldn't be enough to ease the pain that had gnawed on him ever since a witch's emerging powers had exploded, killing Landry's wife and child.

He turned his mind from the memory, deliberately locking his loved ones away into the otherwise empty darkness of his heart. Landry was no longer that man who had loved his family. Now he was a hunter. Pure and simple. And this witch, Teresa Santiago, was his target today.

If they had gotten better intel, he told himself, they'd be stationed around this town at all of the witch's haunts. But no, the powers that be had only just found out about the witch and who the hell knew how. Their information was sketchy at best and all Landry's superiors had been able to come up with on short notice was her damn address. A neighbor had told them about her stealing off to the desert a few hours ago. Seems the witch often went into the desert to be alone. So one team was out there in a chopper, using high-tech magical tracking devices to home in on the witch's position—for all the good that had done them. There were still more agents combing the streets of Sedona for her, just in case she gave the chopper boys the slip, and Landry and the college boy were here.

Well, College Boy was welcome to his safe and warm cubbyhole. Landry was a boots-on-the-ground kind of guy. He preferred being as close to his target as possible, even if it meant standing in the rain waiting for the supernatural bitch to show up.

And she would, he knew. Yes, she'd gotten away from the team in the desert, but she wouldn't run without coming home first. Witches were, after all, *women*, and she would need to pack before doing a disappearing act.

Then he'd have her.

Chapter 6

Bolting from the alley, Teresa forgot about stealth and gave in to the pressing need to hurry. She ran down the darkened, rainy streets, not caring who might glance out a window and notice her. Panic chewed at her insides. She couldn't afford to go slowly. Her instincts were screaming that she was in danger and she wasn't about to ignore those feelings.

"Hey! Freeze!"

The voice came from behind her. She stumbled, then hunched her shoulders and kept going, pretending she didn't know that voice was aimed at her.

"Lady, stop or I shoot." The order came—deep, sharp.

Teresa had no choice now. She skidded to a stop only a block away from the house where she'd left her Eternal. So close to safety—but now that distance might as well be hundreds of miles.

The street around her was dark, houses closed up against the weather and the fear of what moved around in the night. She wouldn't find help here even if she were crazy enough to ask for it. People minded their own business these days—safer that way.

She turned around slowly, clutching Elena's medical

bag to her chest with her left arm. Rain pelted her, cold, icy drops that slapped at her face, making her blink furiously to keep her vision clear. She watched the lone MP stride unerringly toward her, his boots splashing heavily through the wide puddles.

Holding a short automatic weapon in the cradle of his arms, he lifted his chin and demanded, "Where the hell are you running to and what's that you're carrying?"

Fear boiled in her belly and spread throughout her system. The fed was young, but his features were hard and cruel. She wouldn't find any mercy or sympathy in this quarter. "I'm taking some supplies to a friend of mine. A doctor. He's waiting for this bag."

"Uh-huh." He wasn't buying it. "So why doesn't this doctor carry his own bag?"

"It's an emergency," she told him, glancing right and left, futilely looking for help that wouldn't be coming.

"Right. Put it down, lady, and step back."

God. She had to go. Had to get away.

"Come on, soldier," she said, giving him a weak smile that she knew couldn't be convincing. "Can't we talk about this?"

He lifted the weapon in his arms, slowly bringing the barrel up to point at her. That was when Teresa knew she was out of options. Heart racing, fear finally took a backseat to rage. Who were these bastards to hunt her down like a sick dog?

Time to fight back.

Her power trembled to life inside her and she fed it with the fires of her anger. Reaching back for lessons learned from her *abuela*, she found the words and hoped they would be enough. *"Light to dark, dark to light, hide me now from his sight—"*

"Witch!" he shouted, breaking her spell, lifting the gun, aiming it.

Still clutching the medical bag to her chest, Teresa suddenly dropped to one knee, lifted her right hand and aimed her fingers at the sky. No time for spells. She could only hope to focus her aim.

"Stand down, bitch, or I kill you right here and now!"

Before he could train his weapon on her and fire, Teresa gathered her power into a tight knot inside her, prayed for control and then sent that power flying heavenward, her gaze locked on the enemy.

Lightning flashed, thunder boomed.

His eyes went wide as a bolt of skyfire slammed into the street at his feet. Blown backward by the impact, the MP flew through the air and landed with a hard thump on the windshield of a parked car. The glass beneath him shattered and his gun fell from nerveless fingers to the street.

Teresa jolted to her feet and dragged in a quick breath stained with the taste of ozone. Shaking in reaction, she started moving. Once the fallen MP was found, it wouldn't be long before every witch hunter in town arrived, combing the area for her.

As she dashed past her fallen enemy, she snatched up his weapon and ran toward safety.

"We've gotta move, Eternal."

Rune lifted his head to stare at his witch as she raced through the door. She was holding a black bag and a weapon. "Where'd you get that?"

She glanced down at the gun as if she'd never seen it before. Then she set it down gently. "Off the MP who tried to shoot me."

"Damn it." He groaned out the words.

"I threw some lightning at him and then ran for it. Relax, I'm good."

"Lock the door."

"No shit." She did just that, then hurried to him, dropping to her knees at his side. "You look like hell, Eternal."

"Did you kill the man?"

"I don't know," she admitted, trying to help him sit up. "Didn't stick around to find out." She exclaimed with the effort. "It's like trying to move Everest! Sit up, Eternal."

"My name is Rune," he muttered, but he did as she ordered.

"Got it," she said.

He looked up at her. "Were you followed?"

"No." She whipped her soaking-wet hair back behind her shoulders and opened the black bag. "I only saw the one MP and he's not going anywhere for a while. No one else is leaving their houses. Once that storm hit town it's like they rolled up the sidewalks."

"Good," he muttered, fighting the pull of the white gold beneath his skin. "That's good."

"Yeah," she said, kneeling beside him. "It's great. You do look horrible."

He laughed shortly. Just what he wanted to hear from his destined mate. The witch who was to be his other half. His partner, his lover. Looking at her now, he noticed how pale her skin was. How shadowed her eyes. He could feel the chill sliding from her body and cursed himself for being in no position to help her. What kind of Eternal was he, anyway? Belen, the sun god, must be rattling the heavens in disgust with him.

Eons ago, Belen had crafted his Eternals, drawing

heat and fire from the heart of the sun to form his creations. In an effort to please his lover, Danu, by gifting her witch daughters with mates to love and protect them, Belen had breathed life into the Eternals. He gave them fire and strength and immortality, demanding in return their fealty to the witches in their care.

Through the centuries that had been no easy task, Rune thought grimly.

As if the god was listening, a clap of thunder exploded overhead with enough force to rattle the windowpanes.

"Now turn around so I can take the bullets out of your back."

His witch telling him what to do didn't sit well with him. Especially since he was in no shape to argue. "I got two out already," Rune muttered.

"Great," she said sharply. "Only five or six more to go. Now be quiet and let me do this."

He snorted. "I don't take orders from you."

"Fine. Be the big alpha dog. Lie there with white gold in your back so that your powers go to hell and you're no good to me at all. Fabulous plan."

Hissing under his breath, Rune glared at her. She didn't back down. She met him glare for glare, her expression both determined and worried. They could continue the argument, delaying their escape from Sedona, or he could allow her to do what she must to get him on his feet again.

"Fine," he said, giving in to the simple truth that he needed the white gold removed from his body. There was more trouble headed toward them and if he wasn't in top condition, his witch would die and the Awakening would end. He would accept her help, although the decision didn't stop his burning frustration at being brought so low when their time together was just beginning.

He was the protector. It jabbed at him to be lying here, dependent on her help. "Just do it and be done," he ordered, lying flat on his stomach. "But don't touch the bullets with your hands."

"I know," she said and he heard her open the bag she had carried with her. "I've got a painkiller in here—"

"No. Just take them out." He narrowed his gaze on her. "We don't have much time."

She huffed out a breath as she picked up a pair of medical forceps. "You don't have to be stoic."

"Do it." It was an order, plain and simple.

"Fine. Lie still." A moment later he felt the first dig in his back.

Chapter 7

"Talk to me while I do this," she said, already shuddering as she set the tips of the forceps against his back.

He nearly smiled despite himself. His brave, hotheaded witch was feeling a little queasy at the idea of becoming a doctor. "About what?"

"I don't know—" She broke off, took a deep breath to settle herself and said, "Dark zones. The phrase sounds familiar somehow. You said we were in one. What do you mean?"

Her small hand came down on the bare flesh of his back and he felt an instant sizzle that almost dwarfed the pain that began a heartbeat later. Her touch was heat, fire. The cold steel of the forceps digging into his body was ice.

Rune called on his immense self-control to manage the pain shooting through him. Pain was nothing new to him.

Through the eons, he had been stabbed, sliced and shot so many times that pain was as familiar as his own reflection in a mirror. But his witch was daunted by the task at hand. So he talked. To calm her. To take both of their minds off what was happening.

"Dark zones can be found all over the world," he said, pausing as she pulled a bullet from his back and dropped it unceremoniously to the floor. "They're spots where magic is muted."

She took a deep breath. "You mean I can't use my powers while we're here?"

"No, I mean that magic is hard to track in a dark zone. Those who are after you won't be able to use their devices to home in on your position."

She paused and he felt her surprise. "They have devices to track magic?"

Anger shot through him as he looked back at her and saw the expression on her face, the fear glittering in her eyes. Best she know now exactly what they were up against. Their enemies had come a long way from the Salem witch trials.

"They do. The international community has banded together," he told her wryly. "Apparently the fear of witchcraft is enough to make friends of ancient enemies."

"Great," she murmured, digging into his back again. "Peace at last."

He chuckled, despite the situation. "Scientists and engineers have been working together—along with a few captured, tortured witches—to build devices that pick up on a certain type of energy."

"The magical kind."

"Exactly." He hissed when she dug deep, then forced himself to relax when she muttered, "Sorry."

"Doesn't matter," he told her.

"Only a few more." She worked for a moment longer, then asked, "What causes these dark zones?"

"No one's sure," he replied. "Here in Sedona it might be the red rocks—ancient energy formed by wind and sun and rain, trapped within the sandstone. Nature's energy is stronger than any human knows."

"That I believe," she said. "My *abuela* taught me to respect the earth. To treat her with reverence—" She paused.

"What else did she teach you?" Rune asked, knowing that Teresa needed the distraction as she continued to pull jagged shards of white gold from his back.

"How to use crystals, herbs, potions," she murmured. "Mostly, though, she taught me secrecy."

"Wise woman," Rune acknowledged.

"Yes, she is. So tell me how you know where these dark zones are."

"When your power is stronger, you'll be able to feel the difference. It's . . ." He tried to come up with a way to describe it through the fog of pain muddying his thoughts. "It's a little like a thick coating of syrup on the air. Makes things feel heavier to your senses. Once you're in one, you're safe from electronic tracking, but not from the old-fashioned hunter."

"I'm guessing the feds still use plenty of those."

"They do indeed." Another bullet made a *thunk* as it hit the floor. As each piece of white gold left him, a portion of Rune's strength returned. His powers were rejuvenating, though it would take either rest or sex with his mate to bring him back to full strength.

"Great. Okay, then, what do we do once you're patched up?"

"We leave."

"Yeah, I figured that part out. But to go where?"

Rune lifted his gaze to hers and saw the worry flashing behind the bravado she showed the world. Something in him shifted. For far too long he had carried around a taut knot of anger toward her. This soul that should have been his other half and wasn't—because of unwise decisions made eight hundred years ago.

Now he looked at her and felt an easing of that old rage. This woman was not the one who had chosen so poorly. This soul had grown and learned over hundreds of incarnations. Perhaps this time she would be strong enough to right old wrongs. To end the surge of power streaming from the demon dimensions.

"You have the answer to that," he told her flatly. "Our destination is locked in your memories. So tell me, Teresa. Where do we go?"

She blew out a breath and sat back on her heels, dropping the forceps into the medical bag. "That's it. They're all out."

"Yes." He took a deep breath and felt his body begin to regenerate. "Now, lay your hands flat on my back. Cover as many of the bullet holes as you can."

To her credit, she didn't ask questions, just moved to do what he asked. He felt her touch slide deeply into him and relished the blast of heat she brought. Amazing that a being created of fire torn from the heart of the sun could spend so many centuries feeling cold.

But with Teresa's touch, that cold was abated. Magic, he thought with satisfaction. The blending of two mated souls.

"I can't heal with touch," she warned him.

"No, but our powers together will do the job. Concentrate your magic on my injuries."

He watched her over his shoulder, saw her center herself, then close her eyes to focus better. Then he drew on the fire and in an instant, flames jumped to life on his skin. As they danced across her hands and his back, he felt the healing swiftly overtake him.

Teresa's eyes opened wide and she stared down at the

quickening flames covering her hands. She watched as the ragged holes in his body sealed over and became smooth again, as if he'd never been shot at all. And still the flames burned, covering her palms on his back. She took a breath and let it slowly slide from her lungs.

"That's amazing," she whispered. "The fire doesn't burn."

"No," he said, allowing the flames to flicker and fade away as his body was healed. "Not unless I will it. I *am* the fire, Teresa. The flames are what form me. And what I am will never harm you."

She pulled in another deep breath and studied his face as if coming to a decision. Nodding, she said, "I believe you. Your back is healed over. Not even a scar." She trailed the fingertips of one hand across his skin as if checking for flaws she couldn't see. "But your power was drained by the white gold, right?"

"Yes."

Lifting the hem of her shirt, she pulled it up and over her head, tossing it to the floor. "All right, then. We've got to get you healed completely. I know about the sex magic between a witch and her Eternal. My *abuela* told me that sex drives your power. Right?"

"That is true," he said, gaze dropping to the swell of her breasts, hidden behind a plain white cotton bra. Through the fabric, he saw her pebbled nipples and his hands itched to touch her. His mouth watered for the taste of her. "We were made as two halves of the same whole. When we join, our powers grow and our strength increases. We are mates, Teresa. Bound by the fires of creation. Sex is the most intimate of joinings, twining our powers together, creating strength. The Mating ritual binds us even more deeply—but my magic is too depleted at the moment to begin the ritual."

"The ritual is more than sex?"

"Yes. Much more."

"But sex alone will give you back your strength."

"It will."

"Then we're having sex. Right now." She unhooked her bra and tossed it aside, baring her breasts to him unself-consciously. Then she stood and before he knew it, she had whipped off her boots, jeans and panties, standing before him completely naked with the dignity and pride of a young queen.

She was magnificent.

"You amaze me," he said as his body tightened in an agony of need. He'd had no idea his witch was this strong. He had expected her to be afraid and anticipated that she would be hesitant to take hold of their shared destiny. Instead, she had been expecting him. She'd defied him. Helped him. And now she offered herself to bring him back to full strength.

This witch, this woman, had the inner strength of a warrior. She would do whatever was necessary to survive. His admiration for her matched his desire.

He ran one hand up her naked calf and she shivered. Her brown eyes were shadowed, but her expression was determined. "Take your clothes off, Eternal."

With a snap of his fingers, his clothes disappeared and he rolled over onto his back to look up at her. He felt the fire in him roaring at the promise of sex with his mate.

Teresa dropped to the floor, then straddled him to cover his body with hers. Rune grabbed her and pulled her even closer, his hands coming down onto her hips and holding tightly as if to keep her from changing her mind.

But his witch was nothing if not single-minded. She smiled at him and whispered, "I'm not going anywhere."

Then she raised up on her knees and his hands slid from her hips to her thighs, loving the hot feel of her skin beneath his palms. His cock was hard and ready. His breath stilled in his chest. If he'd had a heartbeat, it would have staggered as she slowly lowered herself onto him.

Heat at her center welcomed him. Liquid warmth drew him in, higher and higher as she took all of him inside her. When he was fully sheathed within her, she paused, allowing each of them to experience the sensation of being completely joined.

Everything in Rune roared for completion. To claim this woman. To give. To indulge in the many varied ways he'd dreamed of having her. Instead, he forced himself to be still, to allow his witch to lead and drive them forward. To set their pace. To accept the inevitability of their union.

A moment later, she did just that.

Chapter 8

Teresa struggled for air and fought for control. She hadn't expected to feel so much or so intensely. Her *abuela* had prepared her for the life that she would live once she met her Eternal. What she hadn't been prepared for was the incredible sensations coursing through her. She held him within her body and felt herself stretch to accommodate him. He was bigger than she had anticipated and for a moment she'd felt a surge of panic at trying to take him inside her. But the instant their bodies met, it was as if she had been waiting for that moment all her life.

Their bodies were like pieces in a puzzle. A perfect fit, each to the other. A connection swarmed between them like fireflies in the air. Threads of something old and true and potent wound themselves into a tapestry inside her, as if she knew him. As if she had *always* known him. There was a compelling sense of recognition that became stronger every moment they were joined.

Powerful magic sizzled and burned around them. Outside, rain still slashed at the windows and hammered on the roof like millions of tiny fists demanding entry. Somewhere in the city, hunters roamed through the night, searching for her. But here, in this small house in the middle of a dark zone, magic was alive.

Teresa inhaled sharply, then slowly swiveled her hips on him, creating a delicious sense of friction that bubbled through her veins like champagne. She shivered in response and looked down into pale gray eyes burning with hunger. He felt everything she did. She sensed that.

Yes, their connection was fragile, new, but it was there and time would only strengthen it.

She moved on him again and leaned forward when he lifted his hands to cup her breasts. His thumbs and forefingers stroked and squeezed her nipples, sending jolts of need through her system. She gasped, arching into him. "I feel . . ."

"Yes, you do," he said and rose up to take first one of her nipples and then the other into his mouth. His teeth and tongue worked her already sensitive flesh. She held his head to her breast, pulled free the leather thong holding his hair back and then threaded her fingers through the thick, dark strands. It was too much. The feel of him beneath her hands. The swamping need his body created in hers. All of it.

Danger persisted at the edges of her mind, yet passion was in the driver's seat. She couldn't be bothered with witch hunters. Not now. Now, all she needed was the climax hurtling toward her.

She moved even faster, rocking her hips against his. And still it wasn't enough. She had to have more. Faster. Deeper. Harder. Magic clawed at her. Need trumpeted inside her.

"I can't go fast enough," she finally managed to say, groaning as an agony of suspense clutched at her. Her body was coiled, tensed, and still straining for the orgasm that remained just out of reach.

"I *can*," he promised, his voice a low growl of hunger. Instantly, he rolled her over onto her back and lifted her legs onto his broad shoulders.

Teresa's breath came in short, quick gasps. She looked up into his eyes and saw flames pulsing in their depths. His features were taut, his jaw clenched with the same desperate desire that held her so tightly.

His hands slipped beneath her, lifting her behind, positioning her so that his first thrust went deeper than she would have believed possible. Her back arched and she called out his name on a shriek of pleasure that threatened to tear her in two. He was all. He was everything. And if she didn't get that release soon, he would kill her.

As if he knew exactly what she was thinking, feeling, he moved in her, his hips pistoning, his body retreating and advancing with such speed that everything was a blur of sensation. She'd never known anything like this before. Didn't know if she would even survive it. But if she died, Teresa told herself, it would have been worth it.

Again and again, Rune pushed his way into her body and she moved with him, meeting each and every thrust with a silent demand for more. Until, finally, that long-sought release crashed down on her.

The first shattering explosions shook her to her bones and she shouted his name as her body bucked beneath his. Her hands clutched at his strong arms, holding on for her life while the world as she knew it dissolved into a shower of bright lights and sensation.

"More," he demanded, before her first release had finished, and with his thumb he stroked her center until she screamed again, twisting wildly in his arms, calling out his name as her body did what she wouldn't have thought possible. She felt herself splinter and then some-

how come together again, all within several amazing moments.

She was still trembling, futilely trying to catch her breath, when she heard his deep voice thunder out a howl of victory. Then his body emptied itself into her and all she could see was her Eternal, staring down at her with flames shining in his eyes.

Chapter 9

Kellyn reclined in the oversized tub and idly stroked her fingertips through the mountain of bubbles covering the surface of the water. She'd had a rough month, she acknowledged. Hardly surprising that she needed a little pampering.

A frown curved her mouth as she remembered the bitter conclusion to her last encounter with Shea Jameson and the Eternal Torin. It had ended with Shea throwing a teleportation spell, sending Kellyn to the back end of beyond in the blink of an eye. Infuriated, frustrated, she'd awoken in a muddy field in Ireland, surrounded by cows who looked even more startled than she had felt.

Still feeling the sting of failure, Kellyn reached over to pick up her glass of champagne. She took a long sip, letting the icy bubbles soothe her tattered spirit.

"Doesn't matter," she assured herself, smiling at the way the light glinted off the crystal flute. "All I have to do is turn *one* of the Awakening witches. Just one. Then their plan will fall apart and I win."

Sliding down deeper into the water, she rested her head against the cool porcelain and looked out the window at the skyline of Washington, D.C. She could have been in New Mexico right now, tromping through some hideous desert to deal with Teresa Santiago. But really, a bubble bath in civilization sounded so much better to her battered temper.

"Besides," she whispered, "if he needs help with her, he can come and get me."

When her phone rang, she considered not answering it. After all, hadn't she earned a little relaxation? But the insistent, shrill tone wouldn't be ignored and Kellyn sat up to snatch the phone off the shelf beside the tub. "What is it?"

"We missed her in the desert."

Fury shot through her. "You mean you let those idiot human teams *kill* her?"

"No," the voice on the other end of the line assured her quickly. "They missed her, too. The Eternal showed up and flashed her out."

"Eternals," she muttered, tossing the rest of her champagne down her throat as if it were medicinal. The immortal warriors had been a pain in the ass of every would-be bad guy for centuries. "I thought you said you could deal with him."

"I can," her caller said. "But the point was to not give ourselves away, remember?"

"As this is my plan, do you really feel it necessary to remind me of its intricacies?" Attractive or not, this particular male had begun to annoy Kellyn. She probably shouldn't have agreed to work with him on this after all. But with his special gifts, he had proven just too tempting to ignore.

"No more than you should feel it necessary to remind me what the goal is."

The ice in his tone let Kellyn know he was no happier about this situation than she was. Well, then, fine. She would give him a chance to fix it. "Where's the witch now?"

"We don't know," he admitted. "An MP was attacked, though. Apparently he was hit by lightning."

Kellyn smiled to herself. A powerful witch, this one.

"And there are a lot of dark zones in Sedona," the man was saying. "My guess is the Eternal swept her into one. He was shot up pretty bad, so he's going to need some healing time."

"Then find her while he's weakened."

"That's the plan," he told her and hung up.

He hung up.

On *her*.

Kellyn stared at the phone in disbelief. No one dismissed her. No one. Her fingers closed around the phone until the plastic shattered and shards of it dug into her palm. Then she threw the mess at the wall and watched as pieces fell to the floor like black rain.

Furious both at having her relaxation time interrupted and at the clear disrespect, she poured more champagne and quaffed it. Turning her glare on the window again, she stared at the outside world and promised herself that once this damn Awakening was finished there would be some payback.

Her bathwater had cooled by the time she stepped out of the tub, leaving all thoughts of relaxation behind.

Chapter 10

"He's fried." Landry looked at the dead MP sprawled across the shattered windshield of a sedan. The kid's eyes were wide-open as if he were still surprised.

"What the hell happened to him?"

Landry shot the young agent beside him an incredulous look. "The witch happened to him, you fuckwit. You heard the report from the desert. She can throw lightning, for chrissakes. Looks like she landed a hit on this poor bastard."

While the younger agent muttered to himself, Landry narrowed his eyes against the driving rain and scanned the neighborhood. He knew people were watching him. Knew they were too afraid to step outside and get pulled into a federal investigation. All but one, anyway.

"She ran off down the street there. Just left that guy smokin' on the hood of that car."

The boy couldn't have been more than seventeen and both fear and excitement glittered in his eyes. Landry recognized the look. It was the thrill of the hunt.

"How long ago?" he asked the kid.

"'Bout an hour. I called to report it, but it took you

guys forever to show up." Just a touch of disgust colored
his tone.

Landry agreed with him. But the MPs had to call in
tips, get approval. Hell, even tracking and killing witches
was filled with bureaucratic bullshit these days.

"Fine. Thanks for being a good citizen. Your country
appreciates your help," Landry told him.

"Yeah, can I come with you?" The kid was practically
bouncing in his eagerness to get in on a witch kill. "I'll
stay out of the way. Swear it."

"No. Official business," Landry told him, then cuffed the
kid on the shoulder. "But when you're eighteen, you sign
up for MP Youth Camp. Give 'em my name—Landry—as
a reference."

The kid glowed. "Thanks, dude. Seriously."

But Landry was already moving off, his mind on the
witch. They were in a dark zone, so he knew he wouldn't
be able to trace her magic. His best bet was to return to
her house. To join the others already there. He wanted
this damn witch.

Teresa was shaken.

She'd gone into this with her eyes wide-open. She was
no shy virgin offering herself up on an altar of duty. She'd
had sex before and had assumed that this would
be no different.

She couldn't have been more wrong.

Despite everything her grandmother had told her,
taught her, the old woman hadn't known exactly what a
witch and her mate would *feel*. If just sex with her Eternal was this overwhelming, what, she wondered, would
the Mating sex be like? Mate. She would be this immortal's mate, she knew. Destiny and all that. But Teresa had

promised herself that she would do her duty to her magic, to the world, all while keeping her heart separate.

She'd been in love before and that had turned into a misery the likes of which she was in no hurry to repeat. Miguel, her ex-boyfriend, had been a bastard. He'd hurt Teresa in more ways than she wanted to remember—and he was human. Just imagine what an immortal could put her through. No. She knew now that she had given Miguel power over her by the simple act of loving him.

She wouldn't be making a mistake like that again. Especially with an already extremely powerful immortal.

A flicker of something that might have been fear sputtered into life in the pit of her stomach, then dissolved again a moment later. That was a worry for another day. For now, they needed to get moving.

"My strength has returned," Rune said, lifting one hand and watching as blue and red flames danced across his skin.

"I see that." Teresa moved off him and bent to pick up her clothes, but they were soaking wet and cold as ice. She really didn't want to put them back on.

Looking back at him, she asked, "You have this house ready for me. Any chance there are clothes here, too?"

He snapped his fingers and instantly he was clothed, in black jeans, a black T-shirt and boots that looked as though they could kick their way through hell without a problem. He smiled at her as he stood up.

"Nice for you," she said.

His fingers snapped again and she was suddenly dry and warm and dressed in the very clothes that had just a moment before been lying in a sodden heap on the floor. Even her favorite cowboy boots were dry and tucked securely on her feet. She couldn't help giving him a smile. "Now that's something I want to know how to do."

"You will," he assured her. "In time."

"Right." Time. It all boiled down to time. Her powers needed to be fully unleashed. She and Rune had to fulfill the Mating ritual. They had to find the Artifact that she had once hidden from the world. All they needed was time. Trouble was, the people chasing her were determined not to let them have it.

And just like that, they were back to the business at hand. "So what now? Where do we go?"

"You hold the answer to that question." He came close enough to lay his huge hands on her shoulders. "You've been having visions?"

"Yes," she admitted, staring up into his gray eyes, swirling with power and secrets as old as time. Teresa felt as if he was looking into her mind, though she didn't feel his presence in her thoughts. Was this new connection between them strong enough for him to sense what she was thinking and feeling?

If it was, then he would be able to see everything as she thought of what had been happening in her life the last three weeks. There were signs she might have missed if she hadn't been trained since childhood to be on the lookout for the magical world.

A black dog seemed to be outside her house day and night. Candles melted and the puddles of wax formed symbols that resonated with a part of her she didn't recognize. Ancient whorls and circles and symbols of eternity and rebirth. Storms had rolled into Sedona often enough that the TV weatherman was completely flummoxed by what was happening. He couldn't explain where the storms were coming from or why there were so many of them.

But she could.

The electrical energies were being drawn to her. To her power. Her growing strength and burgeoning magic.

Her dreams were haunted every night, too. Even now, the jumbled images came back to her in a flood. She didn't understand most of them. Cages built of fire, burning ferociously in what looked like a dark cave with ancient carvings on the walls. People she didn't know—two women with long red hair, smiling at her, and tall, powerful men like Rune, covered in flames—holding swords crossed over their chests as they took up protective postures.

In her dreams, she was chased by darkness. She could hear voices whispering behind her and footsteps that raced closer every night. Their pounding beat seemed to resonate within her for hours after she jolted awake, her heart in her throat.

Frowning, Teresa rubbed her forehead, closed her eyes and tried to focus. To sift through the memories choking her. There were more. Snippets of other lives that weren't her own. A woman who was her—and yet not—sitting beside a campfire as coyotes howled and the night sky blazed with stars rarely seen now because of city lights. She saw the woman chased into the desert, saw her running in terror. Saw her stumble and fall, and then a rockslide rattled down a mountainside to cover her body.

And she saw her grandmother's face. Her *abuela* had been in every dream. Every vision ended with those well-loved features smiling at her in encouragement. Whispering, "*Ahora*, Teresa, *ahora*."

Now, Teresa, now.

"Tell me," Rune said, the weight of his hands pressing ever more firmly on her shoulders. "Tell me what you see."

"My grandmother. I see my grandmother. We have to go to her in Chiapas. Mexico."

Chapter 11

E lena stepped outside, key in hand to lock the clinic
  door. It was still raining. Seemed like someone in
heaven had upended a bucket on Sedona.

That thought brought a smile despite the trickle of
icy water that sneaked beneath the collar of her jacket
to roll along her spine. She shivered at the sensation,
like a ghostly finger trailing along her skin—then she
whirled around to look over her shoulder. She had
creeped herself out. Not hard to understand why she
was on edge. She knew there were federal agents crawling all over Sedona at that very moment, looking for Teresa.

Still, she couldn't afford to appear nervous. Or suspi-
cious. If the people who were after Teresa were watching
the clinic, then Elena had to make it look as if nothing
was wrong. As if this was just an average day. Thankfully
no one was around to see the flash of temper on her
features as she quietly fumed.

How had the world come to this? she wondered.
Chasing down women because they were "different."
But she knew the answer as well as anyone else did.
Fear. The strongest motivator in the world. Fear could

turn ordinary people into a raging mob. The very people Elena served at her clinic would probably turn on her like a pack of rabid dogs if they knew her best friend was a witch.

So, to protect herself, she would do as Teresa had asked. She would pretend to loathe the woman she loved like a sister, but all the while she would pray to Whoever was listening that Teresa would survive those hunting her.

A skittering sound reached her and she instantly turned to glance up and down the street, searching the shadows. But she saw only rain and deserted shops and quiet homes.

"Get a grip, Elena," she muttered. "No one's out on a day like this. Just close up and go home."

"I don't think so."

The deep voice behind her startled her enough that she dropped her keys into the puddle at her feet. Suddenly terrified, she turned slowly and looked into a pair of pale gray eyes. "Who are you?"

The tall, impossibly gorgeous man gave her a slow once-over that made her feel as though she was standing there naked. Then he said, "We have to talk."

At that he scooped up her keys, took her arm and ushered her back into the darkened clinic.

Chapter 12

"We can't go until I get my bird."

"Your what?"

"My bird. It's a lorikeet and he's at my house. Alone. I can't leave him there to starve," Teresa told him, silently daring him to argue.

Rune swallowed back a sigh of frustration and fought for patience. "We don't have time to—"

"Nonnegotiable," she said, cutting him off. With her arms crossed over her chest, she met him glare for glare and just for a moment Rune wished that his witch was a timid little thing. Easily intimidated. Willing to take orders.

He laughed silently at the thought. Hell, he'd lived eons and had yet to meet *any* woman who met that description. And he would have been bored to tears with her if he had. This woman would never bore him, he knew. His witch remained hotheaded and stubborn. In every incarnation throughout the centuries, she had tormented him and taunted him. She had gone her own way and the devil take any who didn't approve.

Theirs had never been an easy path.

Rune looked at her now, his body healed and his

blood still humming from the incredible sex they had just shared, and he felt a flicker of anger jolt through him. She watched him and he could almost feel the animosity sizzling between them where passion had burned only moments before. How were they to accomplish what they must if neither of them could bend? But how was he supposed to release centuries of fury overnight?

In lifetime after lifetime, the years they had spent together had never been placid. Never calm and soothing. There had always been fire and ice between them, Teresa always determined to keep him at a distance and he continually battling his rage at her choices.

This was what he had been waiting for—the moment when her powers awoke and they could embrace their destiny. Though he was pleased to at last have the woman meant for him at his side, he didn't dare trust her to make the right choice this time, either.

Centuries of experience had taught him caution. He would commence the Mating. He would find the cursed Artifact that was at the center of their shared misery. But he wouldn't trust her. Wouldn't allow himself to be fooled again. Not when so much was at stake.

He shook his head. "It's not safe for you to return home."

"I know that. I want *you* to get Chico for me."

Her eyes were glittering with the light of battle. She expected him to refuse her and was already planning to fight him on the issue. If they couldn't even leave the bloody city in tune with each other, what were the odds that they could accomplish their quest?

"You can flame over there and be back here again before anyone even sees you," she pointed out.

Their eyes met and clashed, will to will. He might have argued against her wishes if he hadn't seen a quick flare of hope in her eyes. This was important to her—more so than she was ready to admit.

"We leave afterward. No arguments."

"None," she promised—too easily, Rune thought, but he would hold her to her word.

Was he being foolish, giving in to her desire to see her pet to safety? Possibly. But it was more expedient to do as she asked than to stand here arguing with her. He could, of course, simply grab her and flash her out of Sedona. But they were to be mates, this hardheaded woman and him. Was he really willing to begin their time together with a war that could readily be avoided?

Rune would do whatever he had to do to make sure his witch was safe and their quest successful.

"Fine," he muttered. "Wait here."

He called on the flames, let them sweep over him in a cascading, living blanket of blues and reds and yellows. He looked at her through the fire, then vanished.

Chapter 13

"She was here, yes?"

"Who?" There was only one person this man could have been interested in, but she wouldn't let him know she knew that.

He was so big, she thought wildly. He took up so much space that his very presence in the room with her felt like a direct threat. Just by breathing, he seemed to ooze menace, until Elena felt the cold chill of fear sliding into her bones.

Well over six feet tall, he had a thick, muscular build that would have made him popular on a football field. His hair was long, past his shoulders, and the color of new wheat. But it was his eyes that held her attention. Shades of pewter swirled in their depths as he stared at her, and for a moment she thought she saw flames licking at their centers.

When he smiled, it was a mere curve of his lips, as if he was mimicking something he'd seen once but didn't completely understand.

She had no idea who he was, but clearly he was after Teresa. Elena had never seen him before and his appearance minutes after her best friend left was a bit too coincidental. But if he was after Teresa, he wouldn't get any help from Elena. She would never betray her friend.

"Teresa Santiago," he said. "Where is she?"

Suspicions confirmed, Elena hid her fear behind a blank mask. "I have no idea."

"Is that right," the man mused, running one hand across the receptionist's desk.

Elena's breath caught as she noticed the trail of flames following in the wake of his hand's movement. "How—"

He shot her a look and those gray eyes of his went cold, dispassionate. Like a winter sky about to spit snow on unsuspecting people.

"You know how," he said, walking back to her, leaving behind him a line of flames that swept across the desk to devour the paperwork stacked there.

The crackle and hiss of the spreading fire shot ribbons of sheer panic through Elena. *Magic.* And not the Mother-Nature-protect-the-earth kind that Teresa had been born to wield. This was the kind of threatening power that had people terrified of the supernatural. And right at that moment Elena totally understood.

She was alone with someone who could set her on fire at his whim and she had no defense. But she was still safer than her friend. This man knew that Elena was no threat to him. If, on the other hand, he caught up to Teresa, there was no telling what he would do to her. So it was up to Elena to keep that from happening. *She* wasn't a witch. *She* wasn't in trouble with the MPs or the Bureau of Witchcraft. But she had the distinct feeling that this man had nothing to do with the feds.

He was clearly magical himself, so whatever his reason for looking for Teresa, it wasn't to lock her away in prison. There was something else going on here. Elena wondered if Teresa even knew that she had more to worry about than the federal agents assigned to track her down.

Once she got out of this, Elena promised herself, she'd find a way to warn Teresa about the newest danger. And she *would* get out of this. After all, she was a doctor, not a witch. This guy had no reason to hurt her. Neither did the feds. She was no threat to anyone. So all she had to do, she assured herself silently, was to be cooperative—within reason—and then he'd go away.

Please, God, let him go away.

Over the snap and hiss of the fire Elena whispered, "Who are you?"

Before answering, he touched her desk once more and the flames instantly died, snapping out as if they'd never been. She could almost have convinced herself she'd imagined everything—but for the charred pieces of paper and the curled edges of the manila folders. She swallowed hard and tried to find the courage she would need to stand against a man like this. And as that thought whispered through her mind, he turned his head and gave her that cold, empty smile again. As if he knew exactly what she was thinking—and found it amusing.

"Who am I?" he repeated, his voice a deep rumble. "Interesting question. One I've asked myself many times and I've yet to find the answer."

Great. Riddles.

"Seems simple enough to me," Elena said, sidling closer to the desk. If she could just tip the receiver slightly off its cradle and hit 911, she could get help. *Please, God*— she needed help. "You do have a name, don't you?"

"Don't all beings have names ... Elena?"

Her heart kicked into a gallop. Hearing her own

name on his lips was intimate. Terrifying. "So what's yours?"

"Why do you want to know, I wonder." He followed her slight movement across the room. "Could you be stalling? Trying to buy your friend time?"

"Friend?" She glanced around, anywhere but into his eyes. She quickly noted the everyday ordinariness of her clinic. The coloring books scattered across a child-sized table. The baby bottle someone had left behind. The candy-coated air, now smeared with the lingering traces of burned paper.

"Teresa Santiago," he said and all trace of amusement was gone from his features. "Where is she, Elena?"

She stopped. Only a foot or two from the desk and she stopped dead, sensing the danger suddenly erupting between her and the man with the pale storm-colored eyes. She felt the coiled tension vibrating off him and shared it. Her mouth was dry, her palms were damp and panic was scraping at her throat. Still, she found the courage to look right at him and lie. "I don't know."

He sighed and clucked his tongue at her. "You're lying."

"No." She shook her head for emphasis and prayed he would believe her. "I haven't seen Teresa in—"

"Hours?" He finished for her, taking a step closer. "Minutes?"

"No. Weeks." She told the lie and lifted her chin as if to convince both of them that she was giving him nothing but the truth. "She's a witch, you know—"

"Yes," he said softly. "I know."

"Well, when I found out what she was, I tried to turn her in, but she, *um*—" Elena took another half step toward the desk, hoping he would put her movement down to nervous confusion. "She *threatened* me," Elena said, hoping to hell that she was putting just enough surprise in her tone.

"Did she?" He walked toward her and before she could blink, he had his hand on the phone and was shaking his head. "No phone calls, Elena. We're not through talking yet."

Disappointment welled up inside her. She'd been so close to calling for help. And now . . .

"What do you want from me?" she managed to ask. Her abject fear must have been written on her features, because he shook his head again.

"I'm not a rapist, so have no fears there."

One fear down, about a hundred to go, Elena thought wildly. "I can't help you," she said, her voice low, words tumbling over each other in her haste to get him out of her world. "I don't know where Teresa is."

"I know she was here." He reached out to stroke the tips of his fingers along her jawline.

Elena shuddered, half expecting to feel the burning sting of fire on her skin. But his touch was cold. As cold as his eyes.

"I can feel the lingering trace of her magic," he told her, "so there's no sense lying to me."

Oh, God. She swallowed hard and fought to keep her voice steady as she asked again, "Who are you?"

"My name," he said, "is Parnell. And all you need to know is that I'm looking for Teresa. You can either help me and live to tell the tale, or . . ."

He didn't have to finish the threat. Heck, leaving it unsaid did far more internal damage. Elena's mind took over the challenge and filled in that unfinished sentence with any number of horrifying possibilities. And she had no way to defend herself against any of them. She was at his mercy and judging by the cool dispassion in those gray eyes, mercy was not something Parnell was very familiar with.

"Parnell," she said, using his name deliberately, to forge some bare-bones connection with him. To force him to see her as a person and not just an impediment to what he wanted. "I don't know what you think I know, but I can assure you—"

He smiled. "Another lie. I can smell them on you, you know. Your blood chemistry changes. Humans are very . . . predictable in their responses."

"Humans?" Fear ratcheted up inside her. Just when she had thought she was as panicked as it was possible to be and still live, she found out there was more.

Yes, she knew he had magical abilities. But so did Teresa and she was human. How could he *not* be? What was he? If he wasn't human, what exactly was she dealing with and how in the hell was she going to survive? "You're not—"

"No, I'm not. Haven't you already noticed that I'm something a little more than your average male?"

Yes, she had. The trail of fire across her desk had given her that much information. But what was he? Witches were women. Were there other forms of supernatural beings out there that the world hadn't discovered yet? Well, why not? If witchcraft was alive and well, why not a man made of fire?

"Ah," he said, watching her. "I see that I've made my point. Maybe you're ready to be more cooperative now?"

"Yes." She set her purse down on the nearby desk and reminded herself to breathe. "What do you want to know?"

"Where did Teresa go?"

"I really don't know," she told him and waited for his

super-sensitive nose to pick up on the fact that she was telling the absolute truth.

Parnell smiled and nodded. "Very good. Keep being honest with me and we'll get along just fine, Elena."

A rising tide of panic lifted from the pit of her stomach to sweep through her body. That was all the information she had to give him. She couldn't tell him anything else even if she wanted to. So why was he still here? What more could he want from her?

"But I've just told you. I don't know where Teresa went."

"Yes, but you do know the witch," he mused and closed the distance between them in the span of a single heartbeat. "I'm sure if you really search your mind, you'll be able to give me lots of details about Teresa's life. Where she might go. Who she might trust."

Elena's breath caught in her throat as his big hands came down on her upper arms and he lifted her up until she was balanced on her toes, trying to keep her feet.

"Now," he said, locking his gaze with hers, "we're going to have a long talk, you and I."

Elena swallowed hard and tried to look away. But that pale gray gaze was now swirling like liquid silver, glittering with power and secrets, and it held her as if she were a rabbit staring down a cobra.

"I have no wish to torture you," he said.

Good. That's good.

"But make no mistake," he promised as his eyes glowed with a hot brightness that shone like the porch light to hell, "I will. To get what I want, I will do whatever's necessary."

Helpless, Elena did the only thing left to her.

She prayed.

Chapter 14

Rune drew on the fire and flashed himself to the interior of Teresa's house. The moment he appeared, he *sensed* the imminent danger. There were hunters nearby. Probably watching this house and if they were, then he knew they had seen his arrival. He had only moments before an attack came.

Not that he was worried about his own survival. Yes, white gold could bring him down, but he was still a true immortal. The only thing that would kill him was decapitation. And even then, he doubted that his god, Belen, would allow him to die permanently. At least, not until their task was complete and Belen's lover, Danu, was satisfied that her witches had at last corrected the hideous wrong committed so long ago.

He glanced around the small room with its comfortable but worn furnishings and he felt Teresa's essence here. This was where she lived and dreamed and laughed. There was a sense of warmth to the tiny house that told him this was her safe place. The one spot in the world where she felt most comfortable. Her home. And she would probably never see it again.

Dismissing his wandering thoughts, Rune focused his

attention on the damn bird Teresa refused to live without. He would have spotted it instantly even if it hadn't whistled sharply at his sudden arrival.

It looked like a miniature parrot. Sapphire blue head, dark orange beak curved downward, brilliant green ring of color around its neck and spilling down its back. Bright yellow and orange colored its narrow chest and its beady eyes were locked onto Rune as it squawked the same phrase over and over. It took him a minute to understand the bird's attempt at language, but when he did he almost smiled.

Teresa had trained the bird to shout a warning. Over and over again, the pretty rat with wings shrieked, *"Run for it!"*

Amusement aside, Rune gritted his teeth. He'd never liked birds. Probably went back to the Middle Ages, when hawks were kept and trained by noblemen. One of his fellow Eternals, Odell, had kept the damn things and one of the feathered bastards had clawed Rune's face open one fine day.

Later that night, the hawk had made a tasty stew.

Since then, Rune had hated birds. Especially so called "tame" ones. Treacherous creatures.

"Be grateful I'm not roasting you for a snack, you wretched bag of fluff."

The bird screeched again.

"Run for it!"

He was going to regret this—he could already feel it. But there was no hope for it now. Sweeping one hand out, he captured the damn bird before it could take flight off its perch. "It's your lucky day," he told it in a whisper. "Don't push me."

Rune heard the hunters before he saw them. They hit

the front door with a crash and came spilling into Teresa's tiny home like water from a fire hose. Guns lifted. Men shouted. Rune laughed.

Then he called on the fire and disappeared as white-gold bullets shredded the air where he had just been.

Chapter 15

"Chico!"

The ridiculous bird flew right to Teresa, perched on her shoulder and bobbed up and down like it was doing a victory dance. Then it turned to give Rune the evil eye. While it shook itself, ruffling its brilliant feathers, Rune spoke up.

"You've got the bird. Now we get out of here."

"Right," she said with a nod. "Just one more stop to make before we go."

"Are you insane? There were hunters at your house. Waiting for you. You've already fought one and the others have found him by now. We need to leave."

Gently stroking her bird's back, Teresa paled a little, but even as he noted that, Rune saw a spark of defiance shine in her eyes. "Not until we make sure Elena's safe. She gave me the things I needed to help you and I probably took the feds right to her door."

He understood loyalty. Respected it. And in other circumstances would have admired seeing that trait in his witch. But now was not the time.

"If you did, there's no help for it now," he said.

"Your friend knew what she was doing. She chose to help."

"And now I'm *choosing* to do the same." Teresa took a step toward him, the stupid bird still bobbing and weaving on her shoulder. Her gaze was fixed on him and her features were set in a blank mask that revealed nothing of what she was feeling. "I know I said I'd leave after you got Chico, and I'm sorry about that. But I have to make sure Elena's all right. You can either come with me or wait here or, hell, I don't know . . . go ahead to Mexico and I'll meet you there."

"Not going to happen."

"Which?"

"Any." He watched her closely and saw her loyalty warring with her innate sense of duty. Just as she had done so many years ago, Rune noted, she was forcing a choice on herself. Back then it had been simple. Side with Rune—do her duty as she knew it to be—or throw in her lot with the coven and her sister witches in their quest for power and knowledge.

Rune had trusted her then. He had believed that they were one in heart and mind. But she'd betrayed herself, him and everything she had ever believed in.

"You expect me to trust you?" he said, the deep rumble of his voice rolling out around her.

"Yeah," she said. "Why wouldn't you?"

"Because I trusted you once. And you betrayed me."

"What? I—"

Suddenly he didn't care about the feds. Or the need to get out of Sedona. He wanted Teresa to remember. To grab hold of the past and understand who and what she was. And he had no time to wait for all of her memories to return on their own.

He seized her shoulders, his huge hands gripping tightly. His gray eyes bored into hers, delving into her mind, reaching for the past that had been buried for too long. "Think, Teresa. Remember."

She staggered a little under his touch, but her eyes were awash with the flashing shifts of emotion. He felt her tremble as ancient memories were awoken.

"Oh, God," she said softly. "It was us. The coven. We did a spell with the Artifact. We wanted to open the portals to other dimensions. To gather more power. More knowledge."

"Yes," he said, maintaining his hold on her shoulders.

She blinked as a sheen of tears filled her eyes. "The spell went wrong. We . . ." She shook her head and he knew the memory wasn't clear enough for her yet, so he told her the rest of it.

"You opened the gate to hell. Demons poured out of the opening you carved. The Eternals fought back, but couldn't reach you. You were all in a protected circle; you had shut yourselves off from us. We could only watch and fight."

"We did this," she whispered brokenly. "All of it. The spell. The evil in the world. The Awakening. It's all because of what we did that night."

"Yes."

She blew out a breath and wiped one hand across her face, as if she were trying to reconcile herself to this new information. He knew it would take time. He knew she didn't have all of her memories yet and when they returned it wouldn't be easy for her to deal with them.

Belen knew, Rune had had eight hundred years to reconcile himself to the past and still it ate at him. So he wouldn't blindly trust her to do the right thing. Neither of them could afford mistakes this time around, though,

and if that meant he had to protect her from herself—
from misplaced loyalties—then that's just what he
would do.

"I still need to check on Elena," she told him. "And I
need your help to do it."

"Your friend means nothing to this quest," he said,
though the words sounded brutally cold even to him.

"She means something to me," Teresa told him flatly.
"And I swear to God, if you flash me out of here against
my will—"

"You'll do what exactly?" he demanded. "Turn your
back on your duty? Again?"

"Don't do that," she snapped. "Don't compare me to
that foolish woman from so long ago. I'm not her. I'm
Teresa Santiago and I'm damn well going to do what I
think is right whether you agree or not."

When he only scowled at her, she continued.

"Look," she said, reaching out to lay one small hand
on his chest, "I know we have to go. I can feel it, too. But
I can't go not knowing if Elena is safe. She's family to
me and I don't have many people I care for. Give me
that and I'll go."

He couldn't believe that once again he would be
swayed by the very witch who had made his eternity a
misery so far. He was an Eternal. Drawn from the belly
of the sun. He bowed to no one, human or demon.

And yet . . . The feel of her hand on his chest. The
sound of her soft breaths. The trusting gleam in her
eyes. And oh, Belen, the scent of her—earth and sky
and woman. All witches smelled of the earth magic that
bubbled through their veins, but each witch carried a
singular blend of that scent, too. Something that made
her unique. Something that tantalized her mate and
made him consider foolish things.

She was tall, yet beside him she seemed so much smaller and vulnerable. The unbeating heart in his chest clenched with need and he wondered why he was going to allow her what she needed despite knowing that it would be a stupid move.

Because, a voice in his mind whispered, *your body hungers for her. Your heart aches for her. Despite everything. Despite the years, the betrayal, the loneliness—she is yours.*

All true, he told himself. But that didn't mean he would ever trust her. Not this time. Not when the fate of the world hung in the balance.

"I take you to her and then we leave."

She blew out a breath and gave him a fast smile that swept across her features and was gone in an instant. "Agreed."

"Fine," he muttered, reaching out to grab her and pull her in close to his body. He ignored the bird's outraged squawk, focused on the feel of Teresa's body aligned with his, then called on the fire and vanished.

Chapter 16

"Missed him. Damn it, you missed him." Landry Harper's right hand curled into a fist and it was all he could do to keep from smashing it into College Boy's face. The bastard had had one job. Sniper. All he'd had to do was shoot whoever showed up at Santiago's house.

But the sight of a man appearing within a pillar of flames had thrown him for a couple of stinking seconds and the shot went wild. Now God knew where the bastard and the witch were.

"Get off my ass," the kid argued, embarrassment warring with anger in his tone.

"How the hell could you miss him?" Landry demanded, still considering throwing that punch. His entire body vibrated with frustration and fury. This is what happened when the higher-ups recruited out of college instead of the military. Give Landry a good old-fashioned foot soldier who knew how to take orders and he could get the job done any day.

"That fucker had to be six foot five. Made a hell of a target."

"Yeah and he was on fire, all right?" the kid muttered,

wiping one hand across his face as if he could dislodge the memory. "Shocked the hell out of me, okay? How did he do that? What the hell was that?"

Landry didn't have a clue how to explain the man who'd appeared to be on fire. But he knew that only a month ago, two beings just like him had raided the prison on Terminal Island. They had killed several guards and rescued a couple of witches. So in his book the Fire Man was the enemy, plain and simple. And there was only one way to treat the enemy.

Shoot first—ask no questions.

Ever.

"Doesn't matter what he was or how he does it," Landry told him with a sneer. "Your job was to kill him and now we're up shit creek without the proverbial damn boat *or* paddle."

The witch's house was shot to shit and though they'd searched it thoroughly, they hadn't found anything to lead them to her. The Fire Man had appeared, taken her bird and disappeared in the time it took to think that sentence. So now there was nothing for them here. Landry knew the witch was long gone. They had no chance of finding her in Sedona.

It meant the hunt had to be turned over to the Bureau of Witchcraft. BOW's agents would eventually run her to ground. For him and the rest of the MPs, though, this one had been a gigantic waste of time. They would report to their superiors and get the next assignment.

But Landry knew he wouldn't forget the witch. She would forever haunt him as one of those who had escaped him. The memories of failed missions made for some long, sleepless nights and a hell of a lot of rage.

He left the house with the college kid and walked into the stormy weather. Glancing around the quiet street, he watched as neighbors pulled back drapes and peered out into the driving rain. A silencer had muffled the report of the high-powered rifle, but Landry and the other agents had made a hell of a noise when they broke into the witch's house. Naturally, they'd attracted attention from the neighbors.

The people in the tidy houses on this narrow street would sneak peeks from behind closed doors, but they wouldn't come out. No one interfered in a witch hunt. Well, no one except the maniacs in the RFW. The organization Rights for Witches was starting to pick up steam here lately since the daughter of the damn president had joined it. They were getting all kinds of media, and despite the fear that lingered over the very idea of witchcraft, there were now enough bleeding hearts starting to speak up that a man never knew when he'd run into a crazed government protestor. What the hell the world was coming to when a man couldn't kill a damn witch to protect society, he had no idea.

Landry almost hoped for a confrontation with one of the neighbors. It would give him something to do with the anger pumping through him. But as the minutes passed and the street remained quiet, he knew he was doomed to disappointment.

"What now?"

He looked at the younger man beside him. "Now we go back to HQ, report the fuckup and get our next assignment."

College Boy swiveled his head around, as if searching for the very witch they'd already lost. "You mean we just *leave*? We don't try to hunt her down?"

"We leave," Landry said, narrowing his gaze against the darkness and the rain. "This one's out of our reach. Nothing to do about it."

"But—"

For the first time, Landry almost felt a kinship to the kid. He was young, but he was eager to kill witches, so that said something for him, anyway. Turning up the collar of his black and gold MP jacket against the rain, he shrugged. "First thing you gotta remember in this game, kid, is that there's *always* another witch."

Chapter 17

The smell stopped them cold.

Teresa gagged and turned her face into Rune's broad chest. Chico flew from her shoulder to swoop down the hall toward the front of the clinic, but Teresa hardly noticed. She was too busy trying to catch her breath. The stench clinging to the still air of the clinic was overpowering. Rune's arms came around her and for one brief second she allowed herself to lean into him.

She was so accustomed to standing on her own that it went against her very nature to take comfort from someone else. To depend on someone else's strength. But at the same time, being this close to Rune felt . . . familiar in a way that she'd never known before. His body was big, but it felt as though it had been made to fit against hers. And as he held her head to his chest, her own body stirred, despite the situation.

"What is that?" she asked finally, her voice muffled by his body.

He gave her a hard, brief squeeze, then set her back from him. His eyes were narrowed and swirling with energy and power until they looked like two pools of molten silver.

"I'll find out. Stay here." He set off down the hall toward the front of the clinic with long strides.

As if from a distance, she heard Chico's piercing whistle followed by his screech of *"Run for it!"*

"Like hell," she said, following right behind him. "You might as well know right now that I'm not the kind of girl to stay hidden, hoping a big, strong man will come along to save me."

Her bootheels clicked on the linoleum floor, but the sound was almost lost under the *clomp* of Rune's heavier steps.

"Teresa," he said, half turning to glower at her, "you don't want to go in there."

From inside the room, Chico continued to squawk *"Run for it!"* over and over again until her head pounded in time with the bird's voice.

Teresa pushed past Rune and saw—

"Oh, my God. Elena."

She dropped to her knees beside the charred body of her friend. Anguish flooded her and tears spilled from her eyes, her grief shaking her to her soul. Instinctively, she reached out to take Elena's hand in hers but stopped before touching her.

Elena.

A howl rose up inside her, but her throat wouldn't let it escape. There was a huge knot of pain blocking its passage and Teresa knew that this pain would always be with her. She stared down at the body of her friend and wanted more than anything to scream a denial to the universe.

Elena's left side was charred, the skin blackened and peeling. Her right hand was broken, covered in blood, and her arm bent at an impossible angle. But it was her eyes—open, glassy, frozen in pain and horror—that tore Teresa's soul in two.

"Oh, my God. Elena." This time she tenderly lifted her friend's broken right hand and cupped it in both of hers. Elena's skin was still warm. Hope leaped up inside Teresa. Blind, desperate hope. "She's not dead. Not dead. Oh, God. God, she's hurt bad." Her words streamed from her in a never-ending flow of horror. Turning teary eyes frantically to her Eternal, Teresa begged, "Please. Help her. You can heal her. *We* can heal her."

Chapter 18

Rune looked at the body of the doctor and through his pity he felt a sharp stab of worry. One side of her body was burned. The injury was too deliberate. Too . . . perfect. His rage inflamed him as he realized that there was really only one possible explanation for what had happened here.

Teresa hadn't drawn the same conclusion he had and he wouldn't tell her his suspicion. But Rune knew that only an Eternal could have done this kind of damage so precisely.

Could one of his brothers have gone rogue?

Fury pumped raw and fierce throughout his huge body as he considered it, then denied it again immediately. He refused to believe that one of them was capable of such things.

And yet . . .

He locked his misgivings away for now. He would contact Torin as soon as there was an opportunity and talk about this. But at the moment, his witch needed him—and didn't need more to worry about.

This Teresa was a revelation to him. In the last couple of hours, he had seen only the warrior side of his woman.

Fierce, furious, ready to charge the doors of hell itself with no more than a glass of water with which to defend herself against the roaring flames. She had defied him, cursed him, made love with him, healed him and infuriated him.

Now, she had touched him more deeply than he would have thought possible. In her vulnerability, he saw the witch of his heart. His mate. The woman he would do anything for. The woman he would kill to possess. And he wished with all of his soul that he could somehow grant her the miracle she needed so desperately.

"Teresa . . ." He didn't know much about the other dimensions beyond this one. His knowledge was based on centuries of existence. Of seeing countless millions of humans live, love and finally die. He knew of shades, the spiritual essence of those who refused to move on to the next life, instead clinging steadfastly to the one that was over. But Elena was not one of those. She would not be a ghost of herself, futilely trying to speak to the ones she had left behind.

She had moved on already.

"She's gone, Teresa," he said, his voice as gentle as it could be when dealing a shattering blow.

They had to leave. Her friend had been killed as a message to Teresa. Rune's gaze snapped to the wide windows overlooking the narrow rain-drenched street beyond the glass. Somewhere out there, agents—hunters—were tracking her. Planning on locking her away or doing to her what had been done to this harmless woman.

His guts churning with a boiling cauldron of fury and the need for retribution, Rune deliberately kept his voice calm as he said, "We have to go. Now."

At that moment, her bird flew down from the overhead light fixture to land on her shoulder. Rune couldn't even seem to mind. It was as if the little creature sensed that its owner needed comfort.

Seconds ticked past until at last Teresa laid Elena's hand down with a final stroke of her fingertips. Then she turned to Rune. The shock and pain still shone in those chocolate-brown eyes of hers, but the tears were drying and a flicker of anger rose up. "I want to find them. I want to hurt them like they hurt her."

"I know." Rune pulled her to her feet and she went, reluctantly. Pushing his fingers through her hair at her temple, he cradled her head in his palm. "And I feel the same. Your friend didn't deserve this. The bastards who did it will pay, Teresa."

She nodded, lifting her face to meet his. Fascinated, Rune watched her expression shift and change with the fleeting emotions that were charging through her. Misery, despair, hope and determination all showed themselves briefly on her features. And his admiration for her rose higher as she put her pain aside.

"We'll go to Mexico. See my grandmother. We're going to do what we have to do and then I'm going to find who did this to Elena and make them wish they'd never been born."

"*We* will find them," he corrected her.

She studied him for a heartbeat or two, then nodded again. "Yes, Rune. *We.*"

He pulled her in close and wrapped his arms around her.

When she whispered, "Take me away from here," he called on the flames and granted her wish.

Chapter 19

On the other side of the country, President Cora Sterling, first female president of the United States, was having afternoon tea with a group of would-be radicals. As her thoughts wandered, she smiled to herself and wondered if Nixon had felt as out of place when he met with Elvis Presley at the White House. Of course, she thought, all Elvis had wanted was a badge from the Bureau of Narcotics and Dangerous Drugs. Naturally enough, the director of the BNDD had refused Elvis's request. But half an hour later, President Nixon had presented Elvis Presley with the badge himself.

Ironic, she mused, that Elvis had wanted to do his part in fighting the drug culture, only to die as a result of his own excesses seven years later. Still, Nixon had made an important step in meeting the popular singer: The nation had taken note and for one brief moment, the wildly disliked president had looked almost . . . cool.

Cora Sterling was in a different boat altogether. Her approval ratings were skyrocketing every day. Yet it wouldn't hurt for the media to know that she was taking the time to meet with people hungering for change.

Glancing around the small, elegantly set table, she

glanced from one eager young face to the next before finally settling on just one. Her own daughter, Deidre Sterling, was now the public face of RFW. Rights for Witches had been growing in popularity for the last several months, but it wasn't until Deidre signed on that the group had attained any sort of credibility.

Before Deidre, RFW was dismissed as deluded rabble. Foolish people who refused to see the inherent dangers of witchcraft. They were mocked on cable news shows, and social networking pages were continuously throwing verbal stones. But Deidre had changed all that.

Cora looked at her daughter and felt that stir of pride she always experienced around her girl. At twenty-seven, Deidre had a mind of her own and a spine of steel, just like her mother. Which, Cora admitted silently, didn't always make her easy to deal with.

"Madam President." One of the young women spoke up and Cora turned a pleasant smile toward her. The slim brunette's cheeks flushed a bright pink and she opened and closed her mouth a few times, as if she was suddenly too nervous to speak.

Cora waited, since her long-held belief insisted that *He who speaks first, loses.*

"Mom," Deidre said into the stiff silence, "we appreciate you meeting with us. We know how busy you are."

Cora gave her daughter a smile, reached out and patted her hand, then turned back to the brunette. "Of course I'm happy to meet with bright young people filled with ideas."

A couple of the women exchanged sharp looks as if trying to figure out whether or not they were being patronized. But finally, after having found her courage, the brunette spoke up again.

"Madam President, the RFW is determined to shut down the prison camps where women—"

"Internment centers, not prison camps," Cora corrected and the brunette stiffened, but nodded.

"Fine. These 'camps' are dangerous." Her brow furrowed and her eyes took on the glittering light of the true believer. "Men prey on the inmates and innocent women are being swept up in raids when they've done nothing to deserve it."

Cora didn't care for the woman's attitude, but she really couldn't help but admire her spunk.

"I'm sure you all mean well, and I really do respect the fact that you're all so impatient to change the world," Cora started to say.

"Impatient?" The brunette—what was her name? Ah, yes. Susan Baker—interrupted her. Cora frowned, but it didn't keep the woman from continuing. "It's been ten years since magic was revealed to the world and in that time the prejudice and hatred have only grown. If we're not 'impatient,' more people will die."

One of Cora's eyebrows winged up. She wasn't accustomed to being taken to task. And certainly not in her own parlor. As if picking up on her ire, one of the Secret Service agents stationed around the room moved closer. Cora gave him a slight shake of her head to let him know she was fine and could handle one overwrought young woman herself.

"I understand your passion," she said, looking at the woman with the steady gaze that had gained her seventy percent of the popular vote in the last election. "In fact, I applaud it. But you must understand that change takes time. And effort."

"We do, but—"

"Mom."

She shifted her focus to Deidre, expecting common sense and support. She got neither.

Instead, her daughter said, "When you were elected you pledged to close the camps. It's been two years and they've only expanded. All we're asking you to do is to keep the promise you made."

Cora stiffened. She didn't like being corrected. Arguing with Deidre in the privacy of the family quarters, when it was just the two of them, was one thing. But showing a mutinous streak in front of strangers was not acceptable.

"Everything takes time, Deidre. You know that."

She didn't give an inch. Cora wasn't sure whether to be proud or angry when Deidre countered, "But every day that goes by, women are dying."

"Nonsense," Cora said, waving one perfectly manicured hand to dismiss the notion, all the while making a mental note to take this conversation up with her daughter at a later date. For now, she simply said, "We're not barbarians. This is a nation of laws, Deidre. All of our citizens have rights. Have you forgotten?"

Her daughter clammed up at last, but there was still an insubordinate gleam in her eyes.

A chubby redhead with a face full of freckles spoke up then, demanding Cora's attention. All at once she felt as though she was sitting before a congressional hearing. She resented being treated in such a manner when she'd gone out of her way in agreeing to this meeting in the first place. Cora forced a smile as she faced the redhead.

"It's not nonsense, Madam President. I'm from Wyoming and last week five women were killed in a camp outside Cheyenne."

"I read about that accident." In fact, Cora had received a complete briefing on the facts only yesterday. "Terrible. Just terrible. I understand there was a fire?"

"It was arson," the redhead claimed.

"That's a serious charge, young lady," Cora said. At the rebuke, she saw the woman stiffen in insult. Well, she was young. As to whether she was a lady, Cora was less and less convinced of that fact as the meeting went on.

"Do you have proof of your accusation?" she asked, all business now. "My aides have been in contact with the warden and according to him, there was an accidental fire in the laundry area."

"Was it accidental that the door was locked from the outside and the women had no chance of escape?"

Cora frowned and tapped her fingernails against the arm of the Louis XVI chair she sat in. She hadn't heard about locked doors. Was it possible the warden had been less than forthcoming? "I'll certainly look into the matter at once. These camps operate under a federal umbrella and as such are subject to the government's oversight. If you're correct, we'll take action."

"Don't you get it, Mom?" Deidre asked quietly. "There *is* no oversight. These prisons are death traps. You swore you'd shut them down and—"

"Deidre," Cora said, her voice icy, "I'm doing all I can—"

"It's not enough," the brunette said. "I'm sorry, Madam President, but if the government can't take care of things, the people will."

"Is that some sort of threat?" Cora asked, again waving away her ever-present Secret Service agent.

"Of course not." Deidre spoke up quickly, shooting her friend a hard look. "But, Mother, women are dying and we can't stand by and watch."

Cora nodded. "I understand your impatience. I assure you, I will have this matter looked into at the highest level."

Deidre gave her a broad, approving smile, but the other women didn't look as pleased. Well, young and eager was good, but they also had to learn that the wheels of justice turned slowly enough that sometimes it seemed as though they were rolling backward.

Of course, Cora thought as she poured more tea, how things looked and how they actually were were often two very different things.

Chapter 20

Teresa's heart and mind were shattered. She clung to Rune, the last stable point in her universe. She watched through slitted eyes as he called on the flames and swept them out of Sedona and into unfamiliar territory. Again and again, in a series of long jumps. But to Teresa, one stop was much like the other.

For two days they traveled, stopping only long enough to eat and sleep. They rested in the desert for a few hours the first night and then were on the move again early the next morning. When they were hungry, Rune would leave her somewhere safe, flash into a grocery store and help himself to the food they needed.

Teresa had never been much of a camper and this frenzied trip across Arizona and the border area wasn't changing her mind on the subject. But Rune didn't want to head directly to Chiapas. He felt that if they were being followed, it was worth the extra time it would take to throw the hunters off their trail first.

And so it went. On and on. Teresa was exhausted, but she couldn't complain, since he was going to so much trouble to keep her safe. But it was more than being tired. Her heart hurt. She had been prepared for this madness—at least as much as she could have prepared. But her destiny had cost her friend her *life.*

Regret would be with her for the rest of her own life—whether that was a week or eternity.

Clinging to Rune's broad shoulders, Teresa became numb to what was happening around her. A sudden stop, the fires that covered Rune would snap off and then come to life again before his blurring speed sent them back on the run. Again and again, he continued on, long into the night until blackness and fire were all she could see.

That made sense to her. Her soul was dark now, too, with the flames of rage burning at its center. Always she had prepared for this day, for her witchcraft to materialize and for her Eternal to show himself. But she had never expected to gain and lose so much all at the same time.

Rune stopped again and the fire surrounding them died away. This time, though, he didn't flash them forward; he stayed perfectly still, holding her in the circle of his arms. They must be stopping for the night again and she was grateful for the reprieve.

She took comfort from his touch, so she forced herself to step back and away from him. He released her, as if he knew that she needed some space. For an immortal warrior, he was proving to be surprisingly understanding. If only he didn't look at her with eyes that accused her of crimes she couldn't even remember committing.

The moment he let her go, Teresa missed his warmth, his strength, but she had to stand on her own two feet. Regain her inner power. Soon the Mating ritual would begin and to face Rune as an equal, she had to find balance. She must become the witch she was destined to be. So she had to be strong in her own right.

Looking around, she couldn't see anything beyond the star-filled sky overhead and the inky darkness of the desert. "Where are we?"

"Just across the border. We're in Mexico."

Chico lifted off her shoulder and flew in circles above their heads, as if the tiny bird had needed a break, too. She watched him for a second, then nodded to Rune and pulled in a deep breath. Grateful to be away from Sedona, she said, "Good. That's good. How far from Chiapas?"

"Far enough," he told her. "For now, anyway. There's a village ahead." He pointed and Teresa shifted her gaze in that direction. All she saw was a smudge of pale light in the utter darkness ahead of them.

"We're staying there?" Surprise colored her voice because for the last two days he'd deliberately kept her away from people.

"No," he told her. "We'll get some supplies, then head back into the desert. We'll continue on after we've rested."

Sleeping in the desert wasn't something she could look forward to, Teresa thought, her mind filling with images of snakes and tarantulas and God knew what else. At least last night she hadn't actually had to sleep on the sun-baked sand. Instead, Rune had found an abandoned shack for them to rest in.

She looked around again and realized there were no shacks out here. Then she turned her head and looked toward the distant village. There would be people there—so it would be dangerous. She could hope that word of what had happened in Sedona hadn't traveled this far south already. But the reality was that the MPs were probably on their trail and who knew how far their reach extended.

Rune started walking, his long, easy strides forcing her to run to keep up with him. Her boots kicked at dirt and sand, and she had to fight past the fatigue clawing at her. She hadn't slept well last night. Her dreams were haunted not only by her own past but also by images of what her enemies had done to Elena. All she really wanted, Teresa thought, was to find some safe, quiet corner where she could curl up and whimper.

Which sounded so damn cowardly, it made her shudder. In response to that stray wienerlike thought, she straightened her shoulders and lifted her chin.

She looked toward the few lights shining in the desert blackness. "Should be safe enough there, right? I mean, the feds are looking for us in Sedona."

"True. We should have some time before the hunt goes international."

"I need to get some candles, too, if we can find some," she said.

He glanced at her. "For what?"

"Candle magic. I need my memories, right?"

His eyes shuttered as he turned his head forward again. "Yes."

"There's that look again," she muttered, then spoke up louder. "Tell me more, Rune. About that night. The night everything went to hell."

"You should remember on your own."

"And in a perfect world, sure." Teresa reached out to grab his arm and he stopped dead. When he was looking at her, she said, "You already prodded me once. I need the memories. You told me yourself. So help me."

He scowled. "There's not much more to tell."

"Then it shouldn't take long," she argued.

He spoke then and as his voice wove a spell of words

around her, images filled Teresa's mind and the long-dead past came vibrantly to life.

Teresa felt the swell of power surrounding her and her sisters. The moonlight was bright, shining down from a star-studded black sky. A banefire, built on the bones of slaughtered animals, burned brightly in the center of their circle. The Eternals stood just beyond the ring of power, each of them formidable in his disapproval. Each of them trying to fight past the strength of the magic used to keep him out.

Teresa looked at her own Eternal. The immortal man who came to her bed every night and showed her bliss. His features were twisted as he shouted, trying to make himself heard above the cacophony of sound that seemed to shriek from the very air.

She loved him. A part of her always would. She had promised him that she wouldn't join the coven tonight. That she would go away with him. But the lure of power was stronger even than her love. Besides, how could she turn away from the women who were like her own blood? She stood with her sisters and called on the gods to hear them. They focused their combined magics on the Artifact before them and in the wildly flickering light demanded the knowledge of the ages. Demanded that doors closed to mankind would open to them.

Doors to other dimensions. Other worlds open to new possibilities.

She saw it all. Lived it all. She tasted the excitement of magic in the air and swallowed the bitter dregs of regret as a door finally opened and the first of the demons rushed through.

Chaos reigned.

The Eternals fought valiantly. The coven strove to undo the harm they had done. But the screams of the dead and dying were all-consuming.

The coven's wards failed under the onslaught of so much dark energy. Demons and Eternals alike entered the sacred circle and destroyed it. Her sisters were dying all around her. Teresa shuddered under the hideous onslaught of memory. She watched herself as she had once been, struggling to close the gate to hell. But despite her efforts, there were demons who escaped into this world before the gate swung shut. And she saw the fury on the face of the immortal who loved her.

"Oh, my God." She looked up at him, struggling for air. Her lungs were constricted, as if she was still breathing in that awful fire.

"You saw."

"I did," she said, nodding as she looked up into his eyes. "We let demons loose into this world."

"Most of them were hunted down that night," he told her. "My brothers and I saw to that. But yes. A few remained." He swept his gaze across the dark desert, as if expecting for one of the demons to materialize in front of him. "And the doorway you closed wasn't sealed that night. Not completely. Dark energy still spills through the portal. That is why we have to find the Artifact. We have to undo what you and your sisters did."

"And my memories will tell me where the Artifact is?"

"Your piece of it, yes," he said. "After the battle, the coven shattered the Artifact—each of you taking away one piece and hiding it somewhere in the world."

"That narrows it down."

He frowned at her and Teresa said, "Sorry. Sorry. What else?"

"A spell of atonement was cast. The coven would give up their powers for eight hundred years. At the end of that time, the Awakening would come. And you would gather to put right what went so wrong."

"So you've been waiting . . ."

"A *very* long time," he said.

"And the Mating ritual will help open my memories?"

"Yes."

"We weren't mated then, were we?"

"No," he said, starting to walk again. "None of the witches wanted to share power. You all kept us at a distance."

His tone told her that he still hadn't forgiven her that betrayal.

"Well, no more distance, Rune. We have to start the Mating ritual soon. For everybody's sake."

He shot her a look as she hurried to keep up with him and when his gaze landed on her, nerves fluttered in the pit of her stomach.

An inner voice laughed at her. Trying to convince herself that she was ready for sex with Rune only for the greater good wasn't working. No, the truth was, when she was around him, her entire body hungered. She remembered the feel of his body sliding into hers. She wanted to touch him again. To feel the heat of him surrounding her.

On this crazed race across the countryside, the one stable point in her universe had been his solid, muscular presence. He held her and she felt safe. He touched her and the cold inside her drained away, replaced by a relentless need that only he could ease.

She quivered for a release that seemed to be hovering just out of reach. She looked at him and felt heat pool at her center. She touched him and her nerve endings sizzled. Her magic, her body—there was no distinction here. She wouldn't care for him. Wouldn't love him. But if they were fated to mate, would it really be so bad if she enjoyed herself in the process?

She pushed those thoughts aside for the moment, though, and told him, "There's no point in waiting for the memories to show up. We don't have time to waste, right? Well, I can try an unblocking spell and maybe hurry them up a little."

He nodded. "Good idea. We should be able to find what we need here."

As they drew nearer to the village, Teresa wondered if he was right. The place was hardly more than a spot in the road, really. A dozen or so buildings clustered together in the middle of nowhere.

"Then what?" she asked. "Where do we go from here?"

"There are caves near here," he said, swatting at her bird as the small creature made a dive at his head. "I've stayed there before."

"Caves. Great." Mother Nature's version of a shack. Teresa whistled for Chico and he flew to her shoulder, where he bobbed up and down in time with her steps. She lifted one hand to gently stroke his sleek feathers and immediately felt comforted. Her home, her life, her friend were all gone. Chico and this stranger who would be her mate were all she had left.

Except for the grandmother who probably, thanks to her gift of visions, already knew they were headed her way. Teresa suddenly needed to see her *abuela*. She felt a desperate urge to hear the older woman's steady, no-nonsense advice. And she needed to feel that connection to the past that she knew before she walked into a future that was looking more and more terrifying.

He stopped suddenly and asked, "Will you trust me, Teresa?"

"What?"

"Trust. Can you trust me?"

"I have so far, haven't I?" She wanted to trust him, but there was still so much she didn't know. Prepared or not, she had gaping holes in her knowledge and handing her fate over to an immortal wasn't something easily done.

He grabbed her arms and pulled her in close to him. The color of his gray eyes shifted from pewter to steel to the soft gray of storm clouds, all while he looked into her eyes, as if searching for something that he couldn't find.

"Fine," she admitted. "It's hard. I don't know you, Rune. You say you've always been with me, but I've never seen you, so why should I—"

"You were ten," he said, his gaze boring into hers. "At your *abuela*'s. You wandered into the desert and stirred a rattlesnake nest to life."

She remembered. That frozen sense of terror came back to her and it was as if all the years between then and now had fallen away. "There were dozens of them." She shook her head and swallowed. "The rattling, the hissing, it was so loud and—"

"And a coyote saved you," he said. "It jumped into the nest so you could run."

"Yeah," she said, smiling now. "I don't know where it came from—"

"The coyote was me, Teresa," he said. "I used magic, drawing on yours and my own to create the illusion of a coyote."

"You were there?" She looked into his eyes and saw the truth staring back at her. "You saved me."

"I will always be there when you need me. You are my mate."

The simple honesty of his words tore down a bit of the wall she had built around her heart and soul. And that worried her. She didn't want to be vulnerable to him. But how could she hold back from a being who had already saved her life more than once?

"Trust goes both ways, Teresa," he reminded her.

She tipped her head to one side and stared up at him. Saw shadows crouched in his eyes. She felt his power rippling out around her, drawing her in even as he held a part of himself back.

Something told her that the memories she hoped to draw out of the locked closet in her mind wouldn't all be puppies and rainbows. There was more between them than he was saying. She knew it.

He might pretend to be keeping the past where it belonged, but at his heart, at his soul, he was holding on to feelings that threatened to destroy the very link they were supposed to forge. He expected her to blindly trust him when it was clear he couldn't do the same with her.

"Look," she said, covering a sudden burst of nerves with a stiff, calm voice, "we're stuck with each other, right? We have the Mating ritual to complete. This quest to finish. So it doesn't really matter if we like each other, does it?"

"I suppose not," he agreed.

Oddly, she was almost disappointed to hear him say that. Despite knowing that it was better all the way around this way. After all, she was prepared to go through with the Mating. What she wasn't willing to do was allow herself to love him. Love wasn't part of this package and she had no interest in changing that. Love gave people too much power over you.

Gave them the weapons to hurt you.

So, no thanks. She wasn't interested in eternal love. She was prepared to do her duty. To complete the task her grandmother had prepared her for most of her life. But nowhere was it written that she must love the mate the fates had chosen for her.

When Rune held one hand out to her in a gesture of solidarity, of alliance, Teresa took it, sliding her hand into his. The instant their skin met, a sizzle of something ancient and hot and delicious skittered through her system. Her whole body shook with desire, with quickening passion. She looked into those incredible eyes and saw that he had felt it too and she knew, like it or not, this Eternal was hers.

The question was, what was she supposed to do with him once the quest was over?

Chapter 21

He released her and reached beneath his black coat to the small of his back. He pulled out a wicked-looking knife with a blade that was at least six inches long, sharp on one edge and jagged on the other. The shining silver glinted with menace in the starlight.

She looked from him to the knife and then to the village. Cheerfully bright mariachi music from a radio drifted to them on the night wind. Other than the loud, cheerful tune, the small town might as well have been deserted. Teresa knew all too well how easily sound traveled in the desert. But there were no voices. No laughter. Just . . . silence, and suddenly the village looked more ominous than welcoming. She couldn't stop the shiver as a thread of cold slithered along her spine. "Do you think you're going to need that knife?"

"Better to have it and not need it than the other way around." He stabbed the blade through a belt loop on his jeans and pulled the edge of his coat over it. "Let's go." He paused and glared at Chico. "And keep that bird quiet."

She frowned after him, but a moment later she fell in step behind him. They came out of the desert shadows into the light and for a moment or two Teresa was nearly blinded. Not that the lights on the porches and spilling from small homes were bright—but in comparison to the blackness of the night it was like being dropped from outer space into the middle of the Vegas Strip.

"This way," he said and Teresa walked beside him. She felt the gazes of the villagers following them. That unsettled feeling she'd had only that morning was back and she had to force herself to relax a little. If they walked down the street looking like fugitives, that wouldn't exactly help them blend in. Of course, how much blending in could a six-foot-five bundle of pure danger do, anyway?

Teresa kept pace with Rune and smiled at a couple of old women sitting on worn plastic chairs outside a house that looked as if it had occupied that spot since the beginning of time. Neither of the women smiled back, their wrinkled faces blank except for the curiosity in their eyes.

Teresa couldn't shake the sensation of being watched. This wasn't the time to ask Rune about it, though. She simply followed him into the store when they found it. Chico flew off to take up a perch on an overhead beam, but she didn't try to coax him down. She'd get him when they were ready to leave. The important thing now was to take care of business and get gone again. The front door shrieked, wood on wood, as they opened it and the sound was like that of a tormented soul.

She stepped inside and the radio crackled and hissed, reception interrupted by her innate, electrically fueled magic. She moved past the counter quickly and the radio played on.

Another shiver wracked Teresa's body as she caught the eye of a fiftyish man seated on a rickety chair behind a wood plank counter. She gave him a smile, but he only stared at her, much as the old women had. She wondered if all strangers were treated this way or if word had already gotten out about an escaped witch and her bodyguard.

Now that was a scary thought, so she pushed it away and helped Rune gather what they needed. Fast.

There were shelves filled with dry goods, canned food and bags of chips and pretzels. A refrigerator held bottles of water, beer and soda. The bright, shiny music they'd heard in the desert piped from the radio behind the counter.

The man behind the counter was smoking a cigar and watching a small television set on mute. The program looked like a *telenovela*, a Spanish soap opera. Teresa recognized it because her grandmother watched the same program religiously. The picture rolled and danced when she got too close, so she kept her distance.

"Señor," she said as Rune walked past her to gather up water, canned beans and whatever else he came across. It distracted her for a second and she wondered just how much he could carry while using his powers to transport them. But she shook her head and focused on the older man looking at her. *"Señor, tiene usted candelero?"*

"Sí." He looked her up and down, then pointed to the far aisle. "Candles are in the back."

Teresa grinned at the unexpected use of English. As much time as she had spent in Mexico with her grandmother, her Spanish was still lacking. Her training had focused mainly on spells, the history of witchcraft and preparing for her destiny. Not a lot of time for language lessons.

"Gracias."

Shooting a quick look at Rune, she hurried down the

aisle and smiled at a boy trying to choose a candy bar. His brow was furrowed with indecision as he studied row after row of goodies and she envied him the simplicity of his life. But she didn't have time to curse the fates or to wish that things were different for her. Life was what it was and now it was up to her to do what had to be done.

The old man called out to the boy and he ran to the counter for a whispered conversation. Teresa frowned as she watched, trying to pick out a word or two, but the old man finished in a hurry and a moment later the child was racing from the store, letting the door screech and slam shut in his wake.

She looked over the shelves, dismissing the tall glass votives covered with pictures of the saints or Our Lady of Guadalupe. These were meant for devotions, she knew, for asking indulgences from heaven. Seemed wrong to her somehow to use those for spellwork. For a moment, Teresa went still and thought about buying one of the tall candles for Elena. But if ever there was a person whose soul needed no help in getting into heaven, it was Elena Vargas.

Blinking back a sudden sheen of tears that blurred her vision, she grabbed a box of plain white votive candles. They were probably for emergency use, for when the power went out. Well, she hadn't really expected to find colored tapers here and she would make do with what she had. On the plus side, she thought wryly, she wouldn't need matches. Even without Rune around, she was still funneling magic drawn from lightning, and fire was becoming a way of life for her, too.

She met up with Rune at the counter and nearly laughed when she saw him pull a wallet and money from his back pocket. Funny, but she hadn't even considered that a magical being would have cash on hand. The old man rang up their purchases without once looking at their faces.

Teresa was starting to get another bad feeling and judging by the tension she sensed coming off Rune in waves, he was experiencing the same thing. She was anxious to get out of the store, leave the village behind and disappear into the desert.

Finally they were finished. Rune took the bag of groceries, held on to Teresa's elbow with his free hand and steered her out of the store. Chico flew right at them, whistling sharply as he dove and swooped wildly.

Rune dropped the bag of supplies at their feet. In the next instant, he dropped into a half crouch in front of her and whipped the knife free in the same movement.

Chico's whistle sounded again as the bird flew into the shadows like a brightly colored missile. Teresa heard someone shriek in pain. She stood behind Rune, looked into the darkness and saw three men running at them. One of them had blood streaking along one side of his face, probably thanks to Chico's claws.

Fear washed over her just as Chico's shrill voice shouted, *"Run for it!"*

Chapter 22

Kellyn was on hold.

On *hold*.

Her fingers tightened around the cell phone until she was surprised the tiny device didn't simply shatter in her hand.

The Presidential Suite at the Ritz-Carlton, D.C., felt claustrophobic as she waited, listening to silence, wondering what the hell was going on at the damn lab. The mortals in her little cadre were getting completely out of hand. They were treating her as if she was one of them. As if she didn't have enough power in her little finger to send them all into a caldera.

Which she just might do if someone didn't answer the bloody—

"Henry Fender speaking."

She huffed out a breath as the familiar masculine voice came on the line. "Dr. Fender," she said, congratulating herself silently on the calm, even tone she maintained.

"Kellyn," he replied. "How nice to hear from you."

Nice?

Henry Fender was the head of the Seekers. A national organization that ostensibly existed to find a way to steal magical abilities from the witches it captured. In reality, of course, Henry was looking for so much more.

The fact that the membership of his organization actually believed that Henry would share one iota of power with them only gave credence to just how convincing Henry could be—or, she thought with a smile, just how gullible humans were.

She drew his image up in her mind. He looked like everyone's fantasy version of a lovable grandfather. Though he was only in his fifties, he had a full head of flyaway gray hair that fed into the appearance of geniality. His cool blue eyes were hidden behind round glasses and his voice, always soft and caring, gave the impression of gentleness.

Amazing just how far off impressions could be from reality.

Of course, Kellyn had known just what kind of man Henry Fender was the moment she met him. But then, she had powers of perception that most didn't. Lucky her.

She pushed off the sofa and walked barefoot to the private veranda off her suite. The view of Washington was spectacular and as she stared at the city lights shining below her in the distance, she said, "I've been waiting for an update on your latest acquisition, Doctor. And I'm sure I don't have to remind you that I'm not a patient person."

"No, of course not." He paused, as if measuring his words. "I was preparing my notes before calling both you and our associate."

Careful, she thought. At least he was intelligent enough to be careful about what he said over an open phone line. With federal agencies forever expanding their snooping policies, one just never knew when a line might be tapped. She could spell the line to protect their conversation, but frankly, she simply didn't care enough to do that. If Fender was caught, it wouldn't affect her. And what could any federal agency do to her?

Although no sooner had the thought crossed her mind than she was reminded of how she'd once been captured and imprisoned. She'd needed the aid of an Eternal, of all things, in order to break free. Fine. She would be as circumspect as Fender.

"Excellent," she said, laying one hand on the cool iron railing. "You have news, then?"

"A few nuggets of information, but sadly, our latest . . . guest . . . was devoid of anything interesting involving our ongoing project."

Fabulous, Kellyn thought. The man was the most gifted torturer she had ever known and considering her background, that was truly saying something. If Doc Fender couldn't get information out of a captured witch, then there was nothing to be found. Another dead end. Well, there were plenty of witches running around out there.

"Do you have any other guests scheduled to arrive soon?"

"Yes," Fender told her carefully. "As a matter of fact, I'm expecting two friends later this afternoon."

"Good. Be sure to tell me if they give you anything special."

"Of course," he said and his tone was even more unctuous.

Kellyn rolled her eyes and told herself she wouldn't have to deal with him forever. "You'll see that your current guest is taken care of?"

"Naturally," he said, a whisper of insult creeping into

his voice. "My assistant will see that she gets to her destination safely."

Translation: One of Fender's henchmen would kill the witch and dispose of the body. Apparently this latest witch wasn't even worth holding on to at Fender's lab. She knew very well that the good doctor had a holding area where at least a dozen witches were kept in captivity. They were the rare few whose genetic memories could be mined again and again through the judicious use of drugs and physical encouragement.

Those unfortunate witches would be held indefinitely as Fender searched for clues that would lead Kellyn and her partner to their own holy grail.

The focus needed to channel demonic power.

The Artifact forged by witches and fired by the flames of hell itself.

Once that priceless relic was recovered, there was simply no limit to what Kellyn would be able to accomplish. The world would be hers. Billions would kneel in supplication. Adoration.

And all that stood between her and her goal was a few paltry earth witches.

Chapter 23

"*B*ruja!" A shout in Spanish that needed no translation. *Witch.*

Rune instinctively grabbed his knife and crouched between Teresa and whoever was coming at them out of the darkness. His blood pumped furiously and if his heart could have beaten, it would have been pounding against his rib cage. Eyes narrowed, he split his attention between the witch he must protect and those who meant her harm.

He didn't feel the presence of another immortal and that was good. At least he knew there was no Eternal lying in wait with the mortals determined to kill Teresa.

Three men charged from the shadows. Armed with knives, silver blades shining in the pale light that poured from the store windows, they came at Rune and Teresa in a rush.

Rune caught the first man with a shoulder in the stomach, then stood up quickly, tossing the attacker into the air to land hard on the dirt. He spun around to face the next man, big, with a scar on his cheek and dark eyes slitted in determination. Rune braced himself, all the while hearing his witch shouting in fury and her damn bird screeching.

He caught the man with the jagged edge of his blade but didn't have time to enjoy the spread of red across his shirt. Already the fallen attacker had regained his feet to join in the strike again. The third man was heading around him toward Teresa, but the bird screeched, flew up and came at the guy's eyes, claws extended. The man howled and dropped, lifting both hands to protect his face.

Rune grunted in appreciation and threw himself wholeheartedly into the fight. In hand-to-hand combat, his immense strength was an advantage that mortal men couldn't hope to match. In his peripheral vision, he saw people racing into the narrow street to watch—or to help their fellow villagers. He didn't know which. All he knew was he had to protect Teresa.

How had they all discovered so quickly that he and Teresa were there? Fixing his gaze on those still threatening them, Rune realized how it had happened. It was the old man in the store. Teresa's magic had set off the radio and television and the old man had picked up on the presence of magic. He had sent the boy out to alert the other villagers. Or maybe there had even been a report about them on the television playing in the store. Word had spread to even this smallest of towns in the middle of the desert, then. Which meant there would be others hunting them. Mexico wouldn't be safe for Teresa.

Nowhere would be safe.

As his mind raced, he called on the flames to cover his hands for the fight. Someone gasped; another voice cursed loud and viciously and yet another voice began to pray. Rune wasn't listening to any of it.

His and Teresa's identities were no longer a secret. There was no reason not to use *all* of the weapons available to him. He threw a ragged bolt of flame at the porch beside him and the fire attacked the desert-dried wood like a starving animal offered a feast. Someone cried out a warning and he knew that the crowd's attention would be diverted, at least temporarily, while they fought to keep that fire from spreading.

"Skyfire burn and surge with heat!" Teresa shouted a spell at the heavens and Rune felt the ripple of her magic sliding across his skin. She hadn't used a spell to reinforce her power before—he hoped it influenced her aim.

"Magic I call," she cried, her shout rising above the noise of the fight and the roar of the growing fire. "Skyfire burn and race to me!"

Rune took a slice to his biceps and used the fury thus engendered to turn on the bastard behind him.

His opponent grinned now as he sidestepped in a wide circle around Rune. Foolishly, the man tossed his knife from hand to hand, as if Rune would be impressed. Instead, Rune ended his taunts by flinging one arm toward him and allowing flames to leap from his fingertips to the man's filthy shirt.

Instantly, fire raced over the man's body and he threw himself to the ground, rolling over and over in the dirt.

The storekeeper stepped outside, carrying a shotgun that he lowered and aimed at Teresa's back. Rune threw fire again, but before the flames reached the old bastard, Teresa's spell erupted.

Lightning forked from the sky, slamming into the earth with an electrical charge that lifted the hair on Rune's head and sent several people crashing to the ground, including the treacherous old man. His shotgun fell harmlessly from his hands as those still standing screamed and ran for the relative safety of their homes.

But not everyone was alarmed by the jagged bolts of lightning that slashed and burned the village. There were still two attackers, ready to risk all for the reward of trapping a witch. Teresa's body arched gracefully toward the sky as she sent her power heavenward to call down the energy of the gods.

Even in the fury of the moment, Rune was struck by her beauty. Arms lifted high, her long, black hair twisting and writhing in the wind created by her magic, she looked like a young goddess. And while his mate worked her spell, Rune was left to take care of the most immediate threat.

He squared off against the first man, who came in low with a long swipe of his blade, designed to gut Rune and leave him bleeding out on the dirt. Rune stepped quickly to one side at the last moment and made a hard jab of his own. His knife cut the other man down and he dropped like a stone. The second man cursed him in Spanish and slashed his knife in an arc that caught Rune's shoulder and sent a low hum of pain firing through him.

The old man's reinforcements were falling fast.

Bolts of lightning continued to illuminate the night. Again and again, the slashing streams of white-hot power crashed to the ground, and though Teresa didn't actually hit anyone, she kept the village distracted.

Losing patience with the skirmish, Rune finished the last of their attackers with a knife to the heart, then let him fall. Standing in the middle of the street, surrounded by the bolts of energy pummeling the earth, Rune felt his own powers recharging through his connection to Teresa. His hair lifted in the wind and his body thrummed with the prickling sensations of millions of volts sizzling the air.

"Rune!" Her shout reached him over the clamorous noise and the powerful bolts of electricity. His head came up and his eyes fixed on her in time to see the old bastard once again lifting his damn shotgun to point at her.

Instantly, Rune called on the flames again, flashed out and reappeared behind the duplicitous old man. He snapped the man's neck and dropped him to the dirt. Without a backward glance, Rune grabbed Teresa, who automatically reached down and snatched up their bag of supplies.

"Willful woman!" he muttered and flashed them from the village, leaving only the dead and the suddenly still, silent night behind them.

Chapter 24

"Chico!" Teresa exclaimed the minute Rune flashed them to the entrance of a cave. She looked back over her shoulder at the wide expanse of desert stretching out between them and the village. All she saw was darker shapes of yucca trees, sage bushes and the occasional saguaro cactus, looking like tall, thin men with arms raised to heaven.

Her heart still racing with the aftereffects of what had just happened, she took a long, deep breath and tried to find balance again. But that, it seemed, was impossible.

"Chico's not with us." She turned her gaze on Rune. "We left him behind in that damn village."

Rune shot her a hard look and clapped one hand to the gaping slice on his arm. "The bird's not an issue. For all we know, the *federales* have been called. Mexican feds could be crawling all over that village right now, looking to track us. And you're worried about that bird?"

"Yes!" Furious, she whipped her hair back out of her eyes and tried to get a handle on the raw nerves still rippling through her.

He muttered something under his breath, but she

didn't catch it. Temper and a million other things combined in the pit of her stomach to build to a roiling mass. Only moments ago they had fought as a team, each of them feeding off the other, creating more powerful magic between them than either of them could claim singly. Maybe she should give them both a minute or two to breathe. Yes, Chico was out there and she would find a way to get him. She would. But for now . . .

Teresa couldn't help feeling a wash of victory. She'd actually called down lightning out of a clear, starry sky. For the first time since her magic had awakened, she hadn't had to wait for a storm. She'd *created* the storm with her own will. She'd felt the power, the surging charge of strength that held her in its tight, brutal grip. Inside her there was a fire burning that was as hot and fierce as the flames that made up the soul of her Eternal.

Residual magic still washed through her like tiny orgasms, making her tremble as she looked up at the man who had saved her life. As energized as she felt by the surge of magic she had wielded, she knew that if not for Rune, the old man from the store would have killed her.

And that thought was enough to leave her shaken. "You saved my life. *Again.*"

"I did."

Her gaze went to his arm. "You're injured."

He shook his head. "Not injured. Just hurt. It will heal. Are you all right?"

"Yes," she said, though she wasn't sure of that answer. These had been the longest days of her life and the danger wasn't over. Her mind was a tangled mass of thoughts, sensations, fears and worries. And overriding it all was the crushing knowledge of just what she was actually capable of. "Well, I will be. That was . . . awesome." She scrubbed her hands up and down her arms, as if she could ease the chills racing across her skin. "I mean that in the literal sense of the word, too. *Awesome.*" She shook her head, amazed by what she'd done. "There was no storm—no clouds, even—and I still drew down the lightning."

He blew out a breath and nodded before closing the small space separating them. "You did. You were ... magnificent."

She liked the praise but wasn't entirely sure she deserved it. "It was impressive, sure. But I didn't hit anything."

"You didn't have to. Your power terrified them." He took the bag of supplies from her and steered her into the mouth of the cave.

"That's probably not a good thing, either," Teresa said, trying to look around but not seeing much beyond inky darkness and hard rock walls. Good thing they'd bought candles. "When word gets out about us being in the village, it will only be worse for us. They saw us using magic. Your fire, my lightning—"

He pulled her to a stop. In the darkness his gray eyes shone like beacons. The flames that were a part of him danced in their depths, making him look exactly what he was—dangerous.

"You were already hunted as a witch. Now maybe those tracking you will think twice before approaching."

"Do you really believe that?"

He shrugged and gave her a tired smile. "No, but it doesn't matter anyway. We are the magic, Teresa. We won't hide from it any longer. Instead, we will embrace it and do what we're expected to do."

His words, the forceful way he said them, all seemed as though he was asking her to make a pledge of faithfulness to their shared duty. He wasn't just talking. He was looking for confirmation from her that she was with him. And she was. Whatever else was going on around them, she knew that she belonged at this Eternal's side. At least until they had completed their mission.

"What is it you want from me?"

"I want to believe in you. Your loyalty," he ground out. "To me. To this task. I want to know that you'll see it through this time."

She bristled a bit at being reminded again that in her past lives she had been less than trustworthy. And now that she had remembered just enough to make her feel shame for choices long since made, she liked it even less. She hated knowing that in another lifetime she had been . . . dangerous. Paying for your sins was right, she supposed. But paying for sins you committed as another woman entirely just didn't seem fair at all. Still, there was no choice but to move ahead, so she swallowed the emotions nearly choking her and solemnly nodded. "I will."

He studied her for a long minute or two, then finally inclined his head in a nearly regal sign of acceptance. That bristled, too, but it had already been a long enough day and she didn't really have the energy for an argument, so she let it go.

Taking her arm, he steered her deeper into the darkness. She turned back for one last look at the mouth of the cave and the glimpse of the starry sky and the open desert beyond. "But what about Chico?"

"I'm not going back for him. Not now, anyway," Rune said.

"No." As much as it pained her to think of her pet alone in the wild, she could admit that returning to the village immediately was a bad idea. So that was one more thing she had lost on this perilous journey. Her last link with home. With normalcy. With the life she had lived before this huge man had crashed into it.

As she walked beside Rune, she felt fatigue begin to claw at her. With the adrenaline rush draining away, her legs felt like lead weights and just putting one foot in front of the other became a herculean task. "How far back does this cave go, anyway?"

"Just a bit farther."

His voice echoed off the rocks in a low rumble of sound, but despite what he said, it seemed as if they walked miles more. Finally, though, Rune stopped, called on the fire and she watched as blue and yellow flames danced into life around his hand. Then he touched a cold torch stuck into a stanchion on the wall and light surged quickly into life around the enclosure.

"Oh, my," Teresa whispered, walking farther into the spacious cavern.

When she had entered this cave, she had expected to spend the evening huddled around a miserly campfire in a dank, cold space. *This* had never entered her mind.

The room they stepped into was carved out of the rock and it was massive. There were stalactites of purest crystal jutting from the ceiling in a wide array of colors and Teresa could feel the magical energy humming from them. Rune threw fire to other torches ringing the room, tails of flame that danced to his whims and settled over the dry torches with a rush of sound and a quick flare of light. The walls came alive in the flickering radiance and Teresa saw that there were more crystals sparkling in them. As each torch caught fire, smoke drifted toward cleverly hidden holes in the ceiling.

"Won't people see the smoke?" she asked, staring at the rough-hewn rock overhead. "And then find us?"

"No," Rune said, continuing to throw fire at the remaining torches until the last of the shadows were pushed back into the corners and the crystals on the walls burst into glittering life and color. "The holes lead to ventilation shafts that draw the smoke to still more holes and through other tunnels, until by the time the smoke is released into the air, it's so dissipated no one will spot it."

"Impressive," she whispered. She turned in a slow circle, taking it all in, still hardly believing her eyes. Of course, her gaze snapped first to the most imposing piece of furniture in the place. A bed wide enough to comfortably sleep ten people, it was covered in a mountain of pillows and layers of silky throws and quilts that looked lush enough for a pasha's harem. Something inside her stirred to life and she felt heated tingles begin to gather at her center. She took a breath, held it for a second and then blew it out again as she realized that soon she and Rune would be on that bed, sealing their relationship for all eternity.

Nerves jangled through her, but Teresa battled them into submission. There would be time enough for hesitation later. For now ... she shifted her gaze deliberately to take in the rest of the room. There was a fire ring, surrounded by more crystals that shone so brightly in the flickering torchlight that it almost seemed as if they were alive.

And in a way, she knew, they were. Inside those crystals were trapped the energies of eons. They were of the earth and carried at their core the very heart of magic. She felt the pulse in the air, the reverberating beat of power, and drank it in, as she would a glass of water after a long walk in the desert.

Rune started a fire in the ring of crystals and it was only then that she noticed the metal rack spread across the ring for cooking. "Amazing," she whispered, stunned at both the intricate beauty and the functionality surrounding her.

She felt as though she'd stumbled into Aladdin's cave. She smiled in spite of everything that had happened that day and laughingly said, "If only there was a bathroom with a shower, it would be perfect."

"Well, then . . ." Rune set the bag of supplies down and gave her a half smile. Taking her hand, he led her toward the far wall of the sumptuous cave and then behind yet another wall of crystal-studded rock. He lit the torch within to display even more wonderful secrets.

"A hot tub?" She bent over the rocky ledge of a pool of steaming water and dipped one hand into the froth. Heat pulsed through her and she nearly sighed with pleasure.

"It's not a shower," he told her with another smile, "but I think it'll do."

"Are you kidding?" she asked. "It's *great.*"

"Glad you approve. It's fed from an underground spring," Rune told her, then showed her another alcove. "It drains through here . . ."

Teresa looked, realized what she was seeing and laughed, delighted. It wasn't the Ritz, and in fact it looked more like what she assumed a medieval garderobe was like, but at least she wouldn't have to run into the desert at night to relieve herself. "This is so great, Rune. I don't even know what to say."

She turned to smile up at him and found him watching her with amusement and something . . . else in his eyes. Those pale gray depths were awash with secrets and emotions. As if she could sense exactly what he was thinking and feeling, she shivered in response. That low curl of heat and expectation at the very core of her had returned and it was all she could do not to moan softly as need pulsed inside her along with the beat of her heart.

"You feel it, don't you?" he whispered, even that faint hush of sound seeming to echo against the rocks.

"Yes," she said, not bothering to pretend she didn't know what he was talking about. What would have been the point?

"We begin the Mating tonight."

She lifted her chin to meet his gaze squarely, so that he could see her own determination to accept their joined destiny. She only hoped he couldn't read her trepidations as easily. "Yes, we will."

He nodded, reached for her and then let his hand drop before touching her. "Bathe," he said. "Get warm. Then we begin."

Her insides quivered again, despite the lack of anything remotely resembling anticipation in his tone. If he was going to treat what passed between them as all business, then she would, too. Probably better for her if she did. So in a brisk voice, she stopped him as he turned to leave her in the crystal-studded bathroom of rock. "Did you do all of this?"

"Some of it," he said, pausing long enough to bend down, sweep one hand through the bubbling water and then swipe it across his face. "Another Eternal, Finn, lives here when he's in this country. I helped him dig out the bathtub and a couple of us carted in that bed and helped him set it up."

"Where is he now?"

"Keeping an eye on his witch," Rune told her. "She's in the States and he's waiting for her Awakening."

"Like you did."

"Yes." His eyes flashed with hunger as he looked at

her, and Teresa's body responded instantly. As if he could sense her passion rising, his features tightened. Her heartbeat thundered in her chest as seconds ticked past, ratcheting up the tension between them until she was surprised the very air wasn't sparking with the electricity humming in the room. A long, slow breath slid from her lungs as she tried to get a grip on what was happening between them.

She didn't know him. He didn't know her.

And yet . . . there was an undeniable bond between them that was only growing stronger.

Which terrified her.

Teresa was willing to mate with him. Share the magic. Do their duty. But she didn't want love. Didn't want to risk her heart again or give another male—one even stronger than regular mortals—power over her.

How could she do what she must while withholding her heart?

Would it be possible to cast a spell over herself?

While these thoughts and others raced through her mind, her body continued to hum and pulse as if it remembered all too well being invaded by Rune's huge body and couldn't wait for it to happen again.

She shook her head to dislodge that notion and only then noticed Rune cupping one hand across his upper arm. That's when she realized the gash on his arm hadn't completely healed and that he must be in pain. She reached out to touch the wound and asked, "Can I help with that?"

The instant she touched him, heat dazzled them both. His gaze locked with hers, he whispered, "You can."

She licked suddenly dry lips. "How?"

"Lay your hand on my arm," he said, his voice soft enough that it was like a caress on her strained nerve endings.

She did what he asked, feeling the thick, sculpted muscles beneath his flesh, and then she shivered when he laid his own hand atop hers. Sensation flooded her, rocking her thoughts right out of her head and sending her body into a tailspin of need.

"Hold still," he said as the fire within him flared into life, covering their joined hands in blistering heat that didn't burn.

Fascinated, she watched actual *fire* move over her skin with feather-light strokes. They were joined, two pieces of the same whole, and for this one moment it felt . . . right. She didn't wonder about it. Didn't feel any apprehension or try to think about it logically. She didn't expect any logic in this. There was no reason. There was only what she felt.

What *they* felt.

Moments passed, with the two of them locked together before the fire died away in a whisper of sound. Rune said, "It's healed."

He dropped his hand from hers and she stroked his arm, stunned that there wasn't so much as a scar on his skin. Her fingertips moved down his arm, relishing the feel of his incredible strength.

"You keep touching me like that and we're going to start the Mating right now, no matter how tired you are," he warned.

She had been exhausted a few minutes ago, wanting only to sink into that incredible tub of heated water. Now her whole body felt as energized as the bolts of lightning she'd pulled from the sky. Now she wanted to sink into a different kind of heat.

Lifting her eyes to his, she asked, "Who's tired?"

Chapter 25

"**I**diots!" Parnell muttered darkly as he marched down the middle of the village's one dusty street. He had to force himself to keep from throwing out enough fire to burn this hellhole to the ground.

He'd missed them by an hour. One hour. And all because his informant had gotten greedy. Parnell's gaze flicked to the old man lying in the dirt. "You're lucky you're already dead."

When the old fool had recognized Teresa, he'd had his grandson call it in. He'd been told to leave the witch alone. To do *nothing*.

"But you just couldn't stand that, could you?" No, Parnell told himself, humans were, at the core of it, greedy bastards. And the old man was no different than most—though he had met his punishment, surely. He'd seen an opportunity to get out of this flea-ridden spot in the middle of nowhere and had reached for it. Hard to blame him. Though Parnell certainly did.

When his satellite phone rang, he pulled it from his pocket, glanced at the number and answered, saying, "No. We don't have them."

While the woman at the other end of the line ranted, Parnell lifted one hand to the men who had arrived with him. He waved them over to the crowd, watching the proceedings as if they were fascinated by a television program. Fools didn't even realize what was about to happen to them.

When one of his men silently signaled a question, Parnell simply nodded and drew one finger across the base of his neck.

The first volley of machine-gun fire erupted instantly. Bright lights flashed and the sound was a cacophony in the stillness. Yet the woman on the phone was shouting so loudly, Parnell could still hear her.

He paused for a moment and wished the guns were trained on her. But then, she would get what was coming to her eventually. As anyone who crossed him did.

"Witnesses are being taken care of," he told her when she wound down long enough to take a breath.

"Yes, I can hear that," she snapped. "Very subtle, Parnell."

He stiffened at the condemnation in her tone. "You wanted me to handle it? I'm handling it. We'll find the witch."

"In time for it to do any good?"

The guns fell silent and the night crowded back in. He glanced over his shoulder at his men, moving through the crowd. Kicking bodies out of the way, they were simply making sure the dead were *actually* dead. He wanted no survivors slipping away to tell stories about strange men asking questions about witches.

He had enough to deal with as it was.

"Let me do my job," he told the woman and snapped the phone closed. Holding the offending thing on his palm, he called up the fire and held it until the phone was nothing more than a blackened, melted pile of plastic and wire.

Then he brushed his hands free of both the phone and the woman and headed to his car, calling for his men to follow.

He still had a witch to find.

Chapter 26

Rune pulled Teresa close, lowered his head and kissed her until her blood boiled in her veins. She felt as if she had a fever. Her skin was suddenly too tight. She was hot and yet shivering, as if her body couldn't make up its own mind about what to feel.

Rune's hands moved up and down her back, cupping her bottom, holding her close to the hard thickness of him. The fever inside her burned hotter until even breathing became a challenge. His mouth took hers, his tongue sliding inside to taste, to claim. She felt the urgency in him and reveled in it. Her hands moved through his long, thick hair, holding his head to hers. She surrendered herself to what only he could make her feel and trembled with the force of what he was doing to her.

Behind her, the hot water rushed from the underground springs, sounding like the roar of a caged animal. Above her, crystals hummed with energy, spilling all that they were into the already charged air. She felt it all, but mostly she felt *him*.

This was monumental.

This was the moment when the Mating ritual would begin. Once this step was taken, she knew there was no getting out of it. She wanted this to happen and yet a part of her held back. That hesitant part of her would have jumped away from the cliff she was about to leap from with all the judiciousness of a cowardly bunny.

Eternity.

With that word resonating in her mind, Teresa pulled free of his kiss and struggled for air. She was on fire. There were no flames, but she felt the fire, licking at her skin. Burning her so completely that she knew once the Mating began she would surely be nothing but ash.

When she looked up into his eyes, she saw the fire there, too. Swirling in the liquid silver of his eyes. She was caught for a long moment, just looking at him, feeling the power shimmering around them.

"You're scared?"

His voice was rough, strained, as though he was fighting an inner battle to get control of himself. She knew what he must be feeling.

"A little," she admitted. "My grandmother didn't know much about the Mating. Only that it would seal Eternal and witch together for eternity. That's a long time."

His hands dropped from her arms and he took a step away from her. His already familiar eyes narrowed and in the dancing torchlight, he looked every inch the deadly warrior that he was.

"I've already waited an eternity for you," he said. "This time I thought it would be different. This time, I had hopes that you would have learned from the past. Grown. But now is no different than before. Other lives, other times," he whispered with a shake of his head. "But always the same."

"What are you talking about?"

"You, Teresa," he ground out. "I'm talking about what you're doing right now. Do you not see it?"

What Teresa saw was the frustration glinting in his eyes and she fired the same look right back at him.

"What?" she demanded. "I want to take a minute, think about this, and that makes me the enemy?"

He laughed, but there was no humor in the sound. "Centuries it's been, Teresa. Countless lives and opportunities wasted, because *still* you refuse to make that leap of faith."

Stunned, she simply stared up at him. Her body was still buzzing, but her brain was taking over and it was getting pissed. Didn't seem to matter that he had said pretty much what she had been thinking just before he pulled away. She hadn't been trying to start a fight, for heaven's sake. She had just needed one damn minute.

"What happened to all of the 'your past lives have nothing to do with now' stuff you fed me a couple of days ago?" she countered.

"I tried, but you are proving to be the same woman. You have no faith."

"What am I supposed to have faith in?"

"Me," he told her. "Us. And if not that, then at least in yourself. You say you know about the Mating, but still you stall, you stand back, clinging to your old life, unwilling to accept the new."

"I think I've done a hell of a lot of accepting," she shouted, stabbing his broad chest with the tip of her forefinger. "Do you even realize what's happened to me lately?"

"Yes," he said tightly, glancing down to see sparks of energy snapping from her finger to his chest and back again. "You lost it all. I know. But now, when you could gain so much, you turn your face from it. You turn from *me*. Just as you always have," he finished with a mutter.

"I'm not—"

He was on her in a heartbeat. His hands gripped her upper arms and he lifted her right off the floor as if she were no bigger than a child. When they were at eye level, he said, "I opened some of your memories to you. Can you deny what I'm saying? You've always done this, Teresa. Chosen yourself over your duty. Over *me*. Am I to stand by and watch you throw away our last chance to make right what you and your sisters fucked up so long ago?"

"I didn't ask you to step back," she argued. "I just wanted a minute to catch my breath. Is that so terrible?"

"You wanted the chance to back away."

"You don't know me," she told him, bracing her hands on his shoulders, digging her fingers in for purchase. "All of this talk about who I was, the lives I don't even *remember*—that has nothing to do with me. With who I am *now.*"

"Who you are now comes from what was before. How can the past not matter?"

Furious, mainly because a part of her wondered if he wasn't right about all of this, she shoved him, putting all of her strength into her hands as she pushed at his massive chest. Sparks of light swept from her fingertips, like droplets from sparklers on the Fourth of July, singeing his shirt. Instantly, she was horrified and patted at him to make sure she hadn't set him on fire.

"Damn it, what good is this magic if I can't control it?"

"You will gain control through the Mating," he told her, ignoring the flash of light sparking at the tips of her fingers. "We are meant to join. To balance each other. To focus our magic into one honed force."

It sounded right, she told herself, but that small, doubting voice in the back of her mind still shrieked out warnings. It had always been this way. Through the years of training, of studying, she had prepared for her duty and dreaded its arrival.

She could see his point of view, even if she didn't want to. She had known him less than a week, yet her entire life had been leading her to him. So maybe she should allow for the fact that he knew more about this whole thing than she did. Damn. She really hated being rational.

"Put me down, Rune. Please."

He did and she wobbled a little unsteadily for a second. Not surprising, really, since desire, fury and magic were mixing into a thick, debilitating stew inside her. Hard to straighten out just what she was feeling, what she was thinking, when a pair of gray eyes were fixed on her, waiting for her to make the mistakes another woman had made in another time.

She knew those memories were locked away inside her and she would do all she could to free them. But even if the time came when she could recall every moment of each of the lives she'd lived before this one, she would still be Teresa. And he had to realize that.

"I don't remember those lives you're still holding against me," she said finally. "The images you showed me earlier were hard for me to accept. But I still don't *remember* them. It's more like watching a movie starring a completely selfish heroine. *This* is my life. This one, Rune. And despite all the years of training, what you're asking of me is all new."

He folded his arms across his chest and stared down at her. "I know that."

"So blaming me for what I did back in the day is probably not the best way to make friends."

A reluctant smile tugged at the corners of his mouth. "No, probably not."

"Thanks for that much, anyway." She reached up and pushed her hair back from her face. The roar of the water rushing into the hot tub had become just background noise. Steady. Like her own heartbeat. The heat in the room filled her and the steam rising from the surface of the water shone from the colorful brilliance of the crystals in the wall.

This whole thing, she thought, was out of some wildly twisted fairy tale. An immortal and a witch, chased by enemies, stranded in the desert, sharing a magical cave filled with gleaming crystals. But in this story, the hero and heroine were so busy butting heads they weren't getting anywhere. And she was willing to admit to her share of the confrontations.

Sighing, Teresa reached out and took one of his hands in hers. The sizzle and flash that shot through her at his touch was almost familiar in days filled with too much change. "Whoever it is you remember from our past, it's not me. Whatever you think, that's not me."

"We will see," he said.

Irritation rose up and quickly died away. Yes, she'd had a hard time of it, but so had he. Maybe she could cut him a little slack. "Look, I know what we have to do and I'm not trying to back out. I just want to know what you expect from me."

"I expect you to be beside me," he told her, rubbing his thumb across the back of her hand in long, sexy strokes. "I expect you to be my mate as I will be yours. To join our energies, to channel our magic into finding the Artifact and returning it to Haven. I expect you to do what we must."

She nodded and watched his thumb moving over her skin as if she were mesmerized. "That's it? You're not expecting . . . love?"

He laughed shortly. "My heart doesn't even beat, Teresa. If it once knew how to love, it's forgotten now and I've no interest in reacquiring the knowledge."

She didn't know whether to be relieved or disappointed. How could they possibly succeed when neither of them was willing to invest everything? If each of them held back, would either of them be able to do what they had to, together? But what choice did they have except to try?

"All right, then," she said quietly. "How do we do it?"

"We start like this." He snapped his fingers and they were naked. Torchlight flickered over the walls, firing the crystals and shimmering on their skin.

Danger still resonated between them. They weren't safe and wouldn't be until all of this was over. Maybe, Teresa thought, that emotion was feeding into what was sweeping through her now. She had nearly died today. And again in Sedona. And both times this Eternal had saved her, at great cost to himself.

Life was too damn fragile, she told herself. And too short, despite the fact that she had led many lives. Each one of them had been too short; she knew it instinctively.

There was a nebulous connection between her and Rune, yes, but despite what he was thinking, he didn't *know* her. He knew the woman she had been through the centuries, but *this* woman—Teresa of the here and now—was new. And he had no idea who she was.

That would come, she supposed. They had thirty days to complete the Mating and find the shard of the Artifact she had hidden so long ago. One cycle of the moon. As they worked together toward a common goal. As they became physically closer, their bodies bonding, their souls intertwining.

Her heart wasn't involved and she wouldn't allow it to be. But her body burned and she was witch enough, *woman* enough, to accept the sexual pull between them for what it was.

He caught her left hand in his right and folded his fingers over hers. She did the same and then held her breath as her gaze locked with his. This was a moment filled with more tension than she had ever known.

She was about to pledge her life to this Eternal. The step she had been waiting for all her life was here and the reality of it was a little more intimidating than she had expected. *Eternity.* Not just the human version of until death do we part, this was literally *forever.* When that thought settled in, a flurry of images raced through her mind, leaving her clinging to Rune's hand as her world was rocked. The present fell away and the past rose up to claim her.

Chapter 27

*T*eresa felt the bite of the cold wind, the stinging needles of the rain and the sizzling punch of the lightning. And she smiled. It was all so much more than they had hoped. More than they had thought possible. She and her sisters faced the storm and welcomed it. They chanted as power surged through the air, jockeying from their pale bodies to the sky and back again. As if the witches and the universe itself were charging each other with enough power to change the world.

Lightning lanced from the sky, jagged bolts hammering into the earth on the borders of a circle carved into the dirt. Witches filled the circle, as they stood in the center of the tempest, skyclad, their naked bodies arched skyward, as if awaiting a lover.

"Don't do it!"

The woman Teresa had once been turned her head slowly to find the source of that voice. Rune. Standing beyond the circle, forced to be on the outside with his fellow Eternals, locked away from the witches and what they had come here to do.

"Come to me!" he shouted over the roar of the sea and the crash of the lightning. She heard his voice despite the *chants rising from her sisters' throats. She heard it and responded because he was hers. In a way no other man had ever been, Rune was hers.*

But she was more than simply his.

She was a witch. A member of the great coven. She owed her sister witches her loyalty even before him. And she had no wish to stop the events of this night. She knew they were making a necessary choice and that one day Rune would see that, too. Later, she would soothe him with her body and ease him with her touch. And he would see that the coven was right.

"Stay back," she warned. "You cannot enter the circle!"

"Nor should you," he cried. "Come to me now before it's too late."

She gave him a sad smile, knowing he would never understand her and why she did what she did. "You'll see, Rune. This is the way. For all of us."

She turned back to her sisters, lifted her hands toward Heaven . . . and watched, helplessly, as hell came down on them instead.

Shaken, Teresa staggered and found that Rune's grip on her hand was the only stable point in her universe. She clung to him as the last of the memory slid away, hopefully never to return. He had shown her pieces before. Now, though, she had *felt* it all. Lived through it. And the knowledge and fear and pain were so real they were choking her. "How could I have done that?"

"What did you remember?"

She looked up at him, tears swimming in her eyes. He appeared blurred, but steady. Beside her. As he had tried to be then.

"The night hell opened."

His features tightened, but so did his grip on her hand. As if his own memories were fueling his hold on her, he stared into her eyes and asked, "Did you remember more than what I showed you? Can you tell me why? Why wouldn't you listen to me? Why didn't you step away?"

"I don't know," she whispered brokenly, still feeling the chill of that long-ago night creeping through her system.

"I *trusted* you," he murmured, his grip on her hand even stronger now.

Ashamed of what she'd done and what the memory was making her feel, she tried to pull free of his grasp, but he wouldn't let her go. A part of her was grateful. She needed his touch to mitigate the soul-deep chill crawling through her.

"I know." Two words. Not nearly enough, but all she had to give. "I don't understand why I did it. Why *we* did it. But I know it has to be undone. Finally and at last, it has to be undone."

"And so it will," he said, his voice as rough as sandpaper.

"The Mating makes us stronger, right?"

"Yes. Every day our powers will increase until we've gained enough between us to accomplish our task." He paused and added, "We will share a . . . connection. Our minds will be linked."

"You mean like mind reading?" That sounded horrible. How could you ever have privacy if someone else was able to go picking through your thoughts?

"No, not mind reading. It's more a way of touching each other and being able to communicate silently. Our thoughts will remain our own."

"Okay, that's good. And?" she asked, knowing there

was more. "Look, I know the bare bones of this. I know that the Mating will make me immortal. Will give me control of my powers and bind me to you. What do you get out of this, Rune?"

"My heart will at last beat. I will be at last what I was meant to be. A part of you. No longer separate and alone. I'll be more fully human—able to feel more deeply, experience all that has been muted for centuries—and still immortal. And I'll have you. At last."

She flushed at the heat in his eyes, in the tightness of his words. Maybe she was wrong, but she didn't think he looked very happy at the notion of finally "having" her. And that was probably best, she told herself firmly. It would set them on more common ground. Because immortal mate or not, she wouldn't be staying with Rune after their thirty days were over. She'd be spending her eternity alone. In the long run—and eternity was certainly a long run—it would be better for her. Better for him.

"So, a heartbeat," she said, laying her free hand on his chest to feel the stillness beneath his skin. How could any man be so vibrantly alive and still have nothing pounding in his chest? "Experiencing a full range of emotion and sensation. Is that it? Is that all you want out of this Mating?"

"No." He caught her hand in his and held it tightly. "There's more. There's redemption."

Redemption.

That single word seemed to reverberate throughout the cave, only to hang in the steamy air between them.

"You don't need redemption, Rune," she told him, pulling one hand free of his grasp. "That night, it wasn't you who totally screwed up the world. It was us. My God, I don't even know what to say to that. But you and the other Eternals tried to stop us. At least you can say that. We have no excuse for what we did." Shaking her head, she whispered, "I know it was me, but I don't see how I could have done that . . ."

He rubbed his hand against hers, palm to palm, flesh to flesh. Sparks shot from their joining, flashed brightly and disappeared, winking out like the sparks from fireworks.

"If the Eternals had been able to get through to all of you, the gates of hell would never have been opened in the first place," he said, jaw tight, eyes ablaze. "But we failed you. The bonds we had forged between us weren't strong enough to blast through the coven's thirst for power."

"Why not?" She had to ask. Had to know. She'd had one brief memory of that time, but Rune knew it all. He'd lived through it with her and his memories hadn't been clouded and hidden by generations of reincarnated lives. "Why weren't the bonds strong enough?"

"We hadn't mated," he said, letting his head fall back. Staring up at the crystals shining in the rock face, he added, "The coven refused to mate with the Eternals." He lowered his gaze to hers again. Frustration and old anger radiated off him in thick waves that seemed to reach for her and draw her closer to share in his frustration. As if he believed that she deserved to experience what he had felt that long-ago night. "Sex was all they wanted from us then. You and your sisters closed yourselves off from what we were meant to be together."

She rubbed at the spot between her eyes as if she could massage more memories into life. But nothing came. There were no images filling her brain; there was only the sinking sensation that he was absolutely right. That she and her sister witches had tossed aside everything good and pure in a futile search for more power. Unaware or unconcerned that with that power would come a darkness they couldn't control.

"We were meant to be mated. Two halves of the same whole. Our god, Belen, created the Eternals as equal partners for the witches created by his lover, Danu."

"The mother goddess," Teresa whispered, remembering some of the things her *abuela* had taught her about the origins of witches and witchcraft.

"Yes," Rune said. "She was a bringer of light, knowledge, magic. It's said she gave birth to the witches so that her children could share her with the world."

She shook her head; she couldn't help wondering what Danu would make of her children now.

"Belen was her lover. The sun god. In ancient times, Beltane fires were lit to encourage the warmth of the sun." He smiled, as if remembering those days and, she supposed, he was. "For love of Danu, Belen created the Eternals. He drew us from the heart of the sun itself, molded the fire and breathed life into our bodies."

She looked at their joined hands, and as she watched, fire leaped into life around them. Blue, yellow and red flames danced across her skin and his, joining them in a conflagration of heat without pain.

"We were *meant*, Teresa." He stared into her eyes, his gray gaze swirling now into rich shades of silver and pewter. "But when you needed us most, there was no mating bond to anchor you." Rune's voice came fast and thick, choking with memories that ran soul deep in him. "You stood alone because you wouldn't accept me as your equal."

"If I had?"

"We'll never know," he admitted. "But I believe that

mated souls are stronger together than apart. Otherwise why would we have the Mating ritual at all?"

"Good point." She flexed her fingers around Rune's hand and felt the flames quicken with her action.

The room was hot and steamy. The glow of the crystals shone through the mist and Teresa felt everything in her shiver. She wouldn't again be the woman she had just glimpsed in her fractured memories. She wouldn't risk the world for her own selfish desires and needs.

This bonding would make them both stronger and she knew that in the coming days they would each need that strength. She had to trust in what she was meant to be. Had to give herself over to the cause that was so much greater than her fears and reluctance to be bonded to any man for eternity. She was doing what she had to do, but she knew that she could never offer him all that she was. She couldn't pledge her heart and risk an eternity of pain.

Nodding, she swallowed her uncertainties and looked directly into his eyes. "Then let's do it, Rune. Let's begin the Mating. I'm ready."

He took a breath and studied her as if weighing her words. Finally, he said, "Once the Mating ritual has begun, there's no going back. No changing your mind."

"I understand."

"Each time we come together, the Mating will take a greater hold on us. Entwine our souls more completely."

"I know." She glanced at their joined hands again and saw the fire burning inside their enclosed palms. Felt its heat snaking down through her system, charging her as if a live electrical wire was being threaded through her veins.

"At the end of thirty days, with our quest fulfilled, the Mating will be complete."

"Why thirty days?" she asked. "Why not fifteen or twenty?"

"You know why. Somewhere inside you, you feel it. It is the cycle of the moon, Teresa," he said. "The magic of the coven was drawn from the moon."

"Okay." Harder to talk now. It felt as though the heat filling her was cloaking every doubt and fear inside her. They were still there, but Rune's presence was muffling them somehow. She took strength from his surety about what they were about to do.

But there was one thing she had to know before they began. "And if we don't succeed at this mission? Then what?"

"Then the Mating will be incomplete and our souls will die." His tone was flat, unemotional. He had accepted that this was their last chance—the Eternals' and the witches'—to fix what had gone so wrong. If they didn't succeed, maybe they didn't deserve to go on.

Teresa felt the profoundness in the moment. This was eternal. Trepidation swept through her, but she battled through it. This man—this immortal—was her chance at atonement. The images of that long-ago night were still ripe and rich within her and Teresa knew that she had much to atone for. He was offering that opportunity and more. He offered to risk his own soul for the chance at redemption. Even though their shared past gave him no reason to give a shit if she succeeded or not.

He squeezed her hand hard enough that it should have broken bones, but didn't.

"We begin," he said. "Do you accept me, Teresa?"

She looked up into his eyes and saw how much this was costing him. That he should have to ask her for acceptance when she and her sisters were at the heart of this mess. Teresa felt the first flickering bond between them wrap itself around their joined hands. Though she wouldn't love him, wouldn't stay with him when this was done . . . she would be his partner in this quest. She would be his mate.

"Yes," she said simply. "I accept you."

"And our past?"

"Yes."

"And our future?"

She quailed at that, knowing as she did that their joined future wouldn't go beyond the thirty days of their mating. But a month was the future, too, wasn't it? "Yes," she said firmly. "I do."

That invisible thread of bonding spun tightly around their joined hands.

"Do you take me as your mate? To stand beside you? To do battle with you and to put right what once went so wrong?"

She felt the magic bristling in the air around them. The steam swam and swirled as if stirred by a wind she couldn't feel. The crystals shone more brilliantly and Teresa felt fire rush through her. His words echoed in the cave and rang with the insistence of truth and importance.

This, then, was the most powerful of his questions.

Teresa lifted her chin, met his gaze and said, "Yes, Rune. I accept you as my mate. I accept responsibility for what I did so long ago and I accept you, as my mate, to help me put it right."

The churning flames surrounding their joined hands flared suddenly with the light and heat of a thousand suns. Teresa closed her eyes against the brilliance of it, but in the space of a single heartbeat, the fire was gone.

At that same moment, she felt a sharp, stinging burn in the center of her palm. Then that jolt of heat raced up along her arm until it ricocheted madly inside her chest, like a fireball looking for escape. She stood utterly still, her gaze locked with Rune's as the fire inside her settled behind her left breast. The sizzle and burn focused into a pinprick and jabbed through her flesh above her left nipple.

She swayed, but Rune caught her. Teresa blinked and looked up at him. "What was *that*?"

"The Mating brand," he told her, satisfaction shining in his eyes. "At *last*."

Chapter 28

"B rand?"

"A tattoo, brought on by the Mating, imposing itself on both of us." He lifted one hand and rested the tips of his fingers on her left nipple.

Teresa sucked in a gulp of air. His touch felt so much warmer than the bolt of heat even now searing her skin.

"It will begin here," he told her, caressing a spot directly above her nipple. "Its echo will brand itself into my body as well." He smiled. "Ah, and there it is."

"What? Where?" She looked down and saw a faint red mark above the areola around her left nipple. Her stomach pitched. It had begun. It was real. The biggest decision of her life had been made and as her stomach settled down, she realized she was grateful. It was done. She'd made her choice and now she was on the road she had been preparing to walk her entire life.

Lifting her gaze to his broad bare chest, she reached out to smooth her fingers across the matching red mark on his skin. He hissed in a breath at her touch and she smiled, enjoying the knowledge that Rune was as susceptible to her as she was to him.

"What will it look like when it's finished?"

He pulled her closer to him and it was her turn to gasp as the hard thickness of his desire brushed her core. He felt her reaction to him and smiled. "Each witch's tattoo is different. As individual as each of you are. Drawn from your karma, your heart and soul, so the tattoo will speak to your inner strengths."

He was still talking but she wasn't listening. God help her, she couldn't think. Not with his heavy, hard erection pressed so closely to her aching center.

"The vow we took is just the first part of the ritual," he told her, bending his head low enough to whisper into her ear. She shivered as his breath brushed her skin. "To complete the first step, I must bury my body inside yours and stroke you until you shatter in my arms."

So not a problem. Teresa was on the cusp of shattering just standing here next to him.

Swallowing hard, she met his gaze. "Then we should finish it, right?"

He swept one hand down the length of her, following the curve of her figure. He traced the narrow dip of her waist and the full roundness of her hip and then slid around toward the front of her body.

Teresa held her breath as his big hand splayed across her abdomen and slowly, slowly, drifted lower. Breathing in short, sharp gasps, she gritted her teeth and moaned a need she barely recognized. She had never in her life been so amazingly taut with sexual tension. Even the first time with Rune couldn't have prepared her for this. This monumental, overpowering *need* that slammed within her at every beat of her heart.

When he moved his hand lower, she jolted and parted her thighs to give him easier access. She clung to him, with her free hand since he still had a tight grip on her left. Rocking into his touch, demanding more, needing *more.* Each caress of her damp, heated skin was as much a brand as the fiery tattoo that had burned her body. Again and again, he stroked her, rubbing his thumb across that single bead of pleasure until she was whimpering in his arms. He dipped one finger and then two, deep within her while still using his thumb to tantalize and tease.

He touched her and she burned; he stopped touching her and she ached. The coiled tension ratcheted up inside her and Teresa threw herself into the chase. She pushed herself harder and harder, straining to reach what he promised her. Hungering for the first hard slap of release that would shake her to her toes. It was almost there. She felt it. So close. So ... close ...

He tore his hand from her body and Teresa cried out in mindless hunger, "No, don't stop!"

"I haven't even begun," he promised, his voice a low rumble that seemed to wrap itself around her and shut out all other sensations. Letting go of her hand, he drove her backward a couple of steps until her spine was pressed against the warm rock wall of the cave. Then he dropped to his knees in front of her, pushed her thighs apart and covered her core with his mouth. Teresa gasped one long, shuddering breath and felt everything around her dissolve.

She clenched her fingers in his hair and held his head to her. She parted her legs farther, loving what he was doing to her, needing it more than she had ever needed anything in her life before. Sensations coursed and pooled inside her until she was nothing more than a jangled mass of live nerves. She looked down at him and watched as his clever tongue stroked and tasted her. She saw his lips move on her as he suckled at the very heart of her and she felt the shuddering tension spiral and coil inside her. She had a wild thought of keeping him trapped here, just like this, forever. She wanted this never to stop—even knowing that release would be staggering, she wanted this moment to go on and on.

But the spiraling tension reached a breaking point. Her breathing was hardly more than a whispered plea. Steam settled on her skin. Crystals shone down around her in a kaleidoscope of color. Her vision blurred as her body spun suddenly and completely out of control.

"Rune!" Her shriek resounded over and over again in the cave before losing itself in the rush of hot water pouring into the tub. In the steamy mist that coated their skin. In the glow of the crystals that seemed to shine as a blessing on their mating.

Her body jolted, and she held his head to her, needing the continuing lick of his tongue as her hips rocked and she pulsed with a sweeping roll of orgasms that chased one another through her body.

Breathless, staggered, she held him, watched him through passion-glazed eyes. His name was a whispered cry on her lips, murmured over and over again as if it were a prayer. And he heard her, gifting her with a new barrage of pleasure before the first had even died away. It went on and on until she was mindless, nothing more than sensation with a beating heart.

Just as she thought she'd reached her peak, had come as hard and long as she was capable, he showed her there was more. His hungry, delicious mouth took her again, pushing her higher, faster than before, until his mouth and tongue were as much pain as pleasure and still she wanted more of him.

She stared up at the shining crystals above her head and watched as they seemed to spin wildly along with her body and mind. He continued to taste her, his hot breath on her most sensitive flesh, his tongue tracing strokes of pleasure that rippled on and on and on until Teresa couldn't remember a time when she wasn't a part of this man. This moment. It was all so much more than she had ever expected or ever known.

When he finally pulled away from her, she wanted to weep for the loss of him, but she didn't get the chance. He picked her up, then gently set her down in the rushing water of the hot spring–fed tub.

The heat pushed through her, at once both relaxing and stimulating every one of her nerve endings. She didn't know what was to come next, but she was eager to find out.

"That was . . ."

"Only the beginning," he told her and settled himself in the tub as well.

His big, hard body took up a lot of room, but he reached for her and pulled her onto his lap, and Teresa fitted herself to his body like the missing lock to his key.

The first sweet slide of his body entering hers took her breath away. He was so big, so thick, he pressed on every sensitive nerve she possessed. Her body was still in the final throes of climax when he entered her and set everything afire all over again.

She swiveled her hips, grinding their bodies together. She arched her back, pushing her breasts forward, and Rune took her left nipple into his mouth. Again his talented lips, tongue and teeth worked her flesh with tender, thorough care. He nibbled at the spot where their mating brand had begun and Teresa felt the heat of that tattoo burn into her skin again. She felt the mating brand growing, spreading, claiming her body for Rune.

She looked down at his chest and saw another streak

of red beginning to blossom on his skin, in answer to the new flash of tattoo on her body. She touched his as he had touched hers, claiming him, accepting him—accepting that they were truly meant to be together.

For now.

Chapter 29

Thousands of miles away, Kellyn felt the rise of power shake the boundaries of the universe and she knew the witch Teresa and her Eternal had begun to mate.

Fingers closing around her crystal wineglass, she threw it across the room and watched it shatter against the far wall. The explosion of glass did little to calm her. Nothing much could. Still, her gaze locked on the red wine splattered like blood as its tendrils trailed down the cream-colored wall. That sight did cheer her slightly, but it didn't last.

Inside her, she felt a flicker of something like . . . hope. A foreign sensation fought to rise up within her and Kellyn deliberately pushed it back into the darkness. "I've lost another witch," she muttered grimly, "not the war."

That bright, flickering light within her dissipated and she sighed in satisfaction even as her temper began to burn again. Memories of finding and losing Shea Jameson only the month before to her Eternal and the call of white magic nearly choked her. Now another one had started along Shea's path.

"There's still time, though," she murmured, tightening the slender belt of her silk robe around her waist. Her naked skin was soothed by the kiss of the cool, luxurious fabric, but her spirit was less easily appeased.

Teresa Santiago had taken the first steps in the Awakening, but she wasn't completely out of reach just yet. Of course, Kellyn wouldn't lower herself to traipse through a Mexican desert after the witch, but there were others nearby. There was still time to stop Teresa before she found the Artifact. Before she returned it to Haven like a good little witch.

Kellyn hated not being able to *do* something. She was not accustomed to feeling powerless. She couldn't approach the next witch until she was awakened to her powers. She wouldn't be able to find the next one until her awakening power sent ripples through the magical world. One Awakened witch at a time would be called to her power. So Kellyn was now faced with nearly a month of downtime before she could take up the reins of this chase again. Which only made her more irritable. After all, there was only so much drinking, sex and shopping a witch could do to kill time.

Tapping her finger against her chin, Kellyn smiled softly as another thought occurred to her. There was something she could do after all, while waiting for word from the desert. Tomorrow she would make a trip to Virginia. Maybe it was time to sit in on Henry Fender's interrogations to cheer herself up.

"Babe."

She whipped around and glared at the tall, well-built human standing in the open doorway of her bedroom. As a concierge at this hotel, he was only passably competent. As a lover, though, he had proven to be more than adequate. A dick that seemed to never deflate, indefatigable stamina and a brain with the wattage of a guttering candle.

He yawned hugely, stretched his arms over his chest— the better to display his impressive rippling muscles, no doubt. Then he gave her a grin and reached down to stroke himself. His very impressive cock leaped to attention. "I got something for you right here, babe. You coming back to bed or what? 'Cuz if you don't want it, there's plenty others who do."

No respect, she thought in a sudden fury. This insignificant male thought to bring her to heel? To threaten her with his pathetic human whores? Irritation spiked. Just another pitiful symbol of how badly her day was going, this male was, as the humans often said, the last straw.

In her mind's eye, Kellyn indulged a whim and imagined the man's eyes exploding. She could see his skin peel from his bones. Hear him whimpering, pleading for mercy.

Some of what she was thinking must have shown on her face because he immediately shifted gears. "C'mon, baby. Let me take you on another ride. Let me show you something new."

Slowly, that flash of irritation drained away. Nothing to be gained by killing him now. If she did, she'd have to change hotels and then be forced to spend who knew how many hours finding another lover. And the next one might not be so well endowed. No, she wasn't finished with this one yet.

Still, he needed to learn just who was in charge around here.

Kellyn lifted her right arm, pointed at him and clenched her fist. Instantly, the insolent male's eyes bugged and his mouth dropped open. He lifted both hands to his throat and clawed at whatever was closing off his airway. Desperate, his eyes snapped to her as his skin mottled and his choking, gurgling groans sang into the room like the sweetest of music.

Slowly, she walked toward him, taking her time. She dropped her robe and felt the chill kiss of the air on her skin as she stopped alongside him. She flicked her fingers at his neck and he wheezed in his first easy breath since Kellyn had closed off his throat. Gasping, choking, he bent over at the waist, gulping in air.

As he did, she ran her fingertips down his spine, over the curve of his behind, until she cupped his balls in the palm of her hand.

He went absolutely still.

To make sure she had his attention, she gave a single, hard squeeze. He whimpered, but didn't move. Smart boy.

"Show me what you've got, then," she said, leaning in until she could lick the top of his ear. "But do yourself a favor and don't speak again."

Carefully, he turned his head, looked into her eyes and gave her a sharp nod. When she released him, he followed her into the bedroom like a well-trained puppy.

Chapter 30

Rune looked up into Teresa's eyes and felt something inside him fist around the heart that lay cold and still within his chest. For the first time in centuries, he felt *alive*. With the Mating begun, emotion was erupting inside him. Colors seemed brighter. Every breath was a feast.

It was more than the magic drawing them together. More than the power he felt shifting from her body to his and back again. It went deeper. It went to the heart of her. Who she had been. Who she was now. Who they were—and would be—together.

He still couldn't bring himself to trust her, but damned if he didn't admire her.

She was strong. Even in her vulnerability and pain, strength was what ruled her. She hadn't panicked in that damn village. Instead, she had stood her ground and reached for the nebulous powers just blossoming inside her. She had believed in her magic and used what power she had to take a stand beside Rune. To help him in their fight. To claim all that she was and demand more from the very gods who had first breathed life into their kind.

And she had thrown herself into the Mating with a

wild, sexy abandon that shredded Rune's self-control into rags.

She moved on him, swiveling her hips, drawing his cock higher and deeper into her slick heat. She pulled at more than just his seed. She reached something inside him he hadn't even been aware of.

A last remaining thin trickle of hope.

Hope that they might actually pull this off. Fix the past and face the future together.

He groaned and slid his hands from her waist to her hips. Holding on to her tightly, he moved her, quickening the lazy rhythm she had set. He wanted faster, harder. And one look at her told him she wanted the same. Fire burned in her eyes, as he knew it did in his. The flames of passion. The fire of a deep craving.

The hot water bubbled and frothed all around them, sending steam into the air and clouding their breath. It blurred his vision. But Rune saw her anyway. As she was now, as she had been then. Those snapping brown eyes of hers had remained the same through all the centuries. After haunting his dreams for hundreds of years, they were still powerful enough to pull him in even when he withheld his trust.

"Stop thinking," she ordered sternly. "Be with me. Be *here* with me."

So small, he thought, and yet she was so powerful. He felt her delicate body beneath his hands and shook his head, sending his long, wet hair back behind his shoulders. "I want you too badly. It's taking everything I have to keep myself in check."

"Then don't," she snapped, reaching for his hands and lifting them up to cover her breasts.

He groaned as her pebbled nipples rubbed against his palms. "If I lose control, I could hurt you."

"I *want* you out of control," she said, bracing her hands on his chest now, thumbing his flat nipples until new fire erupted inside him.

"You don't," he warned, fighting his own instincts.

"I do." She reached up again and squeezed his hands on her own breasts, showing him that she was ready for whatever he could give her. That she wanted all he could give her.

Snarling, he kneaded her breasts, his fingers and thumbs tweaking and pulling at the sensitive, rigid, dark tips until her eyes rolled back in her head and she was moaning his name. She writhed atop him, twisting her hips against his, searching for an end to the torment and not finding it.

Rune's instincts warred with caution and won.

He would have flashed her from the tub, but water mitigated the fires that made him. So he pulled free of her body, disregarding her protests, then holding on to her, leaped out of the tub and instantly called on his fire to flash them both to the wide, sumptuous bed in the other room.

There, he laid her on the silken coverlets like an ancient sacrifice. Breath heaved in and out of her lungs. Her eyes were wide as her gaze dropped to his thick erection. Then she smiled in invitation. Her legs splayed, she rocked her hips to him in welcome. He needed no further tempting.

Lifting her thighs, he draped her legs over his shoulders and took her. He shoved his body into hers with one long stroke. She gasped, arched her hips even higher and tipped her head back, baring the curve of her long, elegant neck. As he pistoned his hips against hers, taking her over and over again, he took her scent into his lungs.

The scent of his witch was earth, air and something that

was purely Teresa. Solely hers. She filled him, taking him as he took her. As he felt the mating fire burn in his chest again, he pulled back to watch another splash of red branding claim her luscious coffee-and-cream-colored skin.

Mine.

He watched her shatter. Felt her body contract around his even as she screamed his name. Her fingers clutched at him as he sheathed himself so deeply inside her he wasn't sure where his body ended and hers began. Teresa screamed again as another torrent of pleasure rocked her and in the next moment Rune surrendered to the inevitable and emptied himself into her.

Chapter 31

An hour later, Rune gritted his teeth and called on his immense self-control to withstand the need to touch Teresa again and again. He wanted nothing more than to flip her onto her back and drive himself into her until she was breathless. But there were things they had to talk about. Shaking his head, he said, "Now that the Mating's begun, you need to concentrate on focusing your magic."

"I know," she said, all hints of teasing gone from her expression. "But if we're hiding out, me drawing down the lightning is going to attract attention. Even way out here in the middle of nowhere."

"True," he said, and he didn't like it. "But we'll have to risk it. I'll be with you as you practice, to keep watch. And my presence will help you with your control, too."

"Okay, then what?" She dusted cookie crumbs from her fingers, balled up the used napkins and the apple core and stuffed them into an empty paper bag. "I mean, yes, I work on controlling the magic and you protect me. All good. But what's next? We go to Chiapas, find my grandmother and . . ." Her words trailed off into an unfinished question.

"And we figure out where your shard of the Artifact is," he said, realizing that saying it was a lot easier than finding it was going to be.

"Right. The Artifact. You could start by telling me just what exactly I'm looking for." Teresa pulled one edge of a red silk quilt up to cover her lap as she tucked her legs beneath her, Indian style. "I have the memory of that night when we set the demons loose." She paused to shudder. "But I don't remember the Artifact or what it looked like. I need to know, Rune. Everything you can tell me. What exactly *is* this Artifact?"

Rune leaned back on the mountain of pillows behind him and looked up at her as she watched him. Her features were open, her dark eyes shining with questions. He hated knowing that her eagerness would soon be tempered by fear. But he could see no way to avoid that.

In a quiet voice, hardly more than a hush, he said, "The Artifact was born of fire, breath and blood a thousand years before the birth of Christ. The element that formed it was black silver, created by a coven of powerful witches."

She shivered and took a shallow breath.

"What's wrong?"

"Black silver," she said, her tone breathless, as if even saying the words was difficult for her. "When you said that, I got a cold chill and a seriously uneasy feeling."

"Your memories," he said softly. "They're opening and you're remembering."

"I don't know that I want to," she admitted with a slight nod. "But I know that I have to, so tell me. What was this black silver?"

His gaze was locked on hers as he tried to explain. "The element was drawn from silver itself," he said. "Silver is a conduit for witch magic. It's of the earth and magnifies your powers as well as stabilizing them. But this new dark element was more powerful than that long-ago coven could imagine. It didn't just exist, it . . . *became*."

"What does that mean?"

He swiped one hand over his face and then pushed his hair back. Memories swam before him, thick as flies in summer, as he said, "It wasn't static. It grew. Became something . . . other." Frustrated, he sat up opposite her. "I'm not telling this well. The black silver was created *from* silver, so already it had a connection to the coven. But it was so much more. When the coven poured their power and energies into it, the element exploded with more potency than anyone had thought possible."

"What happened?"

"The black silver couldn't be contained. Not even by magic. Bits of it escaped into the world, beyond the reach of the coven, and it was incorporated into the life of humans."

"That doesn't sound good."

Remembering that long-ago time, Rune frowned. "It wasn't. The element itself was neither good nor bad, just incredibly powerful. But it was drawn to humans of strength—whether evil or decent—and it became whatever they needed it to be. The witches were helpless to gather it all. They were forced to simply witness what they'd wrought on the human world."

Teresa blew out a breath and jumped off the bed. Her hands scraped up and down her bare arms and firelight slid across her light brown skin like a lover's kiss. Her features shone in the dim light. Her steps were quick as she paced to the far wall and back again.

He watched her emotions charge across her features, one after the other, each more compelling than the one before. Fear, fury, worry, excitement and finally, he thought, determination. As she had in all of her previous incarnations, she had found her will. And it was fueled by fury.

"These are the witches I come from?" she muttered. "*This* is the last great coven? They nearly destroyed themselves."

Rune nodded. "Yes."

Whirling around to face him, she snapped, "They could have destroyed the world."

"Yes, but they didn't."

"Out of sheer luck," she argued, then shook her head vehemently. "I had no idea. None. I mean, objectively, you think, magic. I'm a witch. But I never once thought it would be this bad. What am I supposed to do with this? How can I fix it? What could make up for what we did?"

"All we have is atonement," he told her flatly.

"It's not enough," Teresa muttered. "All my life, I thought I was preparing for this. But who the hell could prepare to be faced with hundreds of years' worth of misery and mistakes?" Her insides trembling, she wondered how she ever could have expected to keep her heart out of this. Her heart was *in.* No mistake. She had to care. About Rune. About the past. About the future—if she had any hope at all of succeeding.

"Just . . . tell me what happened next. What did the coven do with the black silver?"

He sighed, got off the bed and walked to her. Resting his hands on her shoulders, he felt her quiver. "The coven took all the black silver they could gather and crafted the Artifact. A series of Celtic knots, entwined together into a crest of sorts. Most of the coven hailed from Eire, so the design was familiar to them."

She frowned as if trying to dredge up the memory to match his words.

"The coven shuddered when they realized the power in the Artifact and vowed to hide it from the world. To protect it—even from themselves." He added, "The Artifact itself was a powerful focus for magic. And they worried what might happen if they lost control of their own will and tapped the Artifact's energies. They kept it hidden in a place known only to them and it was safe for centuries. . . ."

"Until?" she asked, lifting her gaze to his.

The torchlight around the room seemed to swim in the air. A breeze he couldn't feel twisted the flames and sent their shadows dancing across the walls.

"Until the year twelve hundred. The last great coven gathered, reincarnations of the coven that had formed the Artifact. These witches," he said, his voice dropping, "had reached the pinnacle of their knowledge. Arrogant in their power, they lusted for more. They wanted new worlds to explore, new secrets to understand. They wouldn't listen to *us*," he added under his breath. "They heard no one but the voices inside their own minds and hearts. They opened the sealed Artifact, poured their essences into it and—"

"Opened the gateway to hell," she finished for him.

"Yes."

Teresa swayed on her feet as if she'd been dealt a physical blow. She closed her eyes, drew a long, deep breath and whispered, "And the demons raced through the portal. They tore at us, howling, screaming for blood and misery. We tried to fight them, but we couldn't. You fought to get to us, but couldn't enter our sacred circle."

"Yes," Rune said, reliving that night all over again as her whispered words drew up the images in his mind. A part of him regretted the necessity of Teresa remembering the ugliness of that last, awful night.

"Barastat," she said, clearly horrified by what her own mind was showing her. "A demon warlord. He came through the portal we opened and claimed this world for Lucifer."

Everything in Rune fisted and he felt again that long-ago fury and frustration at being magically kept from his witch. Being unable to reach her.

"Oh, God. Several of our sisters died," she said and a single tear rolled down her cheek, shining like a liquid diamond in the torchlight. "Somehow, we dropped the circle and the Eternals—you—rushed in to battle the demons. To force them back through the portal."

"We did," he said gently and with the tips of his fingers he lifted her chin until she was looking into his eyes. "And the coven fought at our side. As you remember the nightmare, remember also that when it mattered most, you and the coven made the right choice. You sent the bastards back to their hell."

She laughed shortly, a harsh sound that ripped free a small piece of his soul. "When it was too late to stop what we'd done, yes. God, the arrogance we had."

"Do you remember the rest?"

Blowing out a breath, Teresa nodded. "We shattered the Artifact magically, breaking it into pieces. Then each of us took one shard and hid it somewhere in the world, covering it with binding magic to protect it. Then we sentenced ourselves to eight hundred years of atonement, cast the spell and . . ."

"Died," Rune said, recalling exactly how he had mourned her, how he had been consumed with rage and grief at her passing. At what she and her sisters had wrought on all of them in a quest for more power. "You died. All of you. Leaving us to wait for your souls to re-incarnate. Again and again, we watched over you. Sometimes at your sides, sometimes no more than a shadow on the periphery of your existence.

"And always, we *waited*, sentenced by your spell as surely as you yourselves were, to a centuries-long agony of a half life." He slid his hands down to her upper arms and held on to her. Staring into her eyes, he felt himself drowning in those dark brown depths. "As immortals, we were forced to continue on through hundreds of dark, empty years. Without you. Without the other halves of our souls."

"Rune," she said, her mouth working as she tried to keep from crying, tried to keep her voice steady, "if we could have gone back and undone it, we would have."

"But you couldn't and so we all paid. As we continue to do."

She sighed heavily, blinked back the tears glistening in her eyes and said, "Centuries of incarnations, waiting for the spell to end with the Awakening so we could get the Artifact back and destroy it. Now we have thirty short days to try to set it all right."

His mouth flattened.

"What do you want from me? What's done is done. It can't be changed. It can't be forgotten. All we can do now is fight *this* fight. To bring the pieces of the Artifact together again so we can destroy it, once and for all."

Rune's gaze moved over her features, from the tear-dampened eyes to the stubborn tilt of her chin. He wanted to believe in her again. But it was hard to move past centuries of mistrust. He'd spent so many years wandering the earth, his soul an open wound because of the magic she had chosen over him. How was he now to turn his back on hundreds of years' worth of rage and give her his faith? His gaze dropped to the beginnings of the brand burned into her skin at her nipple and something inside him eased just a bit.

This was not the same, he told himself. Before, the witches had held themselves separate from the Eternals. Though they had been welcomed as partners in sex, they'd been denied the Mating ritual. The coven hadn't wanted to share magic—not even with a mate.

He touched her tattoo, rubbing his thumb over the physical reminder of her vow to him and his to her. This was more than the two of them had ever shared before. This lifetime was different. The Awakening had come and she was his as she had always been meant to be.

She drew a breath and his thumb dipped lower to smooth the tip of her pebbled nipple. Teresa's eyes slid closed on a sigh and Rune's body thickened to the point of aching.

"Enough talk," he muttered, dipping his head to claim her mouth in a kiss designed to wipe away centuries of misery. "I must have you."

Their mouths met in a frenzy, as if neither of them could ever taste or feel enough. And when she finally broke away, gasping for air, Rune was teetering on the edge of madness.

She lifted both hands to cup his face and looked into his eyes as she said, "I made a vow this time, Rune. We're mates. In this together. This time things will be different."

Her words inflamed him as much as her touch did. If he'd had a beating heart, it would have been crashing against his rib cage. But his hunger was alive and growing and that was all he needed at the moment. He tumbled her back on the bed and let the future take care of itself.

Chapter 32

They spent two days in Aladdin's cave, as Teresa thought of it. And during that time, they pushed the mating brand into showing itself fully.

"Lightning bolts," Teresa murmured, glancing down at the tattoo on her bare breast. There was one complete bolt jutting up from the edge of her nipple and beginning to curl into yet another bolt that was just starting to bloom onto her skin. Linked together, they would make a chain of sorts, like a storm cloud of lightning on her skin.

She smiled at the brand and, running her finger over the tattoo, she felt caged power within her, humming in the design itself. Ancient magic was sliding through her system with every passing moment, settling itself into her body at the cellular level.

Teresa felt stronger, more vibrant somehow. As if she was becoming what she'd always longed to be. She could feel her body waking up. Everything in her was reaching, stretching and growing. Her soul was sparklingly alive for the first time, awakening even as the magic within arose.

And the magic was breathtaking.

Rune had been right. She was gaining control of it, beginning to know how to wield the massive electrically charged bolts that seemed to dance to her whims. The thrill of magic sliding through her was something she thought she would never get tired of. This time with Rune was bringing her closer and closer to the witch she was destined to be.

And she hungered for it.

Just as she hungered to know more. To remember more.

Her Eternal had become the center of her life. She hadn't expected that. But there was more to him than his nature as a warrior. He protected her. Taught her.

She cared for him. His quiet voice. His steely eyes. The patience he showed when he taught her the very magic she needed to survive. His quick smile and fierce lovemaking. He was so much more than she had thought he would be.

Glancing over her shoulder to make sure Rune hadn't returned unexpectedly, she turned her gaze back to the mirror hanging over a low marble-topped table against the cave wall. She looked into her own eyes and realized that she was in some danger here. Yes, she was stronger, and her powers were blossoming like a water-starved flower experiencing spring rain.

But there was something more, too. A seed of something dark that scratched at the edges of her soul. Niggling temptation. Seduction. She felt it every time she called on her powers. Something as dark as the lightning was bright. And it *knew* her. Teresa felt it.

"You won't give in," she told her reflection, lowering her gaze to the tattoo on her mirror image's breast. She had come too far. Lost too much already to surrender herself to the past. Whatever attractions the pull of dark power had over her, they were nothing compared to the need to find justice for Elena and everyone else hurt by those chasing after this Artifact.

Feeling her twisted nerves settle, she pulled up a chair in front of the table. She had already laid out six of the white votive candles they'd gotten at the store what seemed like a lifetime ago.

While Rune was out gathering supplies and checking to make sure no hunters were near, Teresa was going to work a spell. Enlightenment. That's what she needed. Knowledge of the past, and of the future. A smidgen of help from whatever gods happened to be paying attention.

Gently, she reached out and laid one fingertip atop the wick of a solitary candle. Instantly, a spark shot from her skin, setting the wick ablaze. Smiling, she did the same for the other five until the ring of light burned in her reality and in the reflective-glass world as well.

Twice the candle-magic power.

She sat on the chair naked, and curled her legs up beneath her and squared her shoulders. Taking a deep breath, she closed her eyes, waved her open palms over the candle flames and chanted, "Light to light, I call. Remember me and answer. I search the past to gain the future. Light to light, I call."

Eyes still closed, she felt a wind sigh into the room, lift her hair from her shoulders and tangle it around her head. A tingle of awareness prickled her skin when she sensed a presence in the room. It wasn't Rune—she knew that, because if it had been, her body would have simmered with the raw hunger that tore at her whenever he was near. But Teresa couldn't risk stopping her spell and opening her eyes to confront whatever was with her.

If it was a helpful spirit, she would have what she asked. If it was death, she would know that soon enough. She took a breath and continued to move her hands in graceful arcs and designs in the air above the lit candles. If she interrupted the spell now, there was a possibility of a backlash of magic that she wasn't strong enough yet to combat.

So she went on, gathering her strength. Knitting together the tattered ends of her courage and holding on tightly.

"Light to light, I call," she chanted again, her voice louder this time, more insistent. Her hands moved faster now, in intricate patterns over the candles. She felt the heat of the flames against her palms but didn't let that deter her. She knew these hand gestures well. Had learned them from her grandmother when she was a girl.

The gestures represented sacred symbols meant to call down the attention of the old gods. Teresa focused on her task and tried to ignore the unseen presence. She felt the candle flames wavering now with the growing wind. Goose bumps rose on her arms and along her spine. Magic sizzled and snapped. She felt power dancing all around her as the presence came closer, until it was only steps away. The small hairs at the back of her neck stood straight up as she finished the spell.

"I seek answers," she murmured, her voice little more than a whispered prayer. "I seek to know. Let the light guide me to the right path for knowledge and power to fight the enemy's wrath."

The wind abruptly died.

She opened her eyes.

The candle flames *whoosh*ed three feet high, then extinguished in a blink.

And in the mirror someone moved up behind her.

Teresa lifted her gaze, felt tears well and whispered, "Elena?"

Chapter 33

A few hours later, Rune snapped his satellite phone open, hit number three on speed dial and waited impatiently as a distant phone rang. His mind raced and his blood pumped with the need to return to Teresa. Standing on an outcropping of rock a half mile from the cave where she waited, Rune felt more alone than he had in centuries.

He'd had to leave her behind when he returned to the village for supplies and now he was grateful that he had. He had seen the circling flock of buzzards first. Dipping and wheeling in the wind, they performed a dance of death that told Rune he wouldn't have to worry about avoiding the villagers.

Flashing to the middle of the narrow street, he had been surrounded by carnage. Every villager—men, women, and children—was dead. All of them. They had died in a cascade of bullets, their bodies ripped and torn, and now the buzzards were dropping out of the sky like black snow to finish them off.

He had taken what they needed from the store and gotten out of the little town as quickly as possible.

It had been a long time since he had experienced real fear. But it was with him now.

Whoever had annihilated that village was after Teresa. And they clearly didn't care who they had to kill to get to her.

Every protective instinct he had ever possessed was roaring to the surface. His huge body practically vibrated with the need to safeguard her. Hold her in the circle of his arms, safe from anything that might harm her. But more even than the need to protect her was the ancient, pulsing demand to claim her body again and again. To drive the mating brand to completion.

To finish this quest.

Because only then would she be completely safe.

"Rune. Problem?"

Torin's voice shattered his thoughts and jerked him back to the present. An Eternal like Rune, Torin had been the first of them to brand his Awakened witch and find their shard of the Artifact. Together, he and Shea had returned the black silver to Haven—the coven's home in Wales.

Wales, with its lush greenery and crashing waves against timeworn cliffs, was a long way from here, Rune mused. In more ways than one. In Wales, there was safety. The coven's home offered exactly what its name implied—a haven. Here, in Mexico, Rune felt danger creeping ever closer. His sharp gaze swept the dark, empty desert around him. The emptiness was a facade, he knew. There was life out there, behind every rock and bush. Snakes, coyotes, wildcats—not to mention the kind of predator that walked on two legs. Hunters roamed these darkened sands. He could feel it—a hum just under his skin that warned of an encroaching menace.

But from where?

"Lots of problems." Rune's gaze narrowed on the sliver of moon shining down out of a black star-swept sky.

"What?" Torin's voice was taut, expectant.

"I've got Teresa. We're in Mexico, going to head to Chiapas to see her grandmother in a day or two."

"And?"

"Most recently? We stopped in a village for supplies and got made. A couple of the townspeople tried to earn the reward for capturing a witch. I took care of it and got Teresa to Finn's cave."

"Sounds fine. So what happened?"

"Just got back from that village. Went for more supplies. Somebody had been there. Took out the whole place." Shaking his head, he narrowed his gaze on the mountain where Teresa waited for him. "Every last soul dead."

"Fuck. Any idea who?"

"No." Grinding his teeth, Rune continued. "There's more, Torin. I was going to call you about this, anyway, even without the dead village. Elena Vargas, a friend of Teresa's, was killed in Sedona. She was a doctor, Torin. Not a witch. She helped us out and no more than an hour or so later she was dead."

Seconds of silence ticked by before Torin said, "How was she killed?"

"Looked like she was strangled. But not before she was tortured." He hissed in a breath at the memory. He hadn't wanted to show Teresa how her friend's death had affected him, but it had. The woman had died because she had helped *him*. For that alone, Rune owed her justice. "Arm and hand broken—but Torin, one side of her body was burned to a crisp."

"Say again?"

"You heard me right." The image of Elena's body rose up in his mind again and he didn't like what he was thinking. Hard not to go there, though. "There's no way that was done without magic. Unless the guy had a portable blowtorch he carried with him."

"Damn it. What the hell is this?"

"I don't know," Rune admitted. He wiped one hand across his jaw and then scrubbed the back of his neck. "I hate even thinking this, but—is there any chance that one of the Eternals has gone rogue?"

Chapter 34

"No." The answer came back fast, imperious. Torin had long been the de facto leader of the Eternals. He was the one who had kept most of them from losing their minds during the long centuries of waiting. He was the one who had found his mate first. Their union had set them all on the course that had been charted for them eight hundred years ago.

And now Torin was a voice of reason when Rune really needed one. Because ever since he'd seen Elena's body, he'd been half convinced that one of the hunters chasing him and Teresa was an Eternal. How else to explain the controlled burns? If he was right about that, then the Awakening itself was in a world of hurt.

"Not a chance," Torin said flatly. "We've all been tight for centuries. We know each other too well. If one of us went off the reservation, then we'd all know about it. Damn it, Rune, this isn't one of us. There's got to be a sorcerer or a demon working with the hunters. It's the only explanation."

"Maybe." But it hadn't felt like a demon hit to Rune. "I didn't feel any dimensional magic at the site," he said. "No lingering trace of demon energy. And if there's a stray sorcerer out there, why haven't we heard about it?"

"Who the hell knows?" Torin's voice got sharper. "It's a big world, you know? All kinds of bad shit could be hiding out there. Hell, there's always *somebody* trying to stop us and kill our mates. Why would a damn sorcerer be out of line?"

"True enough," Rune acknowledged. A skittering sound caught his attention and he slowly swiveled his head toward it. His gaze swept the nearby area, then searched farther out, looking for a shadow that shouldn't be there. A hint of movement in the blackness. But there was nothing.

"The Eternals are solid, Rune," Torin said, his voice grim and hard as if he was trying to convince not only Rune but himself. "We've waited too long for the Awakening. Now that it's finally here, there's no way one of us would turn at this late date. Not when everything is finally on the line."

Rune wanted to believe. He thought of the immortals, who were his brothers, and he couldn't imagine any of them turning against the group. They had all been stalwart for centuries, banding together for strength. Their god, Belen, had created them for this very purpose. Why would one of them choose to throw his birthright away? And for what?

Still, his mind argued the point. He couldn't come up with another explanation for what had happened to Elena. And a man made of fire was a pretty damn good one whether he liked it or not.

"You think I *like* even considering this? You're crazy, Torin. They're all my brothers, too. But crazy times can push anybody over the edge. And you didn't see Elena's body." Shaking his head, he turned his face into the sharp October wind slicing across the desert, carrying the scent of sage. "The burns were deliberate. One half of her body. No more. Hell, it was like a line had been etched down the center of her. Magic was involved."

"Undoubtedly," Torin agreed. "But that doesn't necessarily make the killer an Eternal."

Rune shook his head again, hearing his old friend but still having doubts. "What about Egan?"

"Are you on crack?" Torin countered. "Hell, we just found out last month from that freak-of-nature witch Kellyn that she *trapped* Egan in a white-gold cage somewhere at the bottom of the fucking ocean. And now you're gonna blame him for this?"

"You think I want to?" Rune's angry shout shattered the quiet of his surroundings and instantly he grimaced and lowered his voice. Sound traveled for miles in the desert and he didn't need to help his enemies find them. "Damn it, I called Egan brother for centuries before he disappeared, but we've only got that 'freak-of-nature witch's' word for it that she's got him trapped. What if he's the one who went rogue?"

"No fucking way. Not a chance. I'll never believe that of one of us. Turning our backs on who we are means turning from our witches. We wouldn't turn on our mates, Rune."

"But we won't know that for sure unless we find Egan. Anybody have anything?"

"No," Torin grumbled and Rune could picture his fellow Eternal, stalking back and forth, scraping one hand through his long hair over and over again in a fit of frustration. "There's nothing. I put Odell and Cort on it a week ago, but we don't even know where to start looking."

"Can't Shea do a locator spell on him or something?"

"Not without a focus. Something that belongs to Egan. And we've got nothing."

"What about his place in Edinburgh?"

"You think we didn't check?" Torin barked. "I sent Cort there to bring something back, but when he got there, the place was empty. Either that fucking witch cleaned it out to prevent us finding him or—"

"Or," Rune finished for him, "Egan's the rogue and he went into hiding."

"No, damn it. It's not one of us."

"Well, who, then?" Rune threw one hand up, called on the fire and watched his hand burn, as if he needed something to focus his rage on. "If it was a dark witch, I would have sensed her presence in Sedona. Demons leave behind trace dimensional residue and a sorcerer leaves astral energy. I could have tracked it."

"Maybe. It's a big city, man."

"Not that damn big and whoever was there at Elena's office was close to Teresa and me." The flames on his hand winked out and again he was surrounded by darkness. All around him, silence reigned but for the small noises made by the creatures whose home he had invaded. "There's something else going on, Torin. Something big—and it's out there alongside the hunters and the feds."

"Fuck me."

A rueful laugh shot from Rune's throat. "Yeah, that about covers it."

He felt Torin's mounting frustration as his own. But Torin was in Wales, on the other side of the damn globe, and wouldn't be able to help even if Rune asked for it.

Torin sighed. "You need me to get a couple of the other Eternals out there to help?"

"No," Rune said. He didn't like thinking it, but damn

if he wanted more Eternals around here until he was convinced they weren't at the heart of this mess. He didn't want to believe that Egan had gone rogue, but not even Torin could deny that it was a possibility. "I can handle things here. I'll keep Teresa safe and we'll accomplish our task. But I do think you should check into this."

"No shit," Torin said. "I'll get Shea and her aunt Mairi on it. They can check the Sanctuary libraries."

"Good." That was something else they'd discovered only last month. The earth's witches had maintained knowledge down through the ages and had stored everything they learned in dimensional libraries that any witch could access through a portal if she was close enough to one of the Sanctuaries. "Hope you've got some ideas, because I don't have a clue what they should be looking for. If it's not one of us—"

"And it's *not*," Torin said.

"Then we're boned." Rune shook his head. "There's something new out there, Torin, and we need to know what it is."

"Agreed," his friend said. "Shea and Mairi will cover this with witchcraft. In the meantime, Mairi's mate, Damyn, and I will hunt down a few of the other Eternals. See what we can find out. And we'll step up the search for Egan. Damned if I'm willing to accept that he or any of us is behind that doctor's death. We'll figure out who the new player is."

Rune slapped his phone shut and tucked it into the pocket of his jeans. He was no closer to an answer, but at least he wasn't alone in his hunt now. Torin and Damyn would check on the Eternals in Europe. Rune would contact Finn and get him to do the same in the States.

He turned his head to stare at the rock formation

nearly half a mile away from him, and he had to smile. It jutted into the sky, sharp and angled, like a fist raised skyward. Naturally Finn would choose to build his home beneath such a rock. The Eternal was always ready for a fight—and, Rune told himself, that would come in handy if this got any uglier.

Beneath that mountain Teresa was waiting for him. She had no idea that her precarious safety had just gotten a lot more complicated. He thought back to the massacre at the village and felt a ball of ice drop into the pit of his stomach.

Federal agents, police, violent civilians, witches, demons, sorcerers, even perhaps a rogue Eternal—they were all out there, just waiting for their chance at her.

But as long as Rune lived, no one would hurt his woman. He would kill any who tried.

Chapter 35

Parnell sat in the shadows, watching his "allies" down shot after shot of tequila. The ramshackle tavern they waited in was hardly more than a hut, but nothing more was needed, anyway. This was just a stop on a long, well-laid-out road. Lifting his beer, Parnell took a sip and set the glass down as his gaze traveled the smoky interior.

Lights were dim, as they were in most bars. There was a fire roaring in a stone hearth on the far wall, dispelling the October chill in the desert night. Hard-bitten men with murder in their eyes gathered around the tables, playing cards and drinking incessantly. They were celebrating the slaughter of the village, he told himself. Proud of having shot down unarmed civilians and telling war stories as if they'd faced down a demon horde.

Idiots.

He had had them kill everyone in the village for expediency's sake. Otherwise he wouldn't have bothered. But he hadn't wanted to risk word getting out about the witch and her immortal bodyguard.

Now he watched the men who worked for him. He knew there wasn't one of them who wouldn't sell him out for the right amount of cash. But knowing that, he paid them well. He hated what they were. Brutality for its own sake served no one. A man without loyalties couldn't be trusted and these men had no fealty to anyone but the person paying them. There was no discipline here. No belief system. No driving ambition beyond the visceral one to maim and destroy.

He reined in his disgust with effort. For now, he needed these men. For now, they were a means to an end that he was determined to reach. For too long he and his brothers had languished in obscurity. Pushed aside and banished without another thought by the very god who had created them. All for the sake of *them*.

The Eternals.

Immortal bastards, all of them. Self-righteous, arrogant assholes who thought that they and they alone were the keepers of the magic. Well, he and the others had a surprise for all of them. After centuries of exile, it was time to show themselves. To reclaim what had been taken. To step up and announce themselves not only to the Eternals but to the world.

And to the witches.

"Any word yet?"

A voice interrupted his thoughts and Parnell flicked a glance at the obnoxious human who had had the nerve to plunk himself down at Parnell's table. With short black hair, whiskered jaws and dark brown eyes, Miguel was probably thought to be a handsome man. Unless one took the time to look deeply into eyes that were as empty as the desert he hailed from.

Parnell could have appreciated the man's dedication to violence if there'd been a reason for it. Instead, this smiling, murderous creature was simply soulless. And the man appeared to be under the mistaken impression that he and Parnell were partners. Equals. When the truth of the matter was that Parnell would have liked nothing better than to see him dead this instant for his treatment of the witch, Teresa.

Instead of following orders and romancing the woman, this boil on the ass of humanity hadn't been able or willing to hide his own abusive nature from her. And so Teresa, being a sensible witch, had tossed him out of her life. Luckily for the bastard sitting opposite him, Parnell had plans for the witch. Personal plans beyond the scope of the strategy that had been laid in place over the last centuries. So if the human male had actually harmed Teresa in any way, Parnell would have ripped his lungs out of his chest and left him gasping for air that would never have come.

Parnell watched the man and felt an inferno rage inside him. Flames leaped to life on his fingertips, flaring blue and yellow and red.

Miguel looked at them, grinned and observed, "Man, if I could do that, I wouldn't be wasting my time in this shithole of a bar." Shrugging, he asked again, "Any word?"

Parnell took a breath and allowed the flames to fade away. He took another slow sip of his beer before trusting himself to speak. "We've heard nothing yet."

Those handsome features twisted into a disappointed pout. "Then how will we know where to go next?"

Parnell's irritation grew by leaps and bounds. To be questioned by anyone went against everything inside him. For those questions to come from a human that he would love nothing more than to execute was even more insulting. But he would play the game as he had laid it out.

"Everything's in place," he said, promising himself

the pleasure of killing this particular human as soon as possible. "Our eyes and ears will keep us informed."

"I still say we should just go to Chiapas," the man whined impatiently. "If you had listened to me, we wouldn't be sitting here in this crappy bar waiting for word that will only tell us what I already said." He leaned back until the rickety wooden chair beneath him rested solely on its back legs. "I know Teresa. She'll go to her grandmother. She was always talking about the old witch. *Abuela* this, *abuela* that. Made me sick. So I know all about the old woman. We could be there right now, waiting. Then we could grab Teresa the minute she shows up." He smiled to himself. "I can't wait to see her again, you understand. I've got some unfinished business with her. And once she's no good to you guys, she's mine. Right?"

"Idiot." Parnell kicked out, sent the chair toppling over and the man in it sprawling. Before he could leap to his feet, Parnell had one foot on his sternum, holding him down.

The bar went suddenly silent, as if even these apelike men understood that a line had been crossed. Parnell took a moment to allow his fire-dazzled gaze to sweep over each and every man in the room until all of them shivered and turned their heads away. Only then did he focus that glare on the man beneath his boot.

"Listen very carefully, you mongrel dog," he said. His voice was low, but the strength of it carried across the room nevertheless. "You get what I say you get and nothing more. If you touch the witch . . ." He called on the flames, watched them race across his palms and fingers, then flicked a stream of living fire down onto the horrified man. Flames licked greedily at the edges of his down jacket and smoke twisted and danced like a basketful of snakes. "You'll die more painfully than your pitiful brain can even imagine. Do you understand?"

Miguel nodded in a jerky movement, hands flailing as he tried desperately to extinguish the fire currently trying to devour him. "I get it. I get it, okay? Put it out!"

Parnell sneered at him, waited an extra moment or two for pure drama's sake, then waved one hand at the flames. Instantly the fire was gone, leaving only the scent of charred polyester dirtying the air.

Once released, Miguel scrambled away, joining the other men and keeping as far from Parnell as possible. Point made, Parnell resumed his seat in the shadows.

Inside him an inferno raged, but he allowed none of it to show on his features. These humans were nothing. Just cannon fodder in a war that had been building for eons. The Eternals were the true enemy—the target of justifiable fury Parnell and his brothers had been harboring since what felt like the beginning of time.

The mere thought of the Eternals was enough to make Parnell want to howl and rage. But cold, clear thinking was better, he reminded himself. His plans for the future were vast and all-consuming and would turn the Eternals' campaign to dust. That knowledge alone was what kept him going. What filled his heart and mind and soul with a black joy.

The Eternals would pay for turning their backs on Parnell and the others. They'd be forced to finally remember *all* of their history. And when it was too late, they would see that they were going to lose. Tradition said that an Eternal and his witch would go alone to find their share of the Artifact.

And tradition would be what finally killed them all.

Chapter 36

"Elena? Oh, my God, is that really you?"

Teresa's breath stopped short in her lungs. It felt as though a cold hand was fisted around her heart, smothering the steady beat until it only whispered anxiously in her chest. In the mirror, her best friend's image wavered and twisted, as if her spirit were trying to gather itself but failing. She was here and yet not here.

Elena looked like a photograph left out in the rain until the brilliance of the colors faded and wept into each other, becoming hardly more than a memory of the original. Smudged, unfinished, Elena smiled at her and Teresa's eyes filled with tears she refused to let fall. She didn't want to risk blurring this vision further. She wanted—needed—this to be real.

In an unseen wind, her friend's white lab coat ruffled and thinned as though tiny fingers were shredding the fabric. But her eyes were the same. Clear. Familiar. A dark, knowing brown that in life had always shone with kindness and humor. Now in those eyes Teresa read only fear.

"Teresa, my killer is coming," Elena said, her voice wavering in and out. "Your *abuela* . . ."

"What?" Teresa felt a jolt of adrenaline spike as fear rose up to grab the base of her throat. "What about my grandmother?"

"Danger, Teresa. So are you—" She stopped and looked over her shoulder at the emptiness as if she'd heard someone approach. When she looked back at Teresa she managed a small smile. "I can't stay. I'm not even sure how I got here. Teresa . . . you have to know . . . Beware of the immortal."

Confusion rippled through her along with the instinctive urge to argue with her friend. Why should she fear Rune? "Elena, he won't harm me. He's my mate."

Elena shook her head and the action caused her image to ripple, like the surface of a still pond after a stone had been tossed in. "The immortal is dangerous. You have to believe me."

"I do." She absolutely believed that Elena had been sent in answer to the candle magic she had performed. Her friend's spirit had come in response to her plea for knowledge, so what she was saying must be believed. It just didn't make any sense at all.

She turned on the stool and looked into the room, but her friend wasn't there. The only thing that met Teresa's gaze was the plush room that had become her haven in the last couple of days. Quickly, she looked back into the mirror and saw that Elena's image was still trapped in the glass, but fading fast.

"He wants *you*, Teresa," Elena said, the words beginning to slur and weaken. "Not just for the witchcraft, but for . . ."

Teresa frowned as she missed that last part. What did this mean? He wanted her for what? If this was about sex, then Teresa could assure her friend that that particular ship had already sailed. Pretty impressively, too.

"He's supposed to want me, Elena. He's my mate."

An otherworldly wind snatched at Elena's short hair and plucked at the hem of her white coat. "Be careful, Teresa. Trust the Eternal, fear the immortal."

"But—" None of this was making any sense. Rune was both an Eternal *and* an immortal. And how could she not trust him? Hadn't he already earned her belief in him by saving her? By beginning the Mating, branding her as his?

"No more time," her friend said hurriedly. "Spell book. Serena. Find it."

Irritation and confusion sputtered together inside Teresa. How would Elena know about a spell book? Who was giving her this information? And why?

"Who? Who's Serena?"

"Find it. Library," her friend urged frantically as her image faded.

"Elena!"

She was gone.

In a breath, the image was gone and Teresa was alone again. Now the tears fell, and as they did, a cold knot of tension settled behind her breast. What the hell was she supposed to do with this? Who was Serena? And where was this library Teresa was supposed to search? What had Elena meant about trusting the Eternal and not the immortal?

Glaring into the mirror, Teresa muttered, "What the hell kind of help was that? I ask for clarity and knowledge and now I'm more confused than ever. Damn it, Elena, come back! Tell me what you meant!"

Not trust Rune?

Impossible. She *did* trust him. And he had earned it. He'd saved her ass a couple of times already, hadn't he? Her gaze dropped again to the lightning tattoo on her breast and she swallowed hard. He was her mate. This relationship was destined. If she couldn't trust him, why the hell had the mating brand shown up at all? And if he meant her harm, why hadn't he just left her to die in the village?

Maybe because he needs me to find the Artifact? Maybe he doesn't want to return it to the witches. Maybe he's got other plans for it that don't include me.

"No," she said, arguing with herself. That idea was ludicrous. He wasn't interested in anything but completing their quest.

But what if his idea of completion was different from hers? What if he had other plans for that ancient chunk of black silver? The knot inside her tightened until she could hardly draw a breath. There was a cold dread settling in the pit of her stomach, no matter how much she tried to convince herself that Elena's warning had nothing to do with Rune. Her mate was honorable. She had seen that firsthand. He had been nothing but honest with her since he had shown up out of nowhere to save her ass from the MPs in the helicopter.

Hell, he had been *shot* saving her.

But why would the gods send Elena to warn her if there was no danger?

"God, how am I supposed to know what to do?" Alone, Teresa felt her mind whirl with the possibilities.

Was Rune the mate and partner he claimed to be? She wasn't stupid. She knew he was holding something of himself back from her. When he watched her, she could see in his eyes that he didn't really trust her.

Was that only because of their long, complicated past? Or was it something else? Was he merely biding his time, waiting for the right moment to make his move? And if he was, how could she defend herself against it?

"Damn it." She had gone into this Mating ritual with her eyes wide open. She had promised to be his mate, even knowing that she wouldn't allow herself to love him. So how was she so different from Rune? She was holding something back, too.

But she *had* trusted him.

Until now.

Suddenly cold, Teresa pushed off the chair, walked to the bed and grabbed the first item of clothing she found: one of Rune's T-shirts. It was black, of course, and when she tugged it on over her head, the hem fell practically to her knees. His scent surrounded her, caressed her and seemed to ease the doubts flooding her mind and heart.

He was her mate. Her partner.

She would trust him because trusting Rune meant trusting her own instincts and if she was going to survive the next few weeks, she'd have to be able to do that.

A whistle in the distance reached her and Teresa whipped her head up. "Chico?"

The whistle sounded again from far away and Teresa raced for the cave entrance. That familiar sound kept coming, making her quicken her steps until she was running down dark, twisted tunnels carved from the rock. She stubbed her toe on an outcropping of stone and saw stars, but she kept going. Now more than ever, she needed her pet with her. She was desperate to have something she could count on. Believe in. Chico had been with her for two years. He was more than just a bird. He was her companion—another heartbeat in the loneliest hours of the night. He was the one she gave her secrets to.

Smiling in spite of her racing, churning thoughts, Teresa hurried on, down what seemed like miles of stone corridors with only the occasional torch to light her way. Somehow Chico had found his way back to her and she was going to take that as a good sign.

She heard the frantic beating of his wings as he flew about the enclosure. His shrieks and whistles came sharper now as she neared him. The closer she got to the main entrance of the cave, the farther behind she left the torchlight. Rune had deliberately kept most of the way dark in order to confuse any pursuers who might stumble across the cave itself.

Her eyes adjusted to the darkness, but the eerie sensation of being on her own in what might as well have been a rock tomb shook her. The stone floor tore at her bare feet, but she ignored the pain.

Alone in the gloom, she suddenly wished Rune was with her—and that told her all she needed to know about her instincts urging her to believe in him. And as her mind began to reassert itself, claiming dominion over her emotional reaction to the sound of Chico's shrill whistle, her steps slowed.

What if that isn't Chico? What if the hunters from the village tracked us to the cave and are pretending to be Chico just to bring me into the open where they can capture me?

Fear walked with her.

The darkness seemed to deepen even though she was nearing the outside world. She could tell because a cold wind was sliding in off the desert and goose bumps erupted on her legs and arms. Rune's scent walked with her and she wished again that he was there beside her. Her feet were cut from the rocky ground and her chest felt tight, but she kept going. She had to. She was alone here and if there was an enemy, better she meet him on her own terms than wait for him to come to her.

She wasn't armed, but she wasn't defenseless, either. She still had her magic. She flexed her fingers, glanced down and watched sparks fire in a blue-white shower from her fingertips. Taking a deep breath, she moved around the last bend in the passage, prepared to defend herself or die trying.

Something rushed at her out of the darkness and she shrieked.

So did Chico.

Then the bird landed on her shoulder, shivered to fluff his feathers and settled comfortably, his claws digging in through the T-shirt. Teresa let out a huge gust of air as relief swamped her. Reaching up, she stroked Chico's yellow and deep orange chest. "Where have you been and how did you find me?"

"An interesting question," Rune said from the mouth of the cave, where he dropped two bags of supplies.

Teresa looked up at her Eternal, backlit by the starry night. He looked formidable, menacing. His black coat stirred around his legs and even in shadow she could see the gray of his eyes pitch and swirl with shades of pewter and silver.

Elena's warning whispered through her mind and Teresa trembled.

Only moments ago she had been wishing he was there with her. Now, she didn't know whether to be grateful to have him back—or to be worried.

As if sensing her hesitation, Chico shrieked, *"Run for it!"*

Chapter 37

Rune looked from the bird on Teresa's shoulder into the eyes of his witch. "How did that get here?"

"I don't know," she admitted with a smile, turning her face to look at the small creature. "But lorikeets are incredibly smart. And loyal, too. It's not the first time Chico's found me like this."

Walking into the cave, Rune studied the brightly colored bird and couldn't quite hide his dislike of the creature. Something about it didn't sit well with Rune. "The village is miles from here. How would it find you across the desert?"

"Beats me," she admitted with another smile. "But he did. Maybe it's a sign of good things to come."

"Maybe," he said, but his voice made it clear that he doubted it.

She looked up at him and her smile slowly faded. "What about you? Did you find anything out there? Any sign of the hunters? Did you have trouble at the village?"

There was no way he could keep this from her. She had to know the kind of dangers they were up against.

"No. There was no trouble at the village. Everyone there was dead."

"What?" She staggered back a step and the bird on her shoulder lifted his wings as if to steady her. "Everyone? When? How? Did you—"

"No," he snapped instantly. "I didn't kill them. Whoever's after us did. That's my guess, anyway. Probably didn't want any witnesses who could identify you or me to the feds."

"Oh, my God." She lifted one hand to her mouth and it wasn't until then that Rune noticed she was wearing one of his T-shirts. She looked like a young girl. Innocent. Hurt. And he hated like hell to add to the burdens already weighing her down.

Then he remembered her inner strength and, as if she recalled it, too, she lifted her chin and asked, "Did they track us? I mean, did you see any sign of them following?"

"No," he said, shifting a quick look to the bright-eyed bird. "There's nothing—for now, anyway. I picked up enough stuff in the village to last us a few days. We'll take it with us when we go."

"When are we leaving?"

"Tomorrow morning," he said, and taking Teresa's arm, he turned her around to walk her back down the long tunnels. When she hissed in a breath, he frowned. "What's wrong?"

"My feet hurt, that's all."

He looked down and muttered, "You came through the tunnels barefoot? You could have cut yourself to the bone on these rocks."

She shrugged. "I was in a hurry. I heard Chico and—"

"The damn bird again." He bent, swept her up into

his arms and held her close while he called on the fire and flashed them to the heart of the cave.

When they appeared in the plush living area, Teresa looked up at him. "Now why didn't you do that the first time we came here instead of making me walk all the way?"

He gave her a quick look before he set her down on the edge of the bed and knelt in front of her. "Because I wanted to walk the tunnels. Make sure there was no one lurking there."

"Ah," she acknowledged. "Good point."

"Thanks." He shook his head as he shifted his gaze from her face to the bird perched on her shoulder. Its beady eyes were fixed on Rune and he had the distinct impression that the creature was watching him with malice. Nothing he'd like better than to get rid of the damn thing. He didn't like it, but more, he didn't trust it. How the hell had it found them? Did Teresa really believe that a small bird like this one could smell her across miles of desert? That it could avoid the raptors and other predators living in the wild?

"What're you thinking?" she asked.

"What?" His gaze snapped back to hers. "Just wondering how your bird found you this far from the village."

Teresa smiled and looked at her pet, bobbing up and down on her shoulder. "He's amazing. He's always been able to find me. I used to leave him at home and go into the desert to practice spells or whatever and after an hour or two, there he was."

Maybe his distrust of the creature was born simply from his dislike for *any* bird. But in any case, Chico wasn't his main concern at the moment. Teresa was.

She was his mate. Under his protection. But even as

he tried to assure himself that his consideration for her was based on mutual respect, he knew it was more.

Teresa had already claimed a small corner of his heart and it would be pointless to pretend otherwise. He held her bare feet in his palms and looked at the dozens of scrapes and deep scratches. She winced and he saw it, hating that she was in pain, even this slight discomfort.

"Hold still."

"Rune . . ."

"Shh." He closed his eyes, called up the fire and let the living flames dance across his hands and the soles of her feet. Warmth spread from him to her and back again in a link that had been destined to be forged. The inevitability of it filled the empty spaces within him and he gave himself up to the rush of it.

"The cuts are healed," he finally said.

"Thanks." She tried to pull free, but he held on to her. Need swamped him and he yielded to the draw of the Mating ritual. To claim her again and again. To hold on to her despite the danger building around them.

He rose up, took her mouth with his and felt her surrender as her body answered his call.

A low, throaty growl erupted from his throat as he looked into his woman's eyes. Her desire raged and fed his own. Her body ached and called to his. The Mating clawed at each of them and the skin around the branding tattoo burned.

Keeping his gaze fixed on hers, he swept one hand in front of his body and his clothing was gone in a blink. He did the same with the T-shirt she wore, baring her luscious, honey-colored skin to him. She sighed and reached for him, dragging her nails along his thighs and up until she was cupping his hard, heavy length in both palms.

Rune hissed in a breath and held perfectly still while

her fingers explored him. Up and back, her hands slid over his rock-hard body and he groaned when her touch smoothed the very tip of him, sliding a single bead of moisture there in tight circles designed to drive him mad.

His thoughts racing, his body churning, Rune couldn't stand another second of not touching her. He pulled her up, tossed her back onto the bed and saw her mouth curve in pleasure as he bent to lower himself over her. Body brushing hers, the tips of her nipples practically scalding his already heated skin, he took one kiss and then another, teeth tugging at her lower lip until she groaned and lifted her hands to cup his face.

Her scent surrounded Rune, pulling him in, drawing him closer to her heat, to the mystical bonds entwining them so completely. He swept his hands up and down her body, coveting every inch, exploring every curve. Every time with her was like the first time. His body ached for release and his soul stirred in recognition of the one woman he would always need.

She whispered to him, her words broken, coming on a sigh, lost in the cavernous room. But he didn't need to hear her to know that she felt as he did. That the fire burning inside him was also engulfing her. She arched up, offering him her breasts, and he accepted the offering. His mouth closed over her left nipple and he felt it pebble and harden with a few quick flicks of his tongue. Desire pumped thick in his veins as he drew back far enough to run the tip of his tongue across the branding tattoo already beginning to encircle her breast.

Lightning bolts.

His witch. His woman of power, dazzling in her strength, humbling in her vulnerability. He wanted all of her. *Craved* all of her.

A roar of something primal and purely male rushed through his system as he stared at that brand. His mark on her skin. A claim staked. This woman was his and no one else's. Her luscious body, strong spirit and quick mind were sworn to his keeping.

"I need you, Teresa," he whispered, bending his head to kiss her neck, the curve of her throat. He felt her pulse beat beneath his lips and wished that his still heart could beat in tandem with hers. To make them even more of a unit. One whole. At last.

"No more talk," she whispered, her gaze locked with his so that he couldn't mistake her hunger. "Take me, Rune. Fill me."

Her sleek thighs parted, baring her center to him, and Rune looked his fill. She was uninhibited, as wild and driven as he. And he loved that she craved him with a raw necessity she was unafraid to show him.

He slid the tips of his fingers over her slick folds and felt her tremble in response. Enjoying the play of emotions on her expressive face, he dipped first one finger and then another into her heat. Her head tipped back and her body bowed gracefully as she strove to meet his touch, to lift her hips to his questing hand.

There was no shyness between them. Only the hunger. The need.

She shouted his name when his thumb pressed down hard on that single bud of sensation at the very heart of her. Her body jolted, her hips rocked as his fingers caressed her inside and out. His own body was screaming, aching for completion, but first he had to watch her tumble over the edge. He needed her release even more than he needed his own.

It was innate. Instinctive. He pushed her higher, faster, his fingers moving over her skin until she twisted and writhed beneath him. She was open to everything and Rune knew that he would never have enough of her. She was deeply sensual, reacting to his touch like a fuse to a match. Explosive. Compelling.

"Damn you!" She shouted again, hips still gyrating in a frantic race toward release. "I wanted you *in* me for this!"

"I will be." He couldn't wait. His cock throbbed with need as blood pumped and pulsed inside him. "First you. Go over, Teresa. Stop fighting it, just go over."

"No, damn it!" She laughed a little wildly and fixed her gaze on him. Dark brown eyes shining with passion and hunger, she stared at him. "I won't let go and you can't make me."

"A challenge," he whispered, grinning at her now as his thumb moved in a tight circle over and over that nub of flesh until she was groaning and gritting her teeth in an effort to hold her own climax at bay. "You're still the stubborn witch."

"Ha!" A short, harsh laugh shot from her throat as her hips lifted again and again. *"I'm* stubborn? You're the one who won't give me what I want!"

"I know what you want, Teresa, and you'll take it."

"You bastard," she whispered, that tight smile still curving her mouth. "Do you want me to beg?"

His free hand snaked up her body to tug and tweak at her rigid nipple. She groaned again, more fiercely this time, as if it took everything she possessed to keep from succumbing to her climax.

"Yes, Teresa," he coaxed her, loving how she gave herself up completely to the sensual give-and-take between them. Loving her stubborn refusal to climax. Loving every damn thing about her. "Beg."

She reared up off the bed, grabbed his face between her palms and kissed him hard and long, chewing at his bottom lip in a frenzy of emotion and sensation. When she finally let him go, she snarled, "I *won't.*"

Rune laughed and withdrew his hand from her body despite her howl of protest. Instantly, he scooped his hands beneath her, lifted her off the mattress and covered the heart of her with his mouth.

She screamed his name as her body immediately shattered in his grasp. Again and again, her body shook and trembled with the force of a series of orgasms that pushed her close to the brink of madness. Every time he felt one climax end, he pushed her into another one, loving the taste of her as her body melted under his tender assault.

Breathless, boneless, she finally collapsed, unable to call his name or shout epithets at him. Only then did Rune release her. He set her back onto the bed, looked into her eyes and saw those dark brown pools flash with defiance. "You win this time. But next time, I'll hold out until I get what I want," she warned him.

"You get it now," he said, his cock as hard as stone and aching from the torturous wait he'd inflicted on himself.

"Finally!" She grinned and reached for him, but Rune shook his head.

He lifted her, flipped her onto her stomach and drew her behind up. She sighed, understanding exactly what he wanted and she wasted no time letting him know she wanted it, too. She got onto all fours, lowering her head to her crossed arms, and spread her legs wide for him.

Looking back at him, she wiggled her hips in invitation. "Take me, Rune. Give me what I want."

"Always," he promised. Grasping her hips, he slid into her from behind and drove himself to the hilt.

That first hard thrust nearly stole his breath as he felt her hot, wet flesh mold itself to his. Her inner muscles still trembled in reaction to the series of orgasms, squeezing his cock in gentle, consistent pulses.

She swiveled her hips, urging him on. Rune didn't need any encouragement. His own need pushed him now. Again and again, he pulled free of her body only to reclaim it in the most intimate way. She groaned and moved with him, taking him deeper at every thrust, and still he wanted, craved, more.

His hips pistoned against her body as he drove them both to the very brink of release and then stopped. Hovering on the edge, he held perfectly still inside her, relishing the hot slide of her flesh on his, the rapid, gasping breaths shooting from her lungs.

"Don't you dare stop now," she ordered, turning her head to fix a dark glare on him.

"I dare much, Teresa. Always have."

She shuddered when he reached around to stroke the bud of her desire at their bodies' joining.

"You're making me crazy," she muttered, moving into him again, helpless to stand against what he made her feel.

"Good to know," he said, running his hands over the curve of her behind before holding her hips tight and pulling her even closer.

She sighed and arched her body into his and that was all he could take. He couldn't wait another moment for the climax hovering just out of his reach. He needed to finish inside her. Needed to stake the claim of the Mating again.

Picking up that hard, fast rhythm once more, Rune

wasted no time driving them each to a feverish peak and this time he gave up control and surrendered to his witch. His body exploded into hers and she held him within her, taking all that he was and giving herself over to him in return.

Chapter 38

"Bastard thinks he's in charge," Miguel muttered, steering his battered jeep down the rutted desert track that passed for a road.

He was still burning over the incident at the tavern the night before. The insult of that prick knocking him to the floor and sneering at him. What the hell was that about? He was supposed to be a partner in this, wasn't he? He had romanced Teresa as he'd been instructed to do. Was it his fault the little bitch didn't fall in line?

Miguel threw himself a look in the rearview mirror and smiled at what he saw. He'd been able to get women to do whatever he wanted since he was fifteen and first realized that women liked the way he looked. Handsome, with an edge of danger, he had women flocking to him like stupid little dogs. And they stayed with him until *he* decided to cut them loose. Nobody disrespected Miguel Hernandez. Nobody.

And that included that pompous prick with the fire hands.

Big deal. So he could do magic. That made him no better than the very witch they were chasing. He was a mutant. Like Teresa. Like the rest of the women with power. And they all thought they were better than humans. Better than *him.*

"Well, fuck that," he said aloud, letting his temper burn unrestrained inside him. He would show them all just how good he was.

They wanted Teresa, fine. He'd show them how it was done. He was finished taking orders. He knew where she was going to show up, so he'd be there. Waiting for her.

"Bastard fire man wants to call the shots, but he's too stupid to listen to *me.*" Miguel had told them all that Chiapas was the secret to catching Teresa. No one wanted to just follow his advice and finish this. So, he was on his own. Fuck the rest of them.

He would do this himself and then they'd realize that he was a man to be taken seriously.

The village tavern was already miles behind him and still Miguel was fuming. He'd slipped out just before dawn when the bastard with gray eyes had left on business. Suited Miguel just fine. He had business of his own and when he was done, they'd all have to admit to his face that he was the one who knew what to do. That *he,* Miguel Hernandez, had come through for them when no one else had.

"When this is over," he promised himself, "I'm not going to take shit from anybody again. I'll have the reward money and I'll get out of this fucking desert and never look back. Then we'll see who's the important guy around here. Fucking Parnell with his fire thinks he's so bad? We'll see how impressive he is with a bullet in the head."

He smiled at the thought. Indulging his fantasies made the miles go by faster. Soon he was deep in the desert, heading for Chiapas. And his destiny.

Chapter 39

"Trust the Eternal and fear the immortal?" Rune repeated, lying back on the bed and crooking one arm behind his head. "What's that supposed to mean?"

"I don't know," Teresa said.

"Focus your power. Aim the lightning at me."

"And if I hit you?"

"You can't kill me."

She threw a white-hot bolt at him. But he had already flashed away. The lightning hit the cave wall instead, making the crystals buried there light up like neon.

"I'm an Eternal *and* an immortal," Rune reminded her unnecessarily when he popped back in just a foot from her.

"That's what I told her." Teresa spun, dropped and threw one hand out, spitting sparks from her fingertips.

Rune grinned and disappeared.

"She wouldn't—or couldn't, maybe; I don't know which—explain any further," Teresa said when Rune flashed back to her side. "She just said that there was danger and that the immortal wanted *me*, specifically. And not just for the witchcraft."

"She was right about that, anyway," Rune whispered, reaching out to grab her.

Teresa jumped away, swung one hand in the air and reached for her magic. "You're not worried?" she asked.

He flashed to stand behind her, wrapped his arms around her middle and held on. "Worried, no. Interested, yes. Now don't depend solely on your magic. Conjure a knife. Like I showed you. You never know what you'll have to fight with."

Teresa held out one hand, focused her gaze on her palm and in a moment a long-bladed knife, gleaming silver in the torchlight, lay in her hand. She smiled, curled her fingers around the hilt, then swung it experimentally through the air.

Admiration for her swelled inside Rune. She'd been practicing. This time together had been good for her. Time to mate. Time to focus on her growing power. Time to connect to each other in a way that they hadn't over the centuries. Her magical skills were impressive. She hadn't needed teaching—only to remember her own past and what she had once done as easily as breathing.

"Good. That's good," Rune said, and crooked one finger at her in challenge. "Now come at me."

She did. She charged across the room, holding the knife blade low and deadly. He swiped her arm out of the way and she spun quickly, dropping into a crouch while swinging her knife in a wide arc. Rune flashed out. If he hadn't, she would have had him.

"That's cheating," she called out to the room.

"If you expect your opponent to fight fair, you'll die," he told her as he appeared again just a few feet from her.

"Then I should just use magic," she countered, walking in a slow, wide circle around him.

"Use whatever you have," Rune told her, dodging her next attack, then smiling when she whirled in time to take another swipe at him. "Stay alive. No matter what you have to do."

She took a breath, looked down at the knife in her hand and said, "That's what this is about? No matter what? Shouldn't there be rules, Rune? Didn't we screw up royally when we didn't believe in rules?"

"Yeah. You did." He flashed out, then appeared again right beside her. He pulled the knife from her hand and tossed it aside. "And we all paid the price. Now we work together and we'll do whatever the hell we have to do to succeed."

"So, then, we learned nothing?"

"We learned what we had to learn," he told her, noting the worry in her eyes. It was good that she considered all sides now. She hadn't once and they had spent centuries paying for it. "Now, tell me. Elena said you should search for new spells? In the library?"

"Yeah. Rune, what library? The one in Sedona? She said search for Serena's spells . . . and I don't know any Serena. We can't go back there even if I knew what to look for and—" She stopped, tipped her head to one side and said, "You know what she was talking about, don't you?"

His eyes were fierce now, flashing with the warrior gleam she was coming to know so well.

"You're sure she said *Serena.*"

"Hard to mistake that name. It's pretty different." She stared into his eyes. "You know who she is."

"So do you," he muttered. Just hearing that name opened up a treasure trove of memories inside him, thick as tar and just as appealing. "You just don't re-member yet."

"What're you—" She stopped and took a breath. "I knew her then? In the past?"

"You could say that," he replied. "You *were* Serena."

Chapter 40

"I was . . . when?"

"Does it matter?" Rune didn't want to talk about that incarnation. The memory pained him. At the moment, he would have liked nothing better than to kick the ghostly ass of Elena's spirit for bringing it up.

"Of course it matters. Elena said it mattered and now, looking at your face, I can see that your memories of Serena aren't exactly cheerful ones, so, yeah. I'd like to know what everyone else knows."

He released her and stalked across the cave, needing to put some distance between them. "You should let your own memories surface. Remember this on your own."

"Do we have time for that?" she countered. "I'm working at dredging up the memories, but so far I'm not getting much. If Elena thinks Serena's spells can help, then wouldn't knowing the truth help, too?"

Irritated and unsettled by the past suddenly encroaching on his present, Rune spun to look at her. The sight of her mating tattoo circling her breast and beginning to spread to her back eased him, though. The past was dead and now they were approaching a future that had been too long in coming. "You want the truth? Fine. Serena was a treacherous bitch. Happy?"

"Thrilled," she said tightly. "Now tell me the rest."

"It was 1530," he told her. "In London. You worked at a tavern there and were drawn to witchcraft even though you had no power. You think the witch hunters now are fierce?" He gave a short, hard laugh. "Back then, they were on a mission from God and were damn relentless about it."

"I've read about it."

He gave her a cold smile. "You lived it, too. You just don't remember it yet."

"So tell me."

"You were separated from your magic because of the atonement, but your soul was still drawn to the craft," he said, bringing it all back in his mind in a churning mass of images. "We were together, until you ran afoul of the tribunal. Someone saw you with a woman of power, trying to learn to do spellwork, and turned you in. To save your own ass, you handed me to them. Set me up to be trapped. You had your witch friend cast a spell to hold me so the 'good people' of London could beat me down."

"Oh, God . . ."

With time and distance, the immediacy of her betrayal had lost the emotional punch it once had. But the bitterness remained. He looked down into her profoundly familiar eyes and saw Serena as she had been that last night. As she had stood with his captors, decrying him as an unnatural "thing."

"Rune . . ."

He shook his head. "Her spell couldn't hold me for

long. I flashed out and later I discovered that once I was gone, the crowd turned on you. I returned the following day to confront you, but—" He hesitated.

"Finish," she whispered brokenly.

"—you were dead. They burned you and the witch at the stake for consorting with demons."

She closed her eyes, took another deep breath and blew it out in a heavy sigh. "Well, that explains a lot."

"Really?" he asked wryly.

"You look at me and see *her*," Teresa said, turning her eyes up to him. "I can't really blame you. But, Rune, I'm not that woman. I made a promise to you. I'm your mate and I'm not going to turn on you like she did."

"Serena didn't *plan* to turn on me, either," he told her flatly.

She walked to him and laid both hands on his bare chest. Rune felt a rush of heat spill from her body into his. It wiped away the chill of his memories and pushed thoughts of betrayal back into the past.

"I can't change what I—*she*—did." She shook her head and frowned. "Every time I find out one more hideous piece of a past I don't remember, it makes me want to scream. But I can't do anything to change it. All I can do is be who I am now. And I'm not that woman."

"I know you're not."

"Do you? Really?" She tipped her head to one side and her long hair swung over her shoulder to cover one bare breast. "I think we're both coming into this with a lot of our own problems strapped to our backs. You don't trust me and I don't—"

"Don't what?" He frowned as her gaze shifted from his. "Teresa." Cupping her chin in his hand, he turned her face back to him until their eyes met once more. "You don't what—"

Steeling herself, she said, "I don't want to love you, okay?"

"Why? Because of that bastard of a boyfriend you had?"

Her eyes went wide in surprise. "You know about Miguel?"

"I know everything about you," he said. "You think it was easy to watch that bastard with you? I saw how he treated you and I wanted to kill him for it. If he had ever struck you or harmed you in any way, I would have."

She smiled at the hostile tone of his voice. "Even though you don't really like me?"

"I do like you," he said and silently admitted that liking her didn't even begin to cover what he felt for her. "I just don't know that I can trust you. And, yes, I would have killed him for daring to harm you. As I would anyone else."

"I know I shouldn't like hearing that, but I do," she said, "so thank you."

"You don't have to love me," Rune said softly.

"But you do have to trust me," Teresa told him. "If this is going to work, if we're to have a chance of succeeding, you're going to have to trust me at some point, Rune."

He nodded because he knew she was right. But knowing and doing were two different things. Still, he was working on it. "I'm trying."

"That's all I can ask for," she said after a long moment. Then she smiled sadly. "You don't trust me and I won't love you. So there are a few strikes against us right off the top."

"Hasn't stopped us so far," he said.

"True," Teresa admitted. "So . . . back to Elena and

what she said. Do you know which library she was talking about?"

"Yeah, I do. It's an interdimensional library."

"What?"

He looked down at her, his gaze moving over her
features while he slid one hand up to cover her left
breast. As if he needed to touch the mating brand, to
link them somehow. To get past the powerful emotions flooding the room. Old pain had no place in his
present and he would have to make a stronger effort
to let it go.

"Torin and Shea," he said slowly, "the first Eternal
and witch to bond during the Awakening, discovered the
library last month."

His hand cupped her breast and the heat wound
through him in a sensual ribbon.

"Tell me," she said, urging him to continue.

"You know that you're the reincarnation of one of
the chosen witches. A member of the last great coven."

She nodded, impatient for him to get to the important part. "Yes, that much I know."

"Well, there are other witches, thousands of them."

"Yeah, and they're being hunted and rounded up by
the feds, and by civilian hunters. But what does this have
to do with—"

He blew out a breath. "For centuries, witches have
been handing down knowledge through the generations.
From one to the other in a long, unbroken link, they've
passed down spells and secrets and legends."

She'd had no idea that women of power had managed to retain all that they were throughout the ages. If
the feds knew about this, she told herself grimly, they

would increase their already rabid efforts to wipe out the witch population.

A shiver wracked her body and as if he understood, Rune dropped a quick, hard kiss on her mouth. She appreciated the kiss for its own sake, and for the reassurance that the awkwardness caused by their conversation was over.

"The witches crafted a 'library' to hold the ancient texts and vital information gleaned through the years. Any witch can access it if she's close to a Sanctuary."

"How close?"

"That wasn't clear," he admitted ruefully. "But I'd guess within a few miles."

"And we're nowhere near one now, right?"

"We are," he said. "We just can't get to it. The closest one is just outside Sedona—but before you say anything, we're not going back there."

"You're right. Going back would be really stupid." She nodded, then asked, "Do you know of any others?"

"There is one outside Veracruz."

On the plus side, she thought, the state of Veracruz was a lot closer to Chiapas, where they were headed anyway. "We should go there, then, don't you think? Let me find a way into the library before we go to my grandmother? Get as much information as we can."

"It's a good plan," he agreed solemnly. "I don't like this 'beware the immortal' warning your friend gave you, though."

"Me neither," she said with a wry smile. Then she reached up to touch his face, drawing her fingertips along the line of his jaw. "But I want you to know, Rune, I *do* trust you."

He kissed her then and before her brain fuzzed over

in an onslaught of sensation, she realized he might never trust *her* in return. She felt a twinge of regret as she acknowledged that a part of Rune was still holding her past against her. He was still keeping himself at an emotional distance from her.

Teresa only hoped that their shared misery of a past wasn't going to doom the future.

Chapter 41

In a soundproofed lab deep below the pretty treelined streets of Arlington, Virginia, a witch finally died screaming.

"You should have gagged her," Kellyn said, her ears still ringing with the echo of the dying woman's wailing.

"Oh, no," Henry Fender said with a jovial wink. "I find their screams quite invigorating."

One of Kellyn's eyebrows lifted into a high arch. She had been in the lab for days already and she'd discovered nothing new—well, beyond the surprising fact that even torture could get boring after a while.

Not to Henry, though, she mused, watching the good doctor as he unstrapped the dead witch from the white-gold torture table. Kellyn kept her distance from the slab of gleaming metal, knowing that if her body got too close to the damn thing, her own powers would be drained. And she didn't trust good old Henry to keep from torturing *her* if he got the chance.

The man was as single-minded as a campaigning politician going after votes.

Dr. Henry Fender had started out his career as a gynecologist. He'd been well respected, with a thriving practice in Richmond. He had given it all up, though, as soon as the world had become aware of witchcraft. He, like so many other humans, was drawn to the promise of power. The only difference between Henry and most of the population was that Henry had no scruples about how he acquired that power.

"She told you nothing," Kellyn said, seating herself on a swivel stool a good distance from the table. She really didn't like this part of the lab. It bothered her to be so close to the power-sucking metal. She much preferred the old-fashioned torture room. After all, Henry had had it stocked with some of the classics. A rack. An iron maiden, thumbscrews and a Judas Cradle, not to mention a few other items that Kellyn remembered fondly from the Middle Ages, all newly made, handcrafted in the mountains of Virginia.

Buy American, she thought with a smile.

Henry waggled his long, bony finger at her as if she were a child in a schoolroom. "Not entirely true. She did reveal that the witches will all eventually head to Wales."

"Yes, well," Kellyn snapped, "I knew that already."

He tipped his head to one side and stared at her. "Did you? Now, isn't that interesting?"

Kellyn shifted uncomfortably. This was what came of being bored to distraction. One slip of the lip and her entire plan could be shot to shit. Once again, she felt that flickering stir inside her, as something fought to surface. Frowning, she buried it even deeper. Covering for herself, she said, "Not very interesting at all, really. Wales is a lot of territory. Their home could be anywhere."

"Hmm . . ." He simply watched her, a curious glint in his deceptively soft eyes.

A change of subject was needed, she told herself.

"Beyond what we already knew," she said sharply, "the witch told you nothing."

"The more of these women I experiment on, the more I learn. Did you know that with their bonding, their powers are stronger?"

"Yes," Kellyn said, "I knew."

"It's fascinating, isn't it?" His pale blue eyes glazed over as new possibilities occurred to him. "If we could get a witch in here *after* her bonding, then her power would be that much greater."

"And that much harder to contain," Kellyn pointed out.

"True, but scientific discovery is not without risk. And think of the rewards. If we could bleed off a bonded witch's power, it would make locating the Artifact a piece of cake."

She chuckled a little and idly studied her nails. She'd actually chipped the polish on that last witch. Now she needed another manicure. "Henry, you've been working on a way to bleed off witch power for ten years now. When are you going to admit it's just not possible?"

One hand snaked out, grabbed her throat and tipped her head back until she was looking up into those pale, haunted eyes. "I will do it. You'll see. You'll all see."

Furious, Kellyn called on her own power and teleported out of his grip to the other side of the room. "You son of a bitch. What the hell do you think you're doing?"

He smiled at her in genuine wonder. "I love that you can do something so incredibly amazing without the slightest effort."

"The effort I'm making now," she told him, "is to keep from killing you."

"Oh"—he waved one hand at her—"you won't do

that. Our common partner wouldn't like it. And besides, we still need each other. The Artifact is out there, my dear Kellyn, and it's up to us to find it. Now . . . would you like to take first shot at our next guest?"

He looked harmless. Affable. Charming. Almost like an absentminded professor of sorts. But underneath it all, he was vicious and, she was beginning to think, dead crazy. But he was right. She couldn't kill him. Their partner wouldn't like it and for right now, Kellyn needed that partner on her side.

Once she had the Artifact, that would be a different story. But for now . . .

"Yes, Henry," she said, giving him the smile he seemed to be expecting. "I would like to take first crack at her. But shall we go downstairs to the other chamber? I'd really like to put the witch on the rack and take it out for a spin. For old times' sake."

Chapter 42

Rune and Teresa spent nearly a week reaching the outskirts of the state of Veracruz. They stayed away from towns and cities, camping in the desert or in valleys as the terrain changed. Veracruz was more of a tropical state, with rivers, waterfalls, jungles and rich meadows. Keeping away from the more populated coastal areas gave them plenty of places to hide. It wasn't only the feds and witch hunters they had to be wary of. There were always humans with nothing better to do than to rob and kill as well. Which made the trip interesting, if nothing else.

He didn't mind roughing it.

Belen only knew, Rune had lived rougher than this for most of his immortal life. But he also knew that Teresa wasn't used to it. Still, he admired that she was game. She didn't complain. Didn't whine. Didn't do anything but practice her magic whenever she had the chance. Using him as a focus, she was becoming unerringly adept with the lightning that she called with a flick of her fingers.

And she was skilled with a knife as well, he thought with an inner smile. He'd been working with her and she was a quick study, her innate grace and speed making her a star pupil. He wanted her to be familiar enough with weapons that she could defend herself if necessary. Of course, he planned to be at her side always, especially in times of danger, but he'd lived long enough to realize that sometimes a plan blows up in your face. And a matter of moments could mean the difference between life and death.

He showed her how to fight—with knife, gun and fist—to win her those few moments. All she had to do, he told her, was to stay alive until he could get to her. Then he'd kill anything that threatened her.

She believed him. Trusted him. He saw it in her eyes.

And he was humbled by it.

The effects of the Mating were racing through them, wrapping the two of them together with mystical bonds that went soul deep. Every time their bodies became one, Rune felt those silken threads winding more inextricably around them. He felt the tattoo in a near-constant burn on his flesh and knew she felt the same. The branding mark was growing rapidly now, curling under his arm to climb up his back, and there was nothing he enjoyed more than tracing her matching tattoo with his tongue.

But there was time to practice honing Teresa's magic as well. Rune had watched her come to grips with the incredible power inside her. Admiration filled him as he saw her work to exhaustion in an effort to remember who and what she had been. To open the memories locked within her mind. To find what they both needed to end this quest.

And as his admiration grew, so did his hunger for her. It was as if that desperate, clawing need for her had a life of its own. She moved and he wanted her. She spoke and

he felt her voice slide inside him. She laughed and his
unbeating heart clenched in his chest. She was so much
more than she had once been, he told himself daily. Her
soul and mind and heart had grown through her many
incarnations.

He had seen that growth personally as he followed
her through time, always near, yet never close enough.
He'd felt her change, felt her progress toward the witch
she needed to be—and still, that silent, doubting part of
him remained.

She was throwing herself into the quest—he could
admit that, but the uncertainty remained with him. He
looked at her and wanted to see only the woman she
was now. But other images flashed across his mind.
Other faces, other times—all her. And in each of them
she had turned away at the last moment. Stepped back
from him when she should have believed in him.

And so now he was the one to step back. Rune wondered if they would ever truly mate if they were separated by centuries of mistrust.

So which of them, he was forced to ask himself,
needed to get beyond the past? Which of them was
clinging to a world that had died out centuries ago?
Holding on to betrayal and pain as a way to keep a risky
future at bay?

Gritting his teeth, Rune pushed that thought aside.
He had reasons for feeling as he did, damn it. The fact
that Teresa was becoming more and more a part of him
only fed the doubts. He'd allowed her too deeply inside
him once before and then the gates of hell had swung
wide and he'd been left holding the proverbial bag.
Damned if he'd do that again.

So he trained her, worked with her, encouraged her
and had sex with her at every opportunity.

But he still didn't trust her.

On the evening of the sixth day of their trip, Rune made camp alongside a roaring river. Trees overhung the campsite, partially hiding the small campfire he allowed them, and dissipating the smoke. It was warmer here, too, as they moved away from the cooler desert into the more humid jungle terrain.

He knew they were close to the Sanctuary, but he also knew he wouldn't be taking Teresa there directly. He remembered all too well his reception at the Sanctuary in the Uinta Mountains of Utah. He had taken three human females there for safety and had practically had to fight his way past a phalanx of guardian witches to gain entry.

Had to admire a woman who was willing to stand up and spit in her enemy's eye, he told himself. But whether it would be safer for them to go or not, they really didn't have the time. As it was, nearly two weeks of their thirty days were up and they were no closer to discovering the whereabouts of Teresa's share of the Artifact.

Not for lack of trying, though, he admitted solemnly. Teresa's magic was blossoming. He could see it, literally, etching itself into her marrow and bone. In the way she held herself, in the more defiant tip of her chin and, most especially, in the cool glint of determination in her eyes.

Now, though, he glanced at her in the snapping firelight and saw her yawn. This constant travel was wearing on her. Even though their combined strength was growing, she was still human and being on the run was taking a toll.

Even her idiot bird wasn't making her smile tonight. It bobbed up and down on a narrow tree limb, shrieking and whistling, but Teresa paid no attention. Rune frowned at the brightly colored creature. Every day the bird flew off on its own and hours later it would return. He kept waiting, hoping the damn thing would run into a hawk or some other wild animal, but it seemed to have an inordinate lucky streak when it came to survival.

As if sensing Rune's thoughts, the bird bristled, ruffling its feathers before hopping up and taking to the air. It banked and wheeled overhead for a minute or two, then streaked off into the night.

"Where the hell does it go?" he murmured.

"Maybe he has a girlfriend," Teresa mused, rummaging in the duffel bag that held their dwindling store of supplies.

Eager to forget all about the bird now that it was gone, Rune asked, "How are the supplies holding out?"

"Really well if we're not very hungry," she told him with a shrug. "We've got enough for tonight and maybe tomorrow. Then we'll need to hit another village."

He didn't like it. Didn't like taking her into rural towns and villages with him, but couldn't really convince himself to leave her alone while he went. He did a slow turn now, letting his sharp eyes scan their surroundings. While the firelight played and danced behind him, he stared into the shadows. At the clumps of trees, the high grasses, the rocks along the river rushing past them. Anywhere an enemy might hide.

Uneasy, he felt a prickling awareness sliding along his spine. Something was out there. He was sure of it. Felt it down to his bones. His protective instincts stirred. He could grab Teresa and flash out—or, he told himself, he could make a stand and get rid of whoever was following them here and now.

Dropping to one knee in the sand, he caught Teresa's eyes across the fire. "I'm going to make a sweep," he said, voice low. "Make sure we're alone out here."

"Why? Did you see something?" she asked, fear overshadowing the fatigue in her voice.

He shot another look over his shoulder at the lush vegetation beyond their campsite.

"No," he assured her, despite the fact that every fine-tuned sense he possessed was tingling. There was definitely something out there. Somewhere. No point in scaring Teresa, though, he told himself. "I just want to check. Do you have your knife?"

She reached into the pocket of the dark blue jean jacket Rune had helped her manifest. For a moment, he remembered her pride, delight shining in her eyes when he showed her how to use her magic to conjure what clothing she needed.

God, was that only a few nights ago? Time with Teresa was ticking past in a frenzy, stealing his breath, niggling at his mind. A constant reminder that their task was unfinished and that there were those out there willing to do anything to see that it remained that way.

Teresa pulled out the knife he'd given her. "I have it."

Firelight played on her features, in her dark, sober eyes. It danced along the blade of the knife she now held with confidence after their intense training sessions. And still he hated to see her with the thing. Hated to think of her having to defend herself without him at her side.

"You won't need it," he told her and meant every word. He wouldn't be so far away that he couldn't flash back to her in an instant. *Nothing* was going to happen to his witch. "But it's a good idea to keep it close."

"I will." Nodding, she then lifted one hand and let sparks fly, shooting up from her fingertips like blue and white showers off a sparkler. "And I've got my powers, too. I'm fine, Rune. Go. Check."

He didn't like leaving her, but better he find whoever was hunting them and take care of it away from her. And the longer he delayed in leaving, the harder it would be. It stunned him to realize just how vital she had become to him in these two weeks. She was more than his mate. She was the very air he breathed.

That realization hit him like a fist in the gut and he wasn't entirely sure how he felt about it. He knew damn well he was still dealing with ancient crap when it came to his feelings for her. But the bottom line was, she was *his*.

"I'll be back soon."

"I'll be here."

As much as he wanted to stay next to her, he could better protect her by locating the threat and eliminating it. Before he could talk himself out of it, Rune called on the fire. He looked down at her through the inferno covering his body, then bowed his head and flashed out.

Chapter 43

He reappeared a couple of hundred yards away from their campsite. Far enough to get a bead on their surroundings without being distracted by the scent and sound of his woman.

The flames covering his body winked out in an instant and he was enveloped by the darkness. Perfectly still, he barely breathed as he listened to the night sounds. The wind sighing through the trees and grass, the soft rustle of an animal slinking through the undergrowth, the sigh of the river. The constant buzz and click of the bugs made for a sort of odd symphony and from a distance came the yowling growl of a panther. Overhead, through the thick branches of trees, he saw the moon shining fitfully as it dove in and out of clouds that washed across the starry sky. He turned and could see just the barest hint of Teresa's campfire, looking like no more than the tip of a fallen star in the blackness.

His mind filled with her, he cursed silently and refocused his concentration on his surroundings, searching for the source of his unease.

Then he found it.

Dropping into a crouch, he pulled his knife free of its

sheath and spun around with a snarl. Every muscle coiled, every cell on alert, his gray eyes narrowed dangerously, Rune muttered, "Come forward and die."

"Nice moves, man," a familiar voice answered lazily. "Thought for a minute you were going to let me get the drop on you."

"Finn." Rune muttered his friend's name and straightened. His muscles remained taut with tension, though. Why was Finn out here? He was supposed to be in the States, watching over his witch. Since he clearly wasn't ... could that mean that Finn was the one responsible for Elena's murder?

That thought tore at him. Hell, he didn't want to think any of his Eternal brothers would turn their backs on their duty and honor. But finding that Finn had turned would be an especially hard thing to bear. The Eternal had always been one of their strongest, fiercest warriors. Driven by his own personal sense of honor, he was the one most of them called on for backup whenever it was needed.

To lose Finn? Unthinkable. But Rune couldn't risk Teresa's safety, so until he knew for sure one way or the other, he would watch his own back and keep his fellow Eternal far from Teresa.

Finn walked in slowly from the darkness of the surrounding jungle, as if a shadow had come to life. Dressed in black head to toe, he blended with the night so thoroughly that he seemed a part of it. He wore his black hair cut military short and he had enough weaponry strapped to his chest and thighs to outfit a small militia.

Despite Rune's doubts, he was glad to see his friend again. It had been more than a year since the last time they'd worked together, to free witches from an internment camp in Joliet, Illinois.

"You son of a bitch, what're you doing here?"

Finn ran the flat of his hand over his brush cut, then shrugged. "Talked to Torin. He says there might be trouble out here. Eternal type of trouble. Hopped in my Gulfstream and here I am."

Rune chuckled in spite of the situation. Nothing Finn liked better than taking up his newest toy, the Gulfstream business jet. He'd even built a runway of sorts near the cave Rune and Teresa had stayed in. The nearly forty-million-dollar price tag hadn't slowed him down a bit, either. Money wasn't a problem for any of the Eternals. And for Finn, cash just made it easier to indulge his passions. He enjoyed flying as much as he relished a good fight, which was saying something.

"So," Finn said softly, "you want to tell me about this? When I spoke to Torin he said you were going to call. Put me on this search. You never did. So what's going on?"

"Yeah, I should have called. Got busy," Rune admitted on a grunt of self-disgust. He'd been so wrapped up in Teresa and the Mating, he hadn't made that phone call.

Finn grinned. "So your witch is keeping you busy, *huh*?"

"You could say that." Rune shook his head and looked out over the surrounding jungle again, though he deliberately kept his gaze from the direction of his and Teresa's camp. No need to point it out to Finn—just in case. He could only hope the other Eternal wouldn't notice the spot of brightness in the black. "What about you? Why're you here? Aren't you supposed to be keeping an eye on your mate?"

"My witch has got a couple weeks before anything happens. The magics are rippling around her, so I know it's almost time," Finn admitted grimly, "and I was going stir-crazy. Hate cities, man. You know that. All those damn humans crawling around."

Rune gave him a sharp look and Finn caught it. At first, insult rippled across his craggy features, but then he laughed, hard and short. "You think it's *me*? You actually think I've gone rogue?"

"You're here," Rune pointed out, tightening his grip on the hilt of his knife. "Elena Vargas was killed with magic and you just said yourself you've never been fond of humans."

"True." Finn tucked his own knife back into its scabbard as a show of good faith, then raised both arms out to his sides. He was opening himself up to an attack, offering no resistance, and Rune didn't know what to make of that, either.

"I don't much like humans. Hate cats, too, but I haven't wiped out that species yet."

Rune rubbed his jaw and looked into his old friend's gray eyes. Like his own, that gray swirled with power and magic and energy. "What the hell am I supposed to think, Finn? You just show up out of nowhere. Hell, for all I know, you've been following Teresa and me around since the beginning."

The slightest flinch showed on Finn's face again and then was gone. When he spoke, his voice was hard and flat. "I didn't call because I figured it'd be easier just to lock in on your trace energy pattern and follow you once I got here. Knew you were in this part of Mexico headed south because Torin told me. I didn't follow you. I didn't kill that woman."

Rune shook his head. He wanted to believe. But the image of Elena's burned body rose up in his mind. "Where were you a couple weeks ago, Finn?"

"You're serious."

"Deadly."

A second ticked past, then another. He still held his arms out at his side, in an open show of trust. He blew out a breath, gritted his teeth and said, "Two weeks ago, I was trying to keep my witch's sweet ass out of a sling when she and her friends decided to stage a breakout at an internment camp."

Stunned, Rune just looked at him. "She did what?"

"Yeah." Finn bristled in memory and shook his head as if even he was still having a hard time believing it. "If I hadn't been there to take out two guards who were coming up behind her, the Awakening would have been over."

The thought of that was a sobering one. After centuries, to be so close to fruition and lose it because a witch was needlessly killed . . . "What the hell is she doing?"

At the implied disapproval, Finn gave Rune a hard glare. "She's trying to save people, you asshole. That so hard to understand? She might not know she's a witch yet, but she feels for the women caught up in this business. And she's trying to help."

Hearing the harsh ring of protectiveness in Finn's tone did more to convince Rune that he was innocent than anything else could have. No rogue would give a shit about his witch, because he'd be in this for whatever he could get. He wouldn't be standing here unarmed and open to attack, either. He'd have tried to take Rune out first thing.

Relief poured through him as he acknowledged that his brother was still just that. But on its heels came impatience. "You *let* her go? Didn't try to stop her? Damn, my man. You were taking a chance."

"Rules of the game, brother," Finn muttered. "You

know that. We can't approach until their powers quicken in times of danger. And she didn't use magic on that raid. Just stupid human emotions."

Rune snorted. "Yeah, never liked that rule myself. Hell, I got shot to shit with white-gold bullets when I swooped in to save my witch as her power erupted."

"That rule blows, all right." Finn looked around. "Anyway, my witch is laying low for a while. Think she got scared. So I figured it would be safe enough for me to come out here and track whoever killed your woman's friend. That is," he added, "if you're done suspecting me."

Rune slid his knife back into its scabbard and nodded. "Yeah, I'm done. And I'm actually glad to see you. There's something going on here, Finn. More than we know. If it's not one of us gone rogue, then there's a new player in the game. Demon. Sorcerer. Some damn thing. And it's deadly."

Finn gave him a cold, confident smile. "Wouldn't be any challenge in it otherwise, now would there?" Folding his arms over his chest, he said quietly, "Tell me everything you know."

Chapter 44

Deidre Sterling turned the stereo down with a click of the remote, then reached for her glass of white wine. She took a long drink and as she felt the icy liquid slide through her system, she hoped to heaven it would help her relax.

But she had to admit the odds of that happening were pretty slim. She hadn't been able to settle down for what seemed forever. Her nerves were jangling, her stomach was in a constant churn and every time the phone rang or there was a knock on her door, she braced herself to be arrested.

The living room in her townhome was dark but for the fire burning in the white-tiled hearth. Firelight spilled through the room in a soothing pattern and she watched the shifting colors chase each other around the room. She sent a quick look at her cell phone again, hoping to see it light up with a text message, but there was still nothing.

"God, you idiot," she murmured to herself as she took another sip of wine.

It had seemed like a good idea at the time. That was all she could cling to for comfort. Staging a prison break at a small internment camp in Omaha should have been simple. They had done all the research. They had had the plans for the place, and a man on the inside, so Deidre's group had known exactly where the guards were stationed and what time they made their rounds. It should have been simple to avoid them. Heck, Deidre had managed to give her Secret Service detail the slip. Anything after that should have been a cakewalk.

She let her head drop to the back of the sofa as she stared up at the ceiling, her gaze tracking the dancing shadows even as she concentrated on the soothing hiss and snap of the fire.

And while she zoned out, her mind replayed the last few moments of the mission she and her group had called Operation Deliverance. Shaking her head now, she sighed at their naïveté. Filled with righteous indignation at their government's treatment of women and witches alike, they had been so sure they could pull it off and give the "justice" system a black eye at the same time.

But it went so wrong.

Everything was going according to plan. They had five witches free of their cells, the white-gold chains off their necks. Six members of RFW were in on the raid and four of them were already out in the vans, having done their part in cutting open the fences to allow Deidre and one other to go inside and get the witches.

Susan Baker, the same woman who had argued with Deidre's mother at their White House meeting, had made all the arrangements. She'd paid off their informers and had vans waiting outside to hustle the women away to where they could hide until RFW could come up with a permanent place to take them.

Deidre, terrified but determined, had led the witches down the dimly lit hallway. In a hurry because the two guards were due back in fifteen minutes, she kept them moving, signaling them all for silence.

She needn't have worried about that, though. These women had been tortured and locked up. They now knew to keep quiet if they hoped to survive. Their bare feet hardly made a sound on the cold cement floor and Deidre ran on her toes, the soles of her ballet flats whispering gently.

Susan waved her on and as Deidre and the others passed her, she pulled a gun from under her jacket.

Horrified, Deidre could only keep going. It was too late to stop and question her friend about what she was up to. But weapons hadn't been part of the plan. No one was supposed to be armed, just in case they were caught. Bad enough to be captured breaking into a federal facility—especially if you were the president's daughter—but to be carrying weapons, too?

Besides, no way was Deidre prepared to kill someone. No one was supposed to get hurt in this raid. Their mission was to save people. Raise the plight of witches in the public consciousness. Garner sympathy for them.

Why did Susan have a gun?

Deidre led the five women down the long hall and through the darkened reception area toward the front door. Then they were outside, darting across the dead grass, puffs of their breath clouding in front of their faces. The cold October night pressed down on them and Deidre felt . . .

Something.

A presence.

She could have sworn that someone was watching her. But she shook off the feeling, knowing that if anyone was

*watching their escape, floodlights would have flashed on
and a warning siren would be wailing. Still, that prickling
sense of something different stayed with her.*

They were at the front gate and Deidre hurried the
witches on, waving her hands, pointing at the two black
vans waiting for them. The women didn't need any further encouragement. They took off at a dead run once
they were free of the compound and Deidre smiled as
they piled into the vans and were driven off.

"Mission accomplished," she murmured just before
she heard a single gunshot from inside the building. It
was inordinately loud in the stillness and the echo of its
report shocked Deidre like a cold hand that fisted around
her heart.

She whipped around and the floodlights snapped on,
nearly blinding her. She ran back to the small enclosure
she had just left, afraid that Susan had been shot and
knowing she had to get her friend out of there before the
guards responded to the noise.

From somewhere close, she heard men shouting and
she realized they didn't have long. Heart pounding,
straining for breath, she dashed down the hall, then skidded to a stop.

"What did you do?" she demanded.

Susan was standing over a guard, the gun still pointed
down at him. A fresh pool of dark red blood had formed
around him and continued to grow, spilling across the cement, tracking toward the toe of Susan's shoe.

"He tried to stop us," Susan whispered, her voice
nearly lost over the sudden shriek of the siren erupting. "I
had to do it," she said, flicking her gaze up to Deidre. "I
had no choice."

"Damn it, Susan," she cried and reached out to grab
her friend's arm. Pulling with all her strength, she tugged

her along behind her, down the hallway, back toward the front of the building and the only escape route they had. "Come on!"

"I had to," Susan muttered, shaking her head, looking back over her shoulder at the dead man lying in a puddle of blood. "I had to. I had to."

Deidre kept running, kept dragging a reluctant Susan along behind her. Heart in her throat now, she could hardly draw a breath. Her nerves were screaming and tears blurred her vision and still she kept running. They were locked in now. They had to get out. If they were caught, they'd all be jailed and it wouldn't be for helping witches escape.

They'd be tried for murder.

And being the president's daughter wouldn't save her.

She bolted around a corner, paused long enough to make sure no one was there, then ran for it, tugging at Susan's arm. She heard a sound behind her. A series of sighs, then a couple of heavy thuds as something hit the floor. Deidre spun around frantically to look. And in that split second, she thought she saw— No.

"Run, Susan! Run!" She yelled it now, no need for quiet and stealth as the sirens wailed and more men shouted, their booted feet crunching on the cold, dead grass.

Susan seemed to wake out of her stupor and suddenly bolted alongside Deidre, the two of them racing for the car they'd left outside the fence. The license plates had been blacked out and there was nothing distinguishable about the plain beige sedan.

They jumped into the car and Deidre put it into gear and stepped on the gas. In moments, they were peeling away from the camp and losing themselves in the darkness.

But nothing would ever be the same again.

*   *   *

Her cell phone rang and Deidre jumped, sloshing wine over the rim of her glass and down her arm. She grabbed the phone, recognized the caller and answered gratefully. "Susan? Are you okay? Where are you?"

"I don't think I should tell you where I am, Dee," she said and her voice sounded distant. It wasn't so much a miles thing as an emotional distance, though.

Deidre set her wineglass down, picked up the remote and turned off the stereo. Somehow, the silky sounds of soft jazz were a discordant note in all of this. "I've been so worried. Are you okay? Tell me that at least."

"I'm fine. Really. I'm just . . ."

Heart aching, Deidre could imagine what her friend was feeling. Guilt. Misery. Fear. She knew because *she* was feeling the same thing and she hadn't killed that guard. Though she might as well have. As far as the courts were concerned, she was as guilty as Susan. Hell, as far as *she* was concerned, she was guilty. If they hadn't broken into that camp, the guard would still be alive.

But, she wondered, would the witches?

"What about—" She broke off, not wanting to ask a question about the rescued prisoners. Cell phone conversations could be overheard or recorded. Hell, in today's world, there wasn't a lot to feel safe about.

"They're good, too," Susan told her. "They're visiting a friend and everyone's okay."

"Thank God."

"Yeah." Susan paused for a long moment, then said, "I'm not going to be coming back to D.C., Dee. I . . . can't."

"Sue—"

"I'm really sorry, but there's just no way I can go back there and pick up like nothing happened." A broken sob carried across the air and Deidre's heart clenched in despair for her friend. "You'll have to take over at RFW, Dee. They'll need a leader and—"

"No," Deidre said quickly, her voice sounding as lost as her friend's. She'd been avoiding the members of RFW ever since that night and still couldn't bear the thought of seeing any of them. "I can't do it, either, Susan. Someone else is going to have to step up to the plate."

"I'm so sorry, Dee," Susan said and her voice broke again on the words. "I ruined everything for both of us. If it hadn't been for you, I never even would have made it out of there. I really owe you."

"No, you don't." Deidre took a breath and blew it out. "I'm not even sure how we got out, to be honest." Their escape was pretty much a blur. She remembered running like mad, terrified, the sounds of men shouting and running feet echoing throughout the building. She remembered feeling someone watching her as surely as if that someone had reached out and touched her.

Frowning, she lifted one hand and rubbed a spot between her eyebrows, where a headache that had been born on the night of the escape was still pounding. As a throbbing, incessant reminder of what she'd done and what she'd *seen.*

Just for a second, she let herself try to remember what had been there in the room with them at the last moment before she and Susan had escaped. But when her friend started talking again, Deidre shook off the memory and listened.

"I don't know yet where I'm going," Susan said quietly. "But once I get settled, I'll call you. Promise."

"Okay. Just . . . be careful, Susan. Take care of yourself, okay?"

"Right. You, too."

When she disconnected, Deidre just sat there, staring at the phone, her last link with her friend gone. She knew Susan wouldn't be calling her again. She would want to cut all ties to that night at the camp. She wouldn't want a reminder of what had happened. Deidre would miss her friend, but honestly, this way was better. How could they ever just go out to dinner or to a movie or laugh over guys together again? With this terrible secret haunting them both, normalcy was not an option.

Reaching for her wine, Deidre took another long sip and sighed. She turned her head to the window overlooking the small park in her Capitol Hill neighborhood, and stared through the rain that slid like tears down the glass—and saw something entirely different.

For just an instant, she let herself go back to that night. To the moment when she'd heard the scuffling sounds and spun around prepared to defend her and Susan against whatever came for them.

She remembered the darkness.

The shadows.

And she remembered clearly one more thing.

The pair of gray eyes watching her.

Chapter 45

Teresa made the best use of her time once Rune took off to do his security thing.

She turned her mind away from the fact that she was all alone out in the middle of a jungle, filled with God only knew what kinds of animals and bugs, and focused instead on the moon overhead. Her grandmother had always taught her that witches were rejuvenated by the moon.

What better time to awaken her own mystical connection to the magic? She had learned as a child that the best time for casting moon spells was when the moon was waxing—growing toward its fullness. The time when the moon was waning, slowly fading away and losing its brilliance, was less powerful.

She glanced skyward and saw the waxing half-moon as a thin layer of clouds parted, displaying its pale creaminess against a black sky. Standing up, Teresa took a step or two away from the fire, then lifted her arms high, cupping her hands as if to catch the silvery light in her palms.

She tipped her head back, watched that moon shining down on her through the dancing limbs of the trees and whispered the long-ago chant she had learned from her *abuela*.

Sister moon, shine for me.
Mother moon, hear my cry.
Sister moon, I call on you
To share your magic and mystery.

She inhaled slowly, deeply, feeling the warm, humid air fill her lungs with the scents of nature. She drew strength from her surroundings as the moon seemed to pulse in the sky. Silvery light dropped like rain to where she stood, enveloping her in a glow that fed her soul and spirit.

Smiling, Teresa sighed as magic slid through her veins, bubbling, frothing, filling her with an incredible wash of something mystical and ancient. She recognized it and welcomed its return.

"Oh, my goddess . . ." she whispered, her voice no more than a sigh on the wind that lifted her hair into a tangle around her head. The stars seemed to spin in the sky as the moon continued to throb along with the beat of her heart.

Such a connection. How had she ever managed to live without this incredible sense of well-being? Her body hummed, every cell bristling with life and burning with need. The wash of moonlight brightened all around her and Teresa felt like a pillar of light in a sea of darkness.

The moon's essence deepened in her, swelling, growing, until she felt like an overfilled bucket and the magic was literally pouring from her in a stream that couldn't be stopped. And along with her power, her body awakened. Her breasts felt heavy, her nipples so sensitive that even the delicate contact with her lacy bra was nearly painful. She hungered for her mate.

Her center was damp and hot and her legs trembled as sensation pumped through her. It was as if she had turned on a faucet, opening herself to the moon, and now she had no idea how to turn it off. More and more of the mystical energies filled her until she trembled with the onslaught and had to fight for breath.

She swayed unsteadily in that pillar of light as the moon reached for its child, as if it were as hungry for the connection as Teresa had been. A door opened in her mind and the past rushed forward, image after image, demanding to be seen, recognized, accepted. She closed her eyes against the frenzied clip show her brain was presenting her with.

But these memories would no longer be ignored. Visions rose up and faded away in a timeless yet hurried slide show. She saw herself across the ages, changing from one lifetime to the next. She watched as the witch she had been took part in that last spell. Watched as demons poured through the opened gate to hell.

Teresa screamed and the images changed. She was a woman in London, a servant in Venice, a wife in Holland. More lives remembered and then cast away. More times with Rune. Always Rune. He was there, in the captured photographs in her memory. Her warrior.

Her mate.

She was so many women in the march through time and yet she was always *herself*. The heart of her, the soul of her remained the same. Then one clear thought screamed into her consciousness and Teresa finally understood why he couldn't trust her. Why he held himself back from her even as they moved forward on the most important quest either of them would ever undertake.

She'd betrayed him in the past. More than once. She had hurt him and cost herself the respect of the man she now loved more than she would ever have thought it possible to love. God, she loved him. Hadn't wanted to. Hadn't planned to. But maybe, she thought, she'd never really had a choice in that at all. They had been destined. And destiny, she was beginning to understand, was not easily fought or ignored.

The moon scrambled her thoughts, its energy creating a tumult inside her that she simply couldn't withstand much longer. She gasped and fell to her knees, bracing her hands on the dirt and grass in front of her. Her back bowed, her head down, she struggled to find the peace she had enjoyed when she first opened herself to the moon. But she had gone past that now and crossed a threshold. There was no peace to be found anymore—there was simply too much chaos churning inside her.

And still the moonlight entered her, like a persistent lover. Pushing into her body again and again even after orgasm had been reached, until pleasure became pain and the two became so entwined that they couldn't be separated. She was heated, gasping, shuddering, pushed into a yearning, desperate need that left her curled on the ground whimpering with the aches rattling her body.

"Rune . . ." She tried to call for him, but her voice was lost in the surging pounding of her own heart. Her blood. Her core burned with an aching need that couldn't be assuaged. Teresa reached to press one hand against her center, hoping to ease the pulsing need that throbbed incessantly within her. It didn't help. Nothing could help, she knew, but his body, driving into hers. She literally burned for it. "Oh, God, Rune. Come back . . ."

"What do we have here?" A man stepped out of the

thicket of darkness and was quickly followed by four more men.

Even through the blinding need, Teresa felt a jolt of fear and shock slap at her. Her eyes wheeled to the hard faces of the men leering down at her like slavering dogs over an unexpected feast. She swallowed hard, tried to scream, but she couldn't find her voice.

The pillar of moonlight still held her in its grasp, saturating her body with the energies of the ages, but she could only moan in response. Twisting and turning on the ground, she reacted to the hunger inside her. She couldn't stop herself. Couldn't ease the longing or her response to it, even knowing that these cold-eyed interlopers were getting off on watching her.

She fought for clarity, struggled to get a handle on the new powers crushing her. Her frenzied gaze flicked from one man to the next and found no comfort in any of their faces. They were dirty, their clothes sweat-stained from life in the jungle. They were smiling, but there was no humor in their eyes. Each of them was carrying knives and guns and two of them wore bandoliers stuffed with more ammunition crisscrossed over their chests.

Bandits.

Teresa gasped in pain, clenched her thighs together against the burning need and shot the first man a wild look as his friends formed a circle around her.

Her body was vibrating, the moonlight filling her beyond her ability to control it. Her powers might erupt at any second. She felt as if she were about to explode and if she did that while these men were close, they'd all die. The way she was feeling at the moment, she wouldn't have a problem with that. But she wasn't a killer, so she gave them a chance.

"Stay away," she said tightly through gritted teeth. She swallowed back another roar of pain and desperation. "I'm warning you, stay away from me."

"If you did not want company, little witch," the man said, his English heavily accented, "you should not have worked your magic. The moon led us to you."

Of course it had, she thought wildly, her body thrashing as it searched futilely for release from the pulse of need crashing inside her. Magic ruled her body now, filling her up so completely that she was helpless when she most needed to be strong. She had had no idea the moon magic would be so powerful. She'd never heard of anything like this before and couldn't explain it even to herself. She had opened her body and mind to a power that was all-encompassing, staggering in its strength.

"Hold her." One sharp command and four men sprang into action. They pulled at her arms and legs, holding her down spread-eagled against the dirt. Firelight danced in the dark. Moonlight continued to stream from the sky. Teresa twisted and turned, trying to break their grip, trying to call down the lightning before they could go through with their plan.

But her power was too knotted inside her to be called so easily. There were too many sensations, too many thoughts, too much fear and no time to sort through it all. She jolted as the leader of the little band knelt in front of her and pulled out a machete stained with old blood.

"Don't!" She groaned the word, unable even to scream for the tight hold the moonlight had on her. "Don't do this. I warn you."

"*You* warn me?" He laughed and slid the razor-sharp tip of the machete beneath the hem of her jeans. With a flick of his wrist, the blade sliced through the denim with a whisper. The man grinned and continued to slice until the blade had reached her hip and her bare leg was open to the kiss of the warm, thick air.

"You are not in charge here, little witch," he promised, his eyes fixed on the expanse of skin he'd displayed.

Rune! She sent out the mental scream, hoping that somehow he would hear it. But she knew in her heart that they were not connected mentally. Not yet. He couldn't hear her thoughts. If he could, he would already be here, tearing into these men like an avenging angel.

Their grasp on her wrists and feet tightened and Teresa's stomach fisted into an icy ball of dread and fear.

The leader ripped off her ruined jeans and warmth snaked across her skin even as the pebbled dirt beneath her scraped at her flesh. Still she fought, battling the moonlight magic for control of her body as she struggled to free herself from the relentless grip of the men holding her down.

The men laughed and Teresa struggled even harder. "Don't do this," she muttered. "You'll be sorry if you do this."

Now the leader laughed, delighted at her threats. "Will you do a spell on me, *bruja*? I don't think so . . ." He reached for the elastic band of her panties, twisting his grubby fingers in the fabric.

In the next instant, the moonlight vanished. The pillar of light was gone as if it had never been and darkness enveloped all of them. She heard one of the men mutter a choked-off prayer, but the leader was not to be denied.

He gave a harsh order in Spanish. Just to the right of them, the river roared. Bugs clattered and a monkey high in the trees screamed. In the blackness, hands fisted tighter around her limbs and Teresa felt as if she had been swallowed by evil. There was no way out. She couldn't fight them. Rune wasn't here. And wouldn't come back in time.

Would they kill her when they were finished with her?

Was she going to die in this jungle, leaving her life, her quest, unfulfilled?

No, damn it.

She wasn't going to die. She was going to find a way to survive, no matter what.

Rune would come.

Holding on to the mental image of him, she called on the last shred of her inner strength, focused her power and screamed, *"Rune!"*

Chapter 46

He felt rather than heard her cry. It was a knife to his chest. He sensed her pain. Her fear. And the danger closing in around her. Looking back toward their camp, Rune saw a towering pillar of moonlight and knew his witch was there at the heart of it. When that light suddenly winked out, he howled in rage, called on the fire and flashed back to his woman.

At the campsite, he found Teresa on the ground, screaming as four men held her arms and legs apart while yet another hovered over her.

He crashed into that man with a body blow that sent the tormenter flying into the jungle. Rune was after him a second later and in a rage beyond anything he had ever known before, he brought his own knife down in a swinging arc, slicing across the bastard's throat. Not pausing to admire his handiwork, he raced back to the camp to find Finn snapping one man's neck only to drop him alongside another of his dead friends.

Teresa had come up on her knees and, trembling with shock and terror, was holding her hands to the sky, waving them frantically. Lightning flashed down and stabbed the jungle floor in an incredible sweep of power and majesty. The night shone with the brilliance of a million candles as lightning bolts pounded the trees, the river, the rocks. Animals screeched and Rune felt the very air burn along with Teresa's frenzied movements. She jumped to her feet and kicked one man's nuts into his throat and he dropped like a stone.

Another of the bandits grabbed at her and Rune threw fire in a river of living flame that raced across the man, wrapping the bastard in what looked like a brilliant, fiery suit. He screamed and fled into the darkness, toward the river, no doubt planning on quenching the flames in the water. Rune smiled grimly. Water wouldn't affect an Eternal's flame. The bastard would continue to burn—he had dealt himself a cruel fate the moment he had touched Teresa.

Rune's fury wasn't abated. He picked up the emasculated prick whimpering in the dirt and gave his head a hard twist, then dropped him like the trash he was. In the next instant, Rune was holding Teresa, pulling her close, running his hands up and down her body as if to assure himself that she was really alive. And safe.

Quickly, he stripped out of his coat and wrapped it around her, giving her back her pride and dignity. He felt her tremble, her entire body quaking, and he hated himself for leaving her alone. If he had been with her, none of this would have happened.

"You came," she whispered, holding on to him and shuddering as if her bones were trying to vibrate out of her skin.

He held her close, cupping her head to his chest with one hand. If his heart was capable of beating, he knew it would have been crashing against his rib cage. Rune had known danger and had always faced it with cool deliberation. But never had he tasted panic like he had just experienced.

"Always, Teresa," he whispered, dropping a kiss on the top of her head. "I will always come. Did they hurt you?"

"No." She shuddered again and lifted her head to look at him. "They didn't have time. But they were going to."

"Well, they won't be trying that again," Finn said, giving one of the bodies a good kick just for the hell of it.

She shook back her hair and stared at him. "Who are you?"

"That's Finn," Rune told her, looking across the fire at his brother. Grateful he'd been here. "An old friend. He's an Eternal. Like me."

One corner of Finn's mouth curved briefly and flattened out again in an instant. "Don't listen to him, Teresa. I'm way better than him."

She actually smiled and Rune felt relief slide through him like a cooling breeze drifting through hell.

"Thanks for the help," he said.

"Not a problem." Finn gathered up their supplies and stuffed them into the duffel bag before tossing it to Rune. "You and your witch ought to be on your way, though. Someone might come looking for this bunch."

"Right." Rune tossed the strap of the bag over his shoulder and said, "You'll take care of the bodies?"

Finn grinned at him, lifted both hands and called on the fire. As the flames burned on his hands and arms, he said, "Cremation special, man. Don't worry about it. Oh, and I'll look into the other thing we talked about earlier."

At the moment, Rune didn't give a flying fuck about the possibility of a rogue Eternal. All he cared about now was Teresa. Seeing that she was safe. Her body pressed tighter to his and he felt her rub her pelvis against his thigh. His cock jerked into action even as he told himself to get a grip. She'd come too close to disaster to be interested in any man—even her mate. So he swallowed back the need crowding him and muttered, "Thanks."

"Don't thank me," Finn told him. "Just find that fucking Artifact, will you?"

"We will." The flames swarmed over the two of them and in an instant Rune and Teresa were gone.

Chapter 47

Teresa was still shaking an hour later when Rune escorted her into a small but clean motel room in a quiet town not far from Tierra Blanca, Veracruz.

"Are you sure?" she asked, still dwarfed by Rune's far-too-big black leather coat. "Is it safe to stay here?"

"Safe?" he muttered thickly, tossing their duffel bag onto one of the two chairs in the room. He rubbed the back of his neck with one hand and said, "I thought the jungle would be safer for you and look what happened."

She spun around to look at him. "It wasn't your fault."

"I shouldn't have left you alone."

"And I shouldn't have done that spell without you close. So we both screwed up."

"But you were the one to pay the price."

"They didn't hurt me," she reminded him, feeling the swell and rush of the mystical moonlight energy swarming inside her still. "You stopped them."

He stalked across the room, grabbed her shoulders and pulled her into a fierce embrace. "I only wish I could kill them again. That they touched you tears at me, Teresa. That I left you alone rips my soul to shreds."

Teresa reached up and wrapped her arms around his

neck. "Don't. Don't take what they did and make it a part of us. It's not. They were evil and now they're dead and that's the end of it."

He lifted his head to look down at her. She watched him search her features, looking for further assurance that she was all right. Unharmed. She understood his need and shared it. She wanted the chance to feel alive and safe. She had survived—she'd fought back and won. Her mate had been there when she needed him. And now, she wanted him.

"Kiss me, Rune."

He did. Tenderly. And that one brief touch of his mouth roused the insistent clamoring need inside her. She pushed her hips against him and felt his erection pressing back. She groaned and swiveled her hips, feeding the fires inside her. "I need you."

"After—" He looked down at her and shook his head. "Teresa, wait. Take a shower. Rest. Then if you still—"

"I opened myself to the magic, Rune, and if I were stronger, I'd have been better able to fight those men off. Being with you increases my strength—and I need your touch."

She grabbed one of his hands and moved it down, down across her bare skin to the very heart of her. Then she pressed his palm to her heated core and sighed at the first contact. She was hot and wet and so ready every nerve ending in her body was screaming for release.

"Ah, God . . ." he groaned, sliding his hand over her sensitive skin, caressing that bud of desire until she let her head fall back on a sigh of bliss. He delved first one finger, then two, into her depths and she rocked on his hand, pumping her hips as she sought release.

He gave it to her.

Teresa lifted her face to his and through passion-

glazed eyes, she watched as he lowered his mouth to
hers. That first brush of his lips lit up her insides and
when his tongue dove into her mouth, she met each caress eagerly. Tongues tangling in a wild dance of desire,
their breath mingled as their bodies went up in flames.

The moonlight magic simmered inside her, pushing
her on, harder, faster. This was what she had needed
from the moment she began her spell. She moved her
hips on his hand, felt his fingers stroking her inner muscles, his thumb caressing her core, and it still wasn't
enough. She wanted to be filled by him. She wanted him
so deeply embedded inside her that he would never be
entirely apart from her again. She wanted his brand on
her skin, his cock in her body, his seed filling her womb.

"Rune, I need you. I need to feel you. Now. Oh,
God, *now.*"

"Take this first," he told her, and she lost herself in
the swirling gray of his eyes.

She groaned his name and continued to move against
his hand as tiny, shuddering explosions discharged inside her. When that orgasm ended, though, the fire was
still there. Still burning, raging out of control. Calling
down the moon had opened her body, her mind, her soul
to the magic that only Rune could complete. *"More."*

Teresa shrugged out of his coat, then pushed at him,
tearing at his clothes until he snapped his fingers and got
rid of his own clothing and what was left of hers as well.

"You're trembling, Teresa," he said, still stroking her
core with steady, driving thrusts of his fingers.

"It's the moon," she whispered, reaching down to curl
her fingers around his hard, thick erection. "It filled me,
lit me up and left me so hungry for you, I don't think I'll
ever get my fill."

He hissed in a breath and held completely still as she

used both of her hands to hold him, stroke him, cup him. Tiny sparks flew from her fingertips and danced across his skin, increasing the heat of her touch, intensifying each caress. He groaned and Teresa smiled with anticipation as his hunger grew to match her own.

"I want you in me," she whispered, suddenly squeezing both hands around his erection, dropping to her knees to take the tip of it into her mouth.

"Damn it, Teresa!" His voice was a snarl of barely leashed passion.

She looked up at him and smiled, loving what she could do to this man. This amazingly strong, fierce warrior. Keeping her gaze fixed on his, she took him deeper into her mouth, letting her tongue and teeth scrape across his sensitive skin until his massive body trembled with the force of his own self-control.

But she didn't want him controlled.

And in the next instant, she got exactly what she wanted.

He reached down, yanked her up against him, then tossed her onto the bed. He was on her in a heartbeat, his huge body covering hers, weighing her down on the bed. She felt the cool glide of the bedspread beneath her heated skin. She felt the hard, muscular planes of his sculpted body atop her and shivered in response. His erection was so close to her center. So near to entering her.

She lifted both legs, gripping the backs of her knees with her hands as she parted her thighs to his gaze. His eyes locked on her and she felt even hotter with him looking at her, naked and vulnerable to him. "Rune, I've been waiting. I can't wait anymore."

"Neither can I." He lifted her hips off the bed, positioned himself and then drove deep inside her.

On that first, hard thrust, Teresa gasped in satisfaction. He filled her as completely as the moon magic had. She was overflowing with what he meant to her. What he could do to her. What he made her feel. He had saved her. He had *always* saved her. She felt it. And the connection between them burned even more brightly.

"Again. God, again." She groaned the words and let go of her knees as he positioned her legs across his shoulders.

She was high off the bed now and she didn't care. This way he could go even deeper inside. In this position, she could take him more completely within her than she ever had before and that was what she wanted. Needed. With a hunger that wouldn't be satiated.

His powerful hips moved against her, claiming her over and over again. He went deep and then deeper still. He rocked into and out of her body like a man possessed and she shared that passion. She reached up, running her fingers across the branding tattoo that was burning into his flesh right before her eyes. She felt the sting on her own skin and knew that she too was being marked more indelibly.

Teresa grabbed hold of his upper arms, digging her fingernails into his skin to hold on tightly. He drove into her relentlessly, furiously. Tension peaked inside her, tightening, coiling into a spring that shivered on the edge of explosion, and still he pushed her.

She was hungry for it, wanted it all, needed it all. When he pulled her legs off his shoulders and then yanked her up to sit on his lap, Teresa went gladly. Now it was she who set the rhythm and she deliberately slowed it down, to torture both of them with the caress of skin against skin.

He kissed her, taking her mouth with his until she was

left gasping for air that wouldn't come. And while his tongue entwined with hers, he set his hands at her hips and moved her faster, quickening their pace.

She was panting now, staring into his eyes, feeling the sweep of release encroach ever faster and still it wasn't enough. Suddenly he pulled free of her body, as if he'd heard her frantic thoughts. Tossing her onto the mattress, he flipped her over as he had once before and Teresa sighed, *"Yes . . ."*

Lifting her hips for his entrance, he pushed inside and Teresa held on to the headboard, bracing herself for each of his heavy strokes. She took him in and released him, feeding the need, feeding the fever clawing at her. Mystical energy pooled inside her, streamed from her body to his and as he reached beneath her to tweak and pull at her nipples, her body shattered.

She screamed his name, and shaking with the tremendous force of her release, she was barely aware of his own shout moments later as he emptied all that he was into her keeping.

Chapter 48

"I remembered," she said, what felt like hours later.

Rune was dazzled by his witch, his body humming with completion and yet already hungering for more. Would he ever have enough of his mate? Would there ever be a time when he didn't want her more than his next breath?

Shaking his head, he pulled out of his own thoughts and shifted on the pillow to look at her. "What?"

Teresa snaked one arm across his chest and he held her there, needing that connection. "I said I remembered. I did that moon spell and . . ." She blew out a breath. "It was like somebody opened a floodgate. Pictures, memories crashed into my mind and I couldn't stand up to the onslaught. It was . . . terrifying."

His hand tightened on her arm when she might have pulled away. This was what they had been waiting and hoping for. The return of her memories. Now she could tap the knowledge they would need to complete their journey of atonement.

The bed was rumpled beneath them. A light burned from the small bathroom and the draperies in the main room were closed, sealing them off from the world. They were alone with the past, and the future was no more than a hazy specter hanging just out of reach.

"Tell me," he whispered, stroking his fingers along her arm in a comforting caress. "What did you remember?"

She shifted until she was lying on top of him, skin to skin, her eyes locked with his. "Everything," she admitted. "I remembered every lifetime in bits and pieces that shattered around my mind like a puzzle that had been shaken and dropped." She frowned, bit her bottom lip and said, "I saw me as Serena. And I saw you—how angry you were with her—*me*—and I didn't blame you. My God, Rune, how did you stand me? Why did you love me? I was like the bitch queen of the universe."

A reluctant smile curved his mouth as he listened to her berate herself for what couldn't be changed. He lifted one hand and smoothed her hair back from her cheek. So soft. Her skin. Her hair. Everything about her was satin covering steel. She was stronger than she knew and he was all too aware that she was going to need all of that strength and more in the coming days.

"You weren't as bad as all that," he said quietly, though his memories were sharper than hers and clearer on the many times in their shared past when this witch had torn the unbeating heart from his chest.

She dropped her forehead to his chest and murmured, "Yes, I was. I lied to you. I turned on you when you needed me. Time and again, I let you—*myself*—down, and it worries me."

"Why?" He tipped her chin up with his fingers, until she was looking into his eyes again. "Why does the past worry you so? It is merely a tool we will use to carve a future."

"You say that, but you don't really believe it."

"Teresa—"

"No. It bothers me for the same reason that you don't trust me," she said, then spoke again quickly when he opened his mouth to argue. "I understand now why you don't. Why you can't. And damn it, Rune, even I don't trust me now. What if I haven't grown enough? What if in all those lifetimes, I still haven't learned what I needed to? What if I fuck this up for both of us?"

"You will not," he said, rolling with her until she was beneath him on the bed and he had braced himself over her. He caught her gaze with his and willed her to believe him. "This is our time. Together, we will do this. The past can't touch us now."

"It can influence us, though," she argued, running her fingertips across the lightning bolts carving a jagged circle around his left nipple and winding their way beneath his arm. "You know that."

"Yes. But its influence is only as strong as you allow it to be." He cupped her face in his palm. "Do you want to succeed in this quest, Teresa? Do you *want* to put right what once went wrong?"

"Of course I do, but—"

"No." He bent his head to her and kissed her hard and deep. When he broke away, he said, "If you want it badly enough, it will happen. The past changes nothing unless you allow it to."

"What about your trust in me?" she whispered, with a sad shake of her head. "Our past keeps you from taking that one last step and you know it. So how can we even think to ignore what came before?"

"I . . . care for you," he told her, though he knew it wasn't what she longed to hear. But in spite of everything he had just said, he knew that his distrust still had a grip on him. That the past lived and breathed in the dark corners of his heart and mind. He couldn't bring himself to take a leap of faith for her, but that was his lack, not hers. "I am your mate. I will be with you on every step of this journey. I will help you to solve the riddle and I will be with you when you return the black silver to Wales."

"But . . ."

"Let it be enough, Teresa," he said softly. "For both of us, here and now, let it be enough."

Grief had etched itself into her eyes, but she nodded, accepting the limitations he felt within himself. Lowering his head, he took her branded nipple into his mouth and swirled his tongue across the sensitive tip. She held him there, her fingers spearing through his hair.

"You taste of moonlight," he whispered against her skin. "Moonlight and magic." Raising his gaze to hers, he saw the flare of desire spark again within her and answered it with a smile. "My witch. My mate. You are in my soul, Teresa."

"As you are in mine," she confessed on a sigh. "Rune, when you appeared in that tower of fire tonight, I'd never seen anything more magnificent in my life."

"I felt your pain. Your fear," he said and thumped one hand hard against his chest. "Here. Inside me, raw and bleeding. I knew you needed me and nothing could have kept me away."

Her fingers moved over the mating brand on his chest again as if she could somehow soothe the ache that lingered there. "I should have waited for you, to do the moon spell. I know that. But once it started, Rune, I couldn't stop it."

Frowning slightly, he asked, "What do you mean?"

"The moon's energies poured into me. Like a water faucet turned on full, it just kept coming. The mystical force of it was staggering and it was all over me. Inside, outside. I felt it sliding through my skin into the air and then wrapping itself around me again and seeping back in." Her voice trembled and he cupped her branded breast with his palm to ground her. "I tapped into something that I wasn't prepared for. I don't know why it happened, what exactly I freed. . . ."

"You freed yourself, Teresa," he said, with a slow smile in the face of her confusion.

"What?"

"You said your memories returned. Can't you recall the reason why the moon reacted so to your spell?"

Her features twisted as she tried to make sense of what was no doubt a spill of information flooding her mind. Eventually, she sighed and admitted, "No. No idea. I told you, the memories are there, but they're all tangled up in knots and I'll probably spend the next fifty years trying to work them free."

"You were the moon's priestess," he said, his own memory nearly choking him now. "In the coven, on that last night so long ago, it was *you* who called down the moon. You who asked her blessing on the magic you all created. You who turned her gift into a weapon."

"Oh, God . . ." She slipped out from under him, rolled off the bed and crossed the room in jerking, halting steps. At the window, she peeled back the edge of the dark red drapes and stared out at the night. Beyond the lamplit emptiness of the parking lot, there was the jungle, with the moonlight glimmering softly over the darkness.

He came up behind her, wrapped his arms around her trembling body and said, "Tonight, you welcomed the moon back into your life, into your spirit. You reclaimed what you had once lost and its power staggered you.

"As it was meant to be." He kissed her forehead, then reached down, grabbed her behind and lifted her, setting her legs at his waist. She hooked her feet at the small of his back and as their gazes met, he said, "The moon has forgiven you, Teresa. It blessed you tonight with the energies it has been holding on to for centuries, in wait for you. Now it's time to forgive yourself. And to remember."

She nodded solemnly and he could see in her eyes that acceptance was growing within her. His witch amazed him anew. Her power was strengthening, as were her confidence and inner control. Her heart was full and ripe and he felt her determination to finally succeed at what they needed to accomplish.

She had withstood tonight what might have broken other women and still held her head high and faced her past with the same resolve that she claimed her future.

Leaning in, Teresa kissed him. Softly. Sweetly. In a benediction of sorts that tugged at Rune's heart and made his soul ache to forever be a part of hers. This one woman had somehow taken his battered, unforgiving nature and turned him into a beast who lived only to protect her.

"You're right," she said, then smiled briefly. "I may not say that often, so you should enjoy it while you can."

"Noted," he answered wryly, tightening his grip on her behind, kneading her flesh until she sighed with pleasure. That one soft sound jerked his cock to life and in an instant his body was ready for hers again.

"In the rush of visions and images I saw tonight," she was saying, "one stood out. My grandmother. I saw her.

She was alone and she was holding something out to me. A twist of metal."

"The Artifact?" Rune asked, suddenly still.

"I think so," Teresa said, frowning as she tried to recapture the image in her mind. "It looked Celtic. And it was black and shiny, like a thousand suns were trapped inside it." She shook her head. "My *abuela* knows something, Rune. Tonight, I'll search the Sanctuary library for Serena's spell book. But tomorrow we should go to Chiapas."

"Tomorrow," he said solemnly. Then slowly, he moved his hands on her behind, stroking her center, running his fingertips across the hot, liquid core of her until she groaned and twisted in his arms.

Touching her wasn't enough for him, though. He wanted to be inside her again, feel her heat lock around his body and hold him deeply within. He wanted that mating connection to burn more fire into his skin and to sear his soul with the same magic.

He walked her to the nearest wall, and slammed her back against it; then, keeping his gaze locked with hers, he pushed his shaft high into her welcoming sheath. She cried out his name as he took her, and Rune knew what the real magic was.

Chapter 49

She lit two of the candles she had left and hoped it would be enough. Dimensional magic wasn't something she was going to take lightly, but it was imperative that she get hold of Serena's spell book.

From the wash of memories still knotted together in her mind, Teresa had learned that most witches kept shadow books—magical journals where they recorded their spells and other important information. Whatever she had once known as Serena would be in that spell book. She had to find it.

"Are you sure you're ready for this?"

She glanced over at her lover, sitting not a foot away from her. He looked worried—and who could blame him. He remembered more clearly than she did the last time she and her sister witches had played with dimensional portals.

"Ready or not, I have to do it," she said as a flicker of apprehension slithered through her.

She wasn't even sure how to do the spell, but she sat cross-legged on the floor, lit her candles and tried to focus on the book she wanted. *Serena's spells.*

She spoke, creating the words to a spell that seemed to echo in the small motel room.

Open dimensions let me see,
A peek back through eternity.
Serena lived and died as me
Find my book in the library.

She felt a rush of comfort and slowly opened her eyes. The air in front of her solidified, bending and twisting as if creating something from nothing. She watched as a shining ball of energy formed and floated three feet off the floor. Her breath came fast and hard in excitement. Despite her crappy rhyming skills, it looked as though she'd done it.

"You opened the portal," Rune whispered.

A swell of pride filled Teresa as she stared into the wobbling sphere before her. It shone with the light of a million suns, yet somehow it didn't hurt her eyes to look at it. The dimensional orb pulsed with power and shimmered with the magic that formed it.

She shot Rune a quick smile and then turned her gaze back on the doorway to the Sanctuary library.

"Now all I have to do is find the book." Steadying herself, she reached out, unsure what to expect. When her fingertips brushed the surface of the sphere, a buzz of energy skittered through her system. It was a little like a static charge, she thought with a grin, and pushed her hand beyond the edge and into the heart of the orb.

She sighed at the contact and closed her eyes as she focused completely on the book she searched for. There were thousands, maybe *millions* of books in the library. She knew that because within the sphere each volume flew past her fingers, allowing her to skim across them, divining their contents. Finally, though, she felt a jolt of awareness when her fingers came into contact with the particular book she sought.

She stopped the slide with a thought, curled her fingers around the book and slowly brought it forth from the dimensional portal.

The moment she had completed the task, the sphere blinked out of existence and the only light left in the room was that of the two candles she had lit before beginning her spell.

"Is that it?"

Teresa held the hand-tooled leather journal in both hands, her fingertips stroking the soft, faded material. She took in the carved sun and moon, the interlinking ribbons of power that streamed back and forth between the two. She felt the sense of ownership zinging in her bloodstream. As if her heart recognized the antique book even if her eyes didn't.

"Yes," she whispered. "This was Serena's."

She untied the rawhide strings that held the journal closed, flipped the book open, and her breath caught in her lungs. The slanted handwriting. The Old English spelling. Even the sight of the faded ink itself. All rose up inside her in a wave of memory so thick, so rich, that her eyes filled with tears that blurred her vision and rained down her cheeks. The woman she had once been called out to her from the heavy vellum pages. Treachery and betrayal flooded her soul along with a nearly tangible sense of hopelessness and regret.

While her heart bled quietly for the doomed woman who had once held this book precious, Teresa could only hope that the answers she needed so desperately would be found in its pages.

Chapter 50

"What's wrong?" Rune glanced at her from the corner of his eye.

"Nothing," Teresa said, waving one hand in dismissal of what she was feeling. "It's just . . . weird, to be riding in a car with you."

He smiled briefly, never taking his gaze off the winding stretch of road spilling out ahead of them. The tires hummed on the cracked asphalt and the wind from their passing was a constant whine. "No choice really. You have to read the book and you can't do that while we're flashing in and out, traveling by fire."

"Yeah, I know," she said, keeping her head down, her gaze fixed on the ink-filled pages in front of her. "It's just weird. So normal, I guess. Even Chico's freaked out."

He scowled as the bird hopped back and forth between Rune's and Teresa's seats. The irritating whistle continuously poured from the creature's throat and Rune gritted his teeth in response. The bird had somehow managed to find them at the motel the night before and Rune's suspicions burned. What the hell kind of bird was it, anyway?

"Well," Teresa added, "normal except for you buying a brand-new car with a suitcase full of cash."

Rune didn't even comment on that. For him, as for every other Eternal, money was no problem. Getting hold of the money hadn't been an issue, either, since Eternals had access to incredible stores of assets through any number of banks. Buying a car from a dealer outside the city had been the only logical choice. Paying cash meant he had avoided certain paperwork and he preferred to leave no paper trail to mark their passing. It hadn't been difficult to get the owner of the dealership to forgo a few legalities in exchange for hard currency.

"Have you found anything yet?"

"I'm not sure," she muttered in disgust. "It's so hard to read her-my-*our* writing." Shaking her head, she flicked him a quick look. "Just the spelling is enough to give you a headache and she-I wrote so damn small. . . ."

"Paper was expensive back in the day," Rune mused. "No one wasted space."

"Great. Just great. So all I have to do is thumb through about a million spells and some petty gossip about Serena's neighbors. No problem." She turned another page gently, as the paper was old and brittle. "This could take forever."

"No, it won't," he said. "You'll find what we need, Teresa."

"You sound confident."

"I am," he said, giving her another quick look.

The road ahead was empty. They drove along a two-lane highway stretching out to the horizon like a dusty gray ribbon tossed down and forgotten. The sky was heavy with clouds, but patches of blue dotted the expanse. The Chiapas landscape spread out on either side of them—lush meadows and green valleys soothed the eye, and in the distance, mountains high enough to be snowcapped jutted skyward.

"Hey," she said a few minutes later, "I think I might have found something." A smile colored her words, and when he looked at her, she was grinning at him. "You were right. I did find it. At least, I'm pretty sure I did. It says . . ."

She broke off suddenly and pointed. "Wait. Turn off here. That dirt road on the right. It leads to my grandmother's village."

He made the turn and floored it, dirt and gravel kicking out in his wake. The ride was a jouncing one, but that couldn't be helped. Rune knew they were in a race—not only against time but also against those who were after them. His instincts were jangling, warning him to hurry. To get this done and get his witch out of Mexico as quickly as possible.

But that warning, he told himself a moment later, had come too late. He saw the first body lying in the street. Blood had seeped into the dirt around the dead man, telling Rune he had been killed at least a couple of hours earlier.

"What?" Teresa said on a horrified gasp. "What happened?" She whipped her gaze from side to side and saw, as Rune did, more bodies.

Outside stores, across open doorways, in the road itself. Survivors wandered the dusty street in a daze, looking around at the fallen, at the twists of smoke lifting from the still-burning homes. A woman wailed beside the body of a man and lifted her eyes to heaven as if asking *why*.

Rune's instincts were screaming. Half the village was dead.

"Oh, my God," Teresa whispered, dropping Serena's journal into the duffel bag at her feet and zipping it closed. She turned horrified eyes on Rune. "My *abuela*. Rune—"

"Where does she live?" His voice was hard with banked rage as he threw the car into PARK and shut off the engine. The air was still, as if haunted by the violence staining the small village. Only the weeping of those left alive shattered an otherworldly silence. Even Chico was quiet, as if he sensed that something was wrong.

"She lives on the outskirts of town. An old cabin."

Nodding, he said, "Get out of the car. We'll flash there. Quieter and faster. No one here will pay any attention to us, magic or not. They're too . . . destroyed."

She grabbed the duffel, swung it over her shoulder and clung to Rune when he came to her side. "Hurry, Rune."

The flames came, carried them away and deposited them just outside her grandmother's home. It looked exactly as she remembered it. Neatly tended flower beds displayed a wild profusion of color. To the side of the house was an herb garden, and surrounding the old cabin were sheltering trees that offered shade from the tropical sun's searing heat.

But the house, like the town, was too quiet.

Teresa broke away from him and headed for the front door at a dead run before he could stop her. Rune's every sense screamed danger. "Teresa! Wait!"

He caught up to her just as the heavy wood door was yanked open. Inside the house, Teresa's grandmother sat, tied to a chair, her wise brown eyes locked sadly on her granddaughter.

"Abuela?"

A man stepped from the shadows, put a gun to the old woman's head and smiled. "Hello, Teresa. Long time, no see."

"Miguel."

Chapter 51

"You son of a bitch," Teresa spat at her ex-boyfriend. "You killed all those people?"

"I had help." He looked to one side, never taking the barrel of the gun from the old woman's temple, and nodded. Three more men stepped into view from the shadows. "We're here for you, Teresa," he said, shifting his gaze back to her. "And the one with you. I know what he is."

She felt a deep chill as soon as she looked into Miguel's eyes. He'd always been an abusive creep. But this was different. He'd moved up—or rather down—the food chain, going from simply dangerous to murderous. Teresa's gaze met her grandmother's and she was swamped by love and helpless agony.

Chico flew into the room in a brilliant display of color and made a diving swoop at one of the men. He swung his gun up in reaction, but the bird shrieked and flew back outside an instant later. The attacked man crossed himself hurriedly.

"For God's sake," Miguel muttered in disgust, "it's just a damn bird." Then he turned to Teresa. "Look, I'll make this easy on you. You tell me where the fucking Artifact is and I let the old woman go."

The Artifact?

Teresa felt Rune stiffen beside her. How did Miguel know about the Artifact?

Miguel smiled. "I know everything. I know that prick with you isn't human. I know the Artifact is the stuff dreams are made of and I know that if I don't deliver you to my superiors, I'm a dead man."

"We can only hope," Teresa told him, enjoying the flash of anger in his eyes.

"Don't piss me off," he warned. "I'll kill this old witch. One bullet and she's gone. Just like those in the village."

Rune's fingers tangled in hers and Teresa held on, feeling his strength rushing through her. She wanted to call down the lightning, but she couldn't risk her grandmother's life. She wanted to simply throw energy at Miguel and watch him light up like a Christmas tree, but again, her grandmother's life hung in the balance.

Beside her, she felt Rune tensing for an attack and she willed him to be still with a silent tug at his hand. She couldn't risk it. As much as it pained her, they would have to go along with Miguel. For now, at least.

"Good girl," Miguel said a moment later, when he read capitulation in her eyes. "You convince the bastard with you to play nice and everybody might live out the day."

He signaled to one of the men with him and the man walked forward cautiously, keeping his gaze fixed warily on Rune. He held two white-gold chains and Teresa heard Rune take a long, shallow breath, hissed in between gritted teeth.

"Hold still, big guy," Miguel said. "You make one wrong move, I'll kill your witch first, *then* the old woman.

I don't care how fast you are with fire, you can't beat a bullet."

Teresa knew what it cost Rune to stand idly by and be hampered by a length of white gold. The man-made alloy would dampen his powers, making him easier to control.

"You risk much, human," Rune said as the man hung the chain around his neck. "There will be payment made for this."

For just an instant, Miguel looked worried, but his own innate sense of self-importance quickly wiped that out. "Right. Big talk for a guy who just got locked down."

"Miguel, don't do this."

"Are you kidding?" he countered with a laugh. Motioning his partner to go ahead and place the second white-gold chain around Teresa's neck, he continued. "They're paying me a *truckload* of money to do this, Teresa. Though to be honest, I'd have done it for free." His mouth twisted and his gaze swept her up and down dismissively. "Bitch. Think you can dump me? Walk away from *me*? Do you know what kind of shit I had to take from the boss when you walked out?"

"The boss?"

He scowled and shook his head. "Never mind." Then to the other man he said, "Do it. Lock her down, too."

She swayed as the effects of the white gold seeped through her. Ice seemed to soak into every pore, flooding every vein and capillary. Her powers were dampened every bit as much as Rune's. She couldn't have called down the lightning now, even if she had been willing to take the risk. The draining wash of white gold had closed off her magical abilities. How completely, she didn't know, but for the moment she was left at Miguel's less-than-tender mercies.

"Now that that's taken care of," Miguel said slyly, "let's get down to business."

He slammed the barrel of the gun against her *abuela*'s face. Teresa gasped as a thin trickle of blood ran along the old woman's deeply lined cheek like a single red tear.

"You bastard! Don't!" Teresa lunged for him, but Miguel only laughed.

Rune stepped in front of Teresa, blocking her from Miguel's sight with his own massive form. "You will die," he said, voice soft and strong and filled with the promise of retribution.

Miguel flinched, but shrugged off the threat. "Everybody dies, fire boy. But if your witch is smart, I'll die rich. So, Teresa, what'll it be? Tell me where the Artifact is or watch your precious grandmother slowly get beaten to death?"

Teresa looked from Rune to her grandmother and felt tight bands of frustrated fury tense around her insides. She couldn't give Miguel what he wanted. She'd only just found a hint of the Artifact's whereabouts in Serena's journal a moment before they stumbled on to the carnage in the village. She wasn't sure yet where it was hidden. And even if she was, she couldn't tell Miguel. Couldn't allow the black silver to be set loose in the world again. Couldn't betray what she was. What her grandmother had taught her to be.

The older woman looked into her eyes and Teresa sensed that her grandmother knew exactly what she was thinking—and that she was proud.

"Teresa," her *abuela* said softly, "it is no use. They will discover it sooner or later. We must tell them."

"What? Grandmother, *no.*"

Rune went utterly still.

"Shut up, Teresa," Miguel ordered, then turned his gaze on the old woman. "Let's have it. You know where the damn thing is, tell me and I let you go."

"Let Teresa go," she said, eyes narrowed on her captor.

"Of course," Miguel lied smoothly. His smile was ingratiating, but his eyes were as cold as the emptiest, loneliest night.

"*Abuela*, don't," Teresa said, knowing now exactly what her grandmother was up to. The old woman didn't know where the Artifact was, but Miguel had no way of knowing that. She was stalling. Offering up information to win their freedom. But Miguel wasn't the type to make deals.

"I must, Teresa," her grandmother said. Then, turning her gaze on the man holding a gun to her head, she muttered, "The Artifact is at Palenque. In the Temple of the Moon."

"The Mayan site?" Miguel asked.

At the old woman's sharp nod, he grinned and said, "Thank you."

Then he shot her.

The report of the pistol boomed into the quiet and Teresa's scream of pain and fury was its echo. Her grandmother's body slumped in the chair, blood staining the fabric of her simple blue dress.

"You bastard!" Teresa screamed, and tried to push past Rune's huge body to get at the man who had just single-handedly ended her family. Clawing and pounding at Rune's immovable back, Teresa was cut off from the very revenge she wanted so badly she could taste it. "I'll kill you myself. I swear to God, I will."

"Temper, Teresa," Miguel said with a grin as he tucked the pistol away at the small of his back. "You should be grateful. Your dead grandmother just bought you a little more time."

Then he motioned for his men to take hold of Rune and Teresa, bundling them out to the van waiting for them behind the small house.

Chapter 52

President Cora Sterling studied her daughter's pinched, pale features and shook her head. "Deidre, you don't look well at all. Are you sleeping?"

"What? Oh. Yes. I'm fine, Mother." She pushed asparagus tips across her plate, the tines of her fork scraping against the fine china.

Cora winced. Here in the family dining room, they didn't really stand on ceremony at meals, but the quiet screech of sound was beginning to get on her nerves. "Could you stop, dear? If you're not going to eat Chef Patrice's meal, simply put your fork down."

"I'm sorry." Deidre did set the heavy sterling silver fork aside, then smiled at the waiter who deftly removed her plate. Once he had left the room, Deidre reached for her wineglass and took a sip. "Honestly, I guess I'm just not hungry."

Cora didn't like this one bit. For more than two weeks now, her daughter had been moody, distant. Completely unlike her normal vibrant self. Which could only mean something was bothering her. "Why don't you tell me what the trouble is? I'm sure it's nothing we can't handle together."

"There's no trouble, really." Her fingers tapped against the Irish linen tablecloth until Cora's gaze landed on her hand. Deidre huffed out a breath and folded her hands together tightly to keep them still.

"This is about Susan, isn't it?"

"What?"

Cora smiled. "Your best friend has moved away and you're feeling a little lost."

"Oh. Yes, I guess so." Standing up, Deidre walked to the wide bank of windows overlooking the pristine White House lawn. Under the soft glow of discreetly placed lighting, the neatly trimmed hedges and flower beds looked, Cora knew, almost artificial in their perfection.

Frowning a bit, Cora watched the slump of her daughter's shoulders and pushed away from the table. A shame to leave such an excellent meal unfinished, but sometimes a mother's duty came first.

She moved alongside her daughter, draped one arm around her shoulders and said, "I know it's hard. Losing a friend is never easy, but Susan may yet move back to D.C."

"I don't think so," Deidre murmured.

"Well," Cora told her, "sadly, I have to say that may be for the best."

"Why?"

Looking into Deidre's eyes, Cora smoothed her daughter's hair back from her face and said, "I think Susan was a little too radical in her beliefs about the witch problem, honey. I saw that easily in the meeting I had here with you and the other RFW members. She was headed for trouble and I'd prefer that you not be with her when she finds it."

A short, sharp laugh exploded from Deidre's throat,

and she lifted one hand to her mouth to stifle her reaction.

"What's so funny?"

"Nothing," Deidre said, shaking her head. "Nothing at all. I'm sure you're right. Susan was . . . passionate about her involvement with RFW."

"A cool head serves you better than misplaced passion," Cora said.

"I suppose." Nodding to herself, Deidre shifted her gaze from the world outside the window to her mother's keen eyes. "And you should know that I've decided to take a step back from RFW for a while myself."

"Have you?" Delighted to hear it, Cora leaned forward and gave her daughter a fierce hug. "I'm so glad."

Deidre hugged her back briefly, then pulled away. "I know my being a part of the organization wasn't easy on you, Mother."

She wouldn't deny it. Even other heads of state had begun to question Cora's authority when her own daughter was a member of what some considered nothing more than a veiled terrorist group.

"No, it wasn't. Especially now," Cora said, her lips thinning into a tight line. "After that raid on the internment camp in Nebraska, the papers are in a frenzy, demanding arrests."

Deidre took a breath and asked, "Have they discovered anything new about that?"

"No." It pained her to admit it, but there it was. Grimly, Cora said, "The missing witches are still unaccounted for. There are three guards dead and the security tapes—which no doubt caught the whole thing—are missing as well."

Beside her, Deidre looked concerned and Cora was grateful for the support. Forcing herself to smile, she hugged her girl again and said, "Now don't you worry, dear. We'll find those responsible. Meanwhile, why don't we see what Chef Patrice has for dessert?"

Deidre was silent throughout the rest of the meal, but Cora consoled herself with the fact that at least her daughter ate every last morsel of the brandied pears and cinnamon mousse.

Chapter 53

Chico swooped into the van to perch on Teresa's shoulder just before their captors slammed the back doors shut. In the dim interior, Rune tried to catch her gaze. "I'm so sorry about your grandmother, Teresa."

She shook her head, silent tears streaming down her face. Quickly, she swiped them away with her fingertips, swallowed hard and said, "It wasn't your fault."

"Nor yours," he pointed out, wrapping one arm around her shoulders and pulling her close. The bird leaped away and sat itself on the bench seat opposite them. Its beady eyes watched their every movement.

The engine gunned into life and the van jerked forward, Rune and Teresa both swaying with the sudden motion. In seconds they were riding back down the rutted track toward the highway.

Rune ignored everything but the woman leaning against him. "I know what she meant to you. If I could change things, I would."

"I know that, Rune," she said and her bottom lip trembled as she fought for control of the emotions raging inside her.

He ached for her, and at the same time he knew she

wouldn't crumble under this latest onslaught of pain. Her strength shone around her like an extra aura, gifting her with the ability to endure, no matter the obstacle.

In that one staggering moment of clarity, his feelings for her deepened inexorably and he knew that loving her completely had always been inevitable for him. Teresa was the other half of his soul. Loving her was as much a part of him as the fire that made him what he was.

Lifting her chin, she blinked away fresh tears, lowered her voice and said, "My grandmother was the bravest woman I ever knew. She wasn't afraid of Miguel. She wouldn't cower and plead with him for anything. Not even her own life. She did what she had to, for *us.*"

Rune flicked a glance toward the front of the van. He had already inspected what he could of the vehicle and as far as he could tell, there were no monitoring devices back there with them. But he would take no chances. Lowering his voice to hardly more than a whisper, he said, "She didn't know where the Artifact is."

"Of course not, but Miguel's too stupid to realize that." Teresa leaned in closer, her voice now no more than a hush of sound. "I think I found the answer in Serena's journal. The Artifact is in Barcelona."

He pulled back, a jolt of excitement shooting through him in spite of the circumstances. "Are you sure?"

"As sure as I can be," she told him. "She—or I—worked dream spells. And in the dreams, there was darkness in Barcelona. A darkness that 'glittered like black magic and shone with the light of a thousand moons.'" Sounds like the Artifact to me."

"It does," he admitted.

"There's something else, too," she said just as quietly. "Remember I told you I saw my grandmother's face, as she held out the Artifact to me?"

He nodded, waiting.

She bit down on her bottom lip to stem another rush of tears and said, "It wasn't my *abuela* I was seeing. I realize that now. It was her sister, Tía Carmen. They look so much alike, it's no wonder I thought it was my grandmother. Tía Carmen *lives* outside Barcelona, Rune. The Artifact has to be there."

He gave her a slow smile, leaned in and kissed her hard and fast. "Well done."

"Yeah. Now all we have to do is get away from these guys long enough to get to Spain and find the damn thing before time runs out on us."

"We will," he said, cupping her face in his palm. He wiped away a stray tear with his thumb, then lifted that tiny bead of moisture to his lips. He drank her tears, swallowed her sorrow and told her softly, "They won't be able to stop us, Teresa. We will complete this task."

Heart in her eyes, she met his gaze and solemnly nodded.

Chapter 54

The damp heat slapped at her as Teresa stepped out of the van. It felt as though she was wrapped in a wet electric blanket. Smothering. Stifling. Chico took wing the moment they were free and she heard his vibrant whistle over the wind that sighed through the dense grove of trees. She hoped he kept going. Hoped he remained free rather than coming back to her.

Teresa took a breath and filled her lungs with the mingled scents of plant and animal life. Just beneath it all, there was a thick undercoating of decay. She had never liked the rain forest, preferring instead the clean sweep of the desert, with its wide-open vistas and sharp, dusty air. The jungle made her feel claustrophobic. Everything was too close. Every tree and bush seemed to be leaning over toward her, cutting off her view of the sky.

She threw a look at Miguel and his men as Rune, held at gunpoint, climbed out of the van to join her.

Miguel's henchmen didn't look too happy about being there. And she knew why.

Even this far from the Palenque site, she felt the threads of magic spilling through the air. This place was sacred. The ground hummed with ancient power and the jungle itself was its living guardian.

"Come on!" Miguel waved his gun to get them moving. "I don't have all day to stand around in this disgusting heat. Move it."

She threw a look at Rune and read the rage burning in his eyes. Teresa understood what it was costing this fierce warrior to be a prisoner to a man so completely beneath him. Her own temper was boiling, demanding to be released, so she could only imagine the depths of her Eternal's wrath. She reached for his hand and with their fingers entwined, they set off down a narrow path, overgrown with so much plant life it was nearly invisible to the eye. One of Miguel's men walked ahead of them with a machete and the constant slap of the blade against the growth became a steady accompaniment to their footsteps.

The jungle closed in around her, making it hard to breathe. Sweat dripped along her spine. The dark mutterings of the men were hardly more than a buzzing distraction.

It rained, a misty soak that drenched their clothes and left them steaming as the sun came out from behind the clouds again. Water dripped from the canopy of trees that stretched high overhead. It was a miserable trek, but through it all, her fury spurred Teresa forward. She would never forget what her beloved *abuela* had sacrificed to give them this chance.

The path led to a clearing and when they stepped into the vast space, Teresa let out a sigh of wonder.

Palenque.

Normally, there was a crowd of tourists wandering the area. How Miguel had managed to keep them all out was a mystery, but one she didn't need to unravel.

"I don't like this," one of the men complained in an undertone.

"Me neither. Place gives me the creeps."

"Shut up," Miguel told them.

Teresa wasn't listening to any of them. Instead, she concentrated on the huge structure in front of her. Her gaze moved over the massive stone palace, covered in dark-green snaking vines and grass crawling up from the well-tended grounds. Smaller structures were staggered around the clearing, with stone steps set into their facades. Everywhere, the jungle pushed forward.

But no matter how hard nature tried to reclaim it, the building remained. Magical energies pulsed from within the structure, the very air resonating with power that fueled the dampened magic inside Teresa. She felt the ancient force of unbridled energies soaking into her skin, feeding what gifts she had with immeasurable abandon. "Amazing," she whispered.

"It is," Rune agreed.

"Yes, yes," Miguel snapped. "It's amazing. Wonder how they built it. Where did the Mayans do their sacrifices? Jesus, you two sound like the tourists our men chased out of here. I don't give a good damn about the stinking temple. All I want is what's inside and you're going to get it for me."

Rune glared at the much smaller man. "You should learn when to keep your mouth shut, *human.*"

Miguel's fist tightened on his pistol. "You should remember that even if I can't kill you with a gun, I *can* kill her."

"Do it and die."

"Tough talk from a guy with a white-gold chain around his neck."

"Rune," Teresa said softly, "let's just do this and be done."

"Good plan, Teresa." Miguel motioned with his gun hand, steering them toward a much smaller building that sat at the crest of a low hill.

It could have been an English country cottage from the lines of it. Until you looked closer and saw the jagged stones making up its skeleton and the sharply pitched roof. Blank doorways and windows stared out emptily at what had once been an arena filled with worshippers.

Teresa stared up at the small temple. "Temple of the Moon," she whispered.

Miguel laughed from behind her. "Actually Temple of the *Dead* Moon. Or Temple of the Skull. Kinda looks like a skull, too."

She threw him a glare, then dismissed him as she shifted her gaze to Rune. He was watching her as if they were alone in the clearing. The men holding them at gunpoint might as well have been on Jupiter for all the notice he gave them.

"Do you feel it?" he whispered.

"I do." It only surprised her that the others couldn't feel the energy pulsing off the moon temple in this amazing place. But their ignorance would help her and Rune.

"Let's go," Miguel ordered, waving them up the side of the grassy knoll toward the temple.

Guns still aimed at them, Teresa went first, with Rune hot on her heels, a living barrier between her and the dangerous men behind them. She slipped, caught her footing and kept on. There was something ahead. Magic. Energy. Power. And it sang to her. Her body, chilled as it was from the white gold, reacted, her cells awakening with every step that brought her closer to the source of that energy.

Heart racing, she smiled to herself and kept climbing, eager now to reach the top. To enter that long-abandoned temple that was somehow reaching out to her.

At the peak, the ribbons of power were stronger, wrapping themselves around Teresa and Rune as they stopped just outside the gaping doorway. She tried to see into the inky shadows within, but with the hot sun behind her, she simply couldn't.

"Okay," Miguel said, "here's the deal. Just in case that old bitch was trying to set me up somehow . . ."

Teresa took one instinctive step toward him, but Miguel just held his gun steadily pointed at her. "You two are going in there first," he said. "And don't get any ideas. I can cover you through the doorway."

Rune grabbed hold of Teresa's upper arm and held her back when she would have charged Miguel, gun or no gun. Logically, she knew he was right. Emotionally, she wanted to rip that arrogant expression off Miguel's face.

"Get movin'," he said, waving his gun again.

Furious, feeling more trapped than ever, Teresa turned and walked toward the temple. She hadn't taken more than two steps, though, when Rune moved in front of her to go first. "Stay behind me," he said quietly.

Again, he was risking himself to save her. Again, Teresa felt a wellspring of love rise up inside her. It nearly drowned the grief for her grandmother and the fear and rage inspired by Miguel. Rune was, in every way she could think of, her *mate*. Without him, she was incomplete. With him, she could withstand anything.

Over the cries of the animals that lived in the rain

forest, Teresa heard Chico shrieking and whistling and she wished he would fly away to safety.

Then she followed Rune into the temple. Deep shadows made the temperature much cooler and the relief from the sun was instantaneous. The stone walls were empty, only vestiges of what they had once been, the grass and vines encroaching even here, beyond the reach of sunlight.

The others followed, just a few steps behind them—and were stopped dead at the open doorway.

"What the fuck?"

Chapter 55

Teresa spun around to face the man who had forced them here. He looked stunned as he once again tried to walk into the temple—and once again came up against an invisible barrier.

Miguel's features twisted in fury as he slammed his hands against air and found something solid. "What is this, Teresa? What the hell are you playing at?"

Teresa didn't answer—she was shocked herself. She just left him shouting furiously as she tugged Rune farther back from the doorway. Everything made sense now. Why her *abuela* had sacrificed her life for them.

"My grandmother sent us here, Rune." She looked around and above her, gaze sweeping over the cold stone as if seeing an old friend after a long separation. "The whole site of Palenque was sacred to the Mayans, but this particular temple is the one built to the moon." She smiled for the first time in hours. "And I was the moon priestess. It's welcoming me, Rune. I can feel the power here strengthening me."

He scrubbed his big hands up and down her arms and the heat of him was a welcome rush.

"The temple is warded magically," she said, shivering

as another wave of mystical power eased inside her. "Protected by powerful magic. Nothing evil can get in."

As her words sunk in, Rune turned to watch Miguel throw one of his thugs against the barrier, only to see the man bounce away like a rock off the surface of a lake. A few more tries were just as unsuccessful. Rune smiled, slow and wide, keeping himself between Teresa and the doorway. "Your grandmother, Teresa, was almost as amazing as *you*."

She grinned back at him, feeling the mystical energies swarming around them. The chilling cold of the white gold was muted as power rushed through her. "Do you feel that?"

Outside, men were shouting and a gun was fired. Bullets, too, bounced off the energy barrier, ricocheting from its surface to other targets. Someone screamed.

"The magic is pure here," Rune said, taking a breath as though a heavy weight had been rolled off his chest. "Rich and timeless. Even the white gold won't hold us in here."

"I know." Teresa could already feel the truth. That her powers were bubbling back to life as though the necklace around her throat didn't even exist.

She looked down at her hands and willed the lightning to life. At first, there was simply a sputter of sparks dazzling the tips of her fingers. But as the power of the temple soaked into her skin those sparks flared and grew, in spite of the white gold's dampening effects.

"Can you get the gold off my neck?" Rune asked.

"Yes." She lifted the chain and felt the cold of the metal against her skin, trying to dwarf what was inside her. But Teresa held on, and with the surge of strength she had gained from the temple's interior, she succeeded.

Concentrating her power, she shot a small blast of lightning at the links of the chain around Rune's neck and sighed in satisfaction as the thing shattered. Quickly, she dropped the white gold and watched as it fell to the dirt at their feet.

He stretched his arms out wide and pulled in a great breath, as if he had been released from a box three sizes too small. Smiling, he said, "Now you."

Rune used the fire of his touch to melt the links at her throat, then brushed the offending necklace aside and let it land on the floor beside the first one.

Only then did he turn to face their enemies again. Miguel hadn't given up. He kept firing at the doorway, despite the ricocheting bullets that continued to endanger both him and his men. The barrier held, permitting no entry. Miguel's men were gathered into a knot, hiding from the bullets and from a power none of them understood but all of them feared.

"We need to leave, Teresa," Rune told her, face grim but determined as he narrowed his eyes on the man still screaming threats and obscenities at Teresa. "I'm going out there to clear the danger. Then I'll come back for you."

But she grabbed his hand and shook her head. "No, there's a better way." Threading her fingers through his, she looked up at him and let him read the idea in her eyes. Rune glanced at the sunlit, grassy area, then back at her. When he nodded, he squeezed her hand tight, stepped to one side and waited.

Teresa inhaled sharply, deeply, and lifted her free hand. With Rune's and her powers recharged from the temple, with the strength of her mate pushing through her as a focus, she drew down the lightning.

A tremendous jagged bolt shot from the sky with unerring accuracy. It slammed into the ground beside the group of thugs huddled together and three of them dropped instantly, dead before they hit the ground. Another bolt chased the first, but by that time the survivors were on the run.

Men screamed.

Miguel cursed.

Chico whistled and shrieked, his cries audible above the furious blast of the lightning.

Teresa filled the area with lightning. Her power sang inside her as it never had before. Magic coursed through her veins, alive, bristling with energy. Rune was her stalwart. Beside her, clutching her hand, he gave her the focus and concentration she needed to target her magic with efficiency. She felt his pride in her abilities. Felt his strength. His faith.

The sizzling bolts crashed to earth one after another, cutting off escape routes, driving the men as if they were being herded. And still she called for more, filling the heavens with her fury. With her need for justice. With the magic that was the very core of her.

As for Miguel, another wicked bolt of energy hit too close to where he continued to attempt to force his way into the temple. He slapped both fisted hands against the barrier keeping him from what he most wanted. "You bitch! This isn't over, Teresa! I'll find a way to end you!"

Teresa watched with a cool detachment and sent another jagged bolt toward him that slammed into the ground by his feet. Knocked over by the powerful blast, Miguel screamed. Fury claimed her and with that emotion spiking inside her, Teresa's ability to aim was compromised.

Finally, he seemed to realize that if he stayed, he

wouldn't survive. So he ran like the dog he was and Teresa's lightning chased after him, crashing again and again into the earth and trees.

When the esplanade was empty, Teresa quieted the lightning and all that was left was the sun, shining down on the ancient site. Hands still locked together, she and Rune stepped outside the temple. The dead lay scattered on the grassy surface and the others—like Miguel—were gone.

She hated that the man who had killed her grandmother had escaped. But she wouldn't waste precious time chasing him down. Miguel had said himself that if he failed, his superiors would finish him. She didn't wish death for anyone—but she couldn't bring herself to feel sorrow for him, either.

"Wait for me here," Rune said tightly, gaze narrowed in the direction that Miguel had fled. "I'm going to finish this."

"No," Teresa told him, releasing his hand long enough to wind her arms about his waist and hold on. Grief for her grandmother was still welling inside her. She felt the burden of what she'd done here with her magic. Men were dead. Yes, they were evil and probably would have killed her with no remorse if given the chance. She had done the only thing she could do to save both herself and Rune. To make sure they lived to complete the quest that was so important, not just to them but to the world. Still, guilt and regret pinged around the pit of her stomach like steel balls in an old pinball game.

Defending themselves was one thing. Deliberately chasing someone down—even Miguel—just to kill him was something else.

"Don't, Rune. Just . . . let Miguel go to whatever end is waiting for him. He'll be in hell soon enough."

He shook his head and blew out a breath. "It's a mistake to let him go. He'll only report to whoever's in charge of this mess exactly what happened."

"Let him," Teresa argued, burrowing closer to Rune's solid strength. Tears filled her eyes and choked her voice. Grief for her grandmother warred with pride in what the old woman had done for them. She'd sent them here, knowing that Palenque's magic would be enough to free them.

Although her *abuela* had known that the cost would be her life, she had set Teresa on the path she needed to walk.

"It doesn't matter what Miguel does anymore," she said, swallowing back the tears. She wouldn't dishonor her grandmother's sacrifice by weeping and wailing over it. Teresa knew that her *abuela* was now on another plane and wherever she was, the old woman was watching.

Teresa would make her proud.

She looked up at her mate and waited until his gaze met hers. Those gray eyes swirling with power and emotion stared back at her.

"Miguel means nothing," Teresa said. "It's more important that we go to retrieve the black silver. The Artifact is out there and until we get it back, no one will be safe."

The warrior in him wanted to argue. She could see that easily in his clenched jaw and the flash of his eyes. But after a long moment of tense, strained silence, Rune bowed his head briefly. "You're right, of course. Your grandmother sacrificed herself to see that we could do what we must do."

Teresa smiled, loving that he understood her so well and that he was willing to set aside his own need for retribution.

Chico swooped in, landed on her shoulder and screeched, *"Run for it!"*

Rune frowned at the creature.

Teresa grinned and reached to stroke its brightly colored chest.

"So," he said, "Spain?"

"Spain," she agreed, hooking her arms around his neck. "Get us out of here, Eternal."

He called on the fire and first took them to the van where their duffel bag had been abandoned. Rune wasn't going anywhere without his knives.

When he was armed and ready again, he flashed them away from the ancient site of death and renewal.

Chapter 56

They didn't go far.

Rune ended the jump just a few miles from Palenque, landing them in a deserted area of the rain forest. Monkeys chattered, a jaguar roared from somewhere nearby and a waterfall surged down a cliff, cool mist spraying into the air.

"Where are we?" Teresa asked, surprised that he'd ended their jump so quickly.

He didn't answer. Instead, his mouth a grim slash, he grabbed the bird off her shoulder and wrung its small neck with a twist of his hands.

Horrified, Teresa screamed and lunged for him just as a thick twist of black smoke lifted from the dead bird and quickly dissipated in the breeze. "Oh, my God."

Rune dropped the dead animal to the jungle floor and reached for her. Instinctively, she took a step back, shaking her head in disbelief. What had she just seen?

"What? What's happening? What was that smoke? How . . . ?"

He let his empty hands fall to his sides. Pity swirled in his gray eyes as he met her gaze. "I'm sorry, Teresa. At the temple, when Miguel tried to get past the barrier—

your bird tried, too. It hit the energy field and bounced away. It couldn't pass."

She looked down at the bright, colorful bird that had been her companion for two years and an empty, hollow feeling opened up inside her.

"It was possessed by a demon. A familiar," he said, his voice so gentle that his words were nearly lost in the rush of the nearby waterfall. "When I saw that it couldn't enter the temple, I knew. Teresa, every time it flew off, it must have been reporting to someone. It explains how Miguel knew exactly where we were."

Shaking her head, Teresa pressed one hand to her churning stomach. The sense of betrayal was so deep, so keenly edged, she felt as if she were bleeding internally. She had talked to Chico, told him her fears, her hopes. She'd had him with her when she went to visit her grandmother and practice her magical skills. He had been with her when she did spells, when she visited Elena— "Oh, God, he must have sent whoever killed her to Elena's place."

"Probably." He reached out for her again and this time she didn't sidestep.

Instead she moved into the circle of his arms and let his strength surround her. Memories flooded her mind. Chico had been a gift from Miguel. Had he known even then what he would do? Of course he had, she told herself. He'd planted the demon familiar with her to keep an eye on her and report on what she was up to.

Then something else occurred to her. She leaned back, looked up into Rune's eyes and said, "Chico was with us in the van. When I told you about Tía Carmen and about Barcelona." She looked down at the broken little body and felt anger stir. "He flew off as soon as we got to Palenque, remember? So he probably already reported what he heard."

"Probably." His expression didn't change, which told Teresa that he had already realized that truth.

"That means—"

"—we'll have enemies waiting for us in Spain." Rune finished for her. "I know. But that changes nothing."

"No," she agreed, "it doesn't. We'll still go. And we'll still claim the Artifact."

"Damn right we will," he murmured, smoothing her hair back from her face with a gentle touch.

Teresa had now officially lost everything. Her home. Her best friend. Her grandmother. Even her pet had been taken from her by an evil that still wasn't finished with her. Her old life was shattered and lay in ruins at her feet.

But looking up into Rune's gray eyes, she could feel his fierce strength and unswerving loyalty surrounding her, and she knew a new life was being born. Rising up from the ashes, her own personal phoenix was becoming something else. Something formidable. Her spirit lifted to the challenge. Her heart soared as she admitted to the deep and abiding love she felt for this Eternal. This immortal who made her feel more alive than ever before.

Whatever came next, she would be prepared for it.

With Rune at her side, no enemy was strong enough to defeat them.

"You ready?" he asked, one corner of his mouth lifting into a half smile.

"Yeah," she said, hooking her arms around his neck. "Take me to Spain, Rune."

Chapter 57

Miguel made it out of the rain forest.

With his skin still buzzing from the electrical charge in the air, he raced down the hilly incline to where they'd left the cars. The van he ignored. If the others survived, they could take it. He jumped into his jeep, fired up the engine and floored it. Spinning the wheels, he did a quick turnaround and headed out of Palenque as fast as he could.

His gaze studied the view in the rearview mirror, but as far as he could tell, no one was following him. And the lightning had stopped. Was Teresa really responsible for that? Damn. The continuous blasts of lightning bolts slamming into the earth had left him partially deaf. His ears were ringing and his heart crashed crazily in his chest.

He wasn't safe. Miguel knew that. He wouldn't put it past the big Eternal to come after him, and if he did, then it wouldn't matter how fast and far Miguel traveled. The man made of fire would find him.

"*Fuck!*" He punched the steering wheel a couple of times and didn't feel any better.

The jeep jolted and bounced over impediments in the road, but kept on going. Just like him, Miguel assured himself. There were problems, sure. But he'd keep going. Parnell still needed him. He'd be able to explain. Hell, who would have known that the damn temple was magically protected?

Teresa, that's who, he told himself with a furious glower. She must have known what was going on. She'd done it deliberately. Her and that fucking old woman. They'd tricked him. Anyone could see that. It wasn't his fault. Hell, if it was anyone's fault, it was Parnell's for not expecting this to happen.

Yeah. That was it. Parnell's fault.

"But I won't tell him that," Miguel murmured. "I won't blame him, so he won't blame me. He'll see I did everything I was supposed to. Not my fault it didn't work. Fuck it—we can catch up to them. We'll stop them. We can still get the damn Artifact."

The Artifact.

Ever since he'd first learned of that magical shard of black silver, Miguel had hungered for it. Who wouldn't? Immeasurable power locked inside a hunk of metal? The key to controlling whatever the hell you wanted to control? If Miguel could only get his hands on it, he could be a king. He could live as he was meant to live.

Not in a damn desert or rain forest, either. He was thinking penthouse. Acapulco, maybe, to start. But with the Artifact, he could go anywhere, do anything.

It was still within his reach.

He would just make Parnell understand the situation.

The farther he got from Palenque, the better he felt. In fact, he could almost convince himself that he'd done Parnell a favor. The lightning had killed off most of Miguel's men and the others wouldn't last a day in the rain forest. *Something* was sure to eat them. Another problem solved.

He drove for hours, finally arriving back at the tavern where he'd left Parnell the day before. In the pit of his belly, nerves were alive and churning, but he didn't let them show. A real man was nothing if not confident.

Miguel wasn't looking forward to this confrontation, but he knew he could talk the boss around. This was the kind of stuff he was good at. Spinning a well-crafted load of bullshit was Miguel's specialty.

Smiling, nodding, he silently encouraged himself and hopped out of the car like a man without a care in the world.

"It's all about attitude," he told himself, plastering a self-assured smile on his face as he headed for the tavern.

Before he had gone more than a few steps, though, he heard powerful engines roaring up behind him. He turned to watch as three black SUVs skidded to a stop behind his battered jeep. Dust flew into the air in waves thick enough to make Miguel cough and turn his face away.

When the dust settled, he turned back and saw men climbing out of the cars. Big men in black suits, wearing sunglasses, carrying automatic weapons. Fear ratcheted up so fast inside him, he thought his heart would jump right out of his chest. And still he fought for calm. For cool.

"I'm here to see Parnell," he said. "To explain."

"Boss ain't here," one of the men said.

"Well, get him on the phone," Miguel argued, looking from one face to the next, finding no sympathy. No sign of mercy.

"He don't want to talk to you. Said he knows what went down and you've failed too many times," one of them said and nodded to his friends.

He *knew*?

How the hell did he know?

"No, wait. I can do this," Miguel said, throwing up both hands as he spoke, fast, panicked. "I know Teresa. I'll get her. I swear."

They weren't listening.

He watched, terrified, as six gun barrels were turned on him. Nowhere to go. Nowhere to run. It was over and the man who would be king was going to die in the dust of this godforsaken desert.

Should have killed that bitch, was his last thought as gunfire erupted and a hail of bullets cut him down.

Chapter 58

They went to Spain by boat.

Of course a plane would have been faster, but with Teresa's magic growing, they didn't want to risk a lightning bolt in midflight. They hadn't had time to look for and procure tickets on a cruise to Barcelona. So Rune being Rune, he had simply purchased a yacht. It was huge and fast, and with a crew paid extremely well to make the best possible time, it was only nine days at sea before they arrived in Barcelona.

And Teresa wouldn't have traded those nine days for anything.

During the long days and longer nights spent in the arms of her mate, Teresa knew she had finally found the one place in the universe where she belonged. With Rune.

As if thinking his name had conjured him, their stateroom door opened quietly. Teresa looked up and he was there. Her warrior, taking up the entire doorway with his muscular bulk. His gray eyes met hers and she saw the quick flare of desire that erupted between them with exhausting regularity.

Despite her body still buzzing from their lovemaking

that morning, Teresa felt fresh need wake and roar inside her. Would there ever come a time when she would be able to look at him and *not* want him immediately?

God, she hoped not.

He braced his hands on either side of the doorjamb. "I told the crew they could go ashore to blow off some steam. They worked their asses off getting us here this fast."

It had been a fast trip, Teresa told herself, but even with that, their thirty days were nearly over. Absently, she lifted one hand to rub her left breast and the mating tattoo that lay just beneath her T-shirt. The Mating was almost complete. And they still had to find the Artifact and return it to Haven.

They were running out of time.

"We should go see Tía Carmen," she said.

"Your aunt won't know where the Artifact is," he said softly. "Only you will as you access the memory."

"I know," she said, feeling the pressure mount. She knew the black silver was here. In Barcelona. But that was a pretty big haystack to find a needle in. "I'm hoping that seeing Tía Carmen will jog something loose. I dreamed about her. There had to be a reason."

Nodding, Rune asked, "Where does she live?"

"Barri Gotic. The Gothic Quarter."

"I know the place," he said and pulled her in tight when she came close. He gave her a hard hug and added, "We'll walk there. Flashing in and out in a city is just too dangerous. Someone would see us."

"Good point." She took a moment to enjoy the feel of his strong arms around her and then they left the ship hand in hand.

Chapter 59

B arri Gotic was the center of the old city of Barcelona. In the hush of moonlight, narrow streets lined
with tall buildings became shadowy cobblestoned laby-
rinths. The walkways felt almost like tunnels with the
sheer walls of the bordering buildings rising up on either
side. This area had been around since before the Romans, and Rune felt ancient times draw close as he and
Teresa made their way past outdoor cafés in the Plaça
del Pi—a square filled with trees boasting tiny white
lights and a line of artists displaying their wares, hoping
for customers.

Teresa took the lead, with Rune's sharp gaze searching for possible danger as she led them down Carrer de
Pi, another narrow, only-for-pedestrians street. The buildings on either side of the street seemed to stretch heavenward, with brilliant splashes of color spilling from flower
boxes and vines trailing around ornate iron railings on
the balconies.

It should have been beautiful, peaceful even, Rune
told himself. Instead, there was an underlying sense of
something dark layered just beneath the beauty. Some-

thing that nibbled at his instincts, prodded him to keep at battle-ready tension.

"God, I remember this place," Teresa murmured, her fingers tightening around Rune's. "And not just from when I was a kid and we visited Tía Carmen. I'm talking about *old* memories. There used to be laundry hanging out here," she said, waving her free hand to indicate the space between the buildings on either side of the street. "People shouting, arguing. Babies crying. And the street was awful. Filthy." She shook her head and lifted her hand to rub at a spot in the center of her chest. "It feels . . ."

"What?" Rune prompted. "What do you feel?"

She looked up at him. "Close," she said. "I feel *close* to the Artifact. It's here. In the old city. I know it."

"Then we'll find it."

Nodding, Teresa said, "First, Tía Carmen. I want to make sure she's okay." She darted through a doorway and up a flight of stone steps.

Rune stayed close, and as they climbed to the third floor, they passed apartments with crosses nailed to the wall. A couple of the doorways were draped in ropes of garlic and Rune's instincts went on high alert. Teresa stopped before a closed door painted a bright emerald green. She lifted her hand to knock, but Rune caught her hand in his.

"Something is off," he said, glancing out a narrow window to the moon in the sky. "Did you notice all the garlic and crosses? People are trying to ward off evil."

She paled a little and looked at her aunt's closed door. "Evil? The Artifact? Or—"

He sensed a presence within the apartment. He held

his fingers to her lips and for the first time reached for her mind with his.

Someone is in there with your aunt, he communicated to her.

What? Her eyes were wide. Terrified. *Who?*

Whoever it is has magic. The swell of power was unmistakable. Was it a friend of Teresa's aunt? Or, more likely, an enemy?

"Wait," he told her, whispering now, not willing to rely on their new mental connection. "Let me go in first."

Her eyes narrowed and her features tightened as she picked up on the tension coiling inside him. "No. We go together."

"We have no idea who might be in there," he said.

"I know. But I'd rather face whatever it is as a team, Rune. I've already lost enough. I don't want to lose Tía Carmen, too. And we've come too far together to split up now, don't you think?"

"I do," he said, his voice hardly more than a breath of sound. "Are you up for it?"

"I am." She lifted her chin and flexed her fingers, sending tiny blue and white sparks flashing from her fingertips. "This is why we've been training, right? I mean, it's not just about the Artifact, is it?"

Her eyes shone in the soft light. "I mean, yes, we get the Artifact, find redemption, all that—but aren't we supposed to be helping people, too? Like my aunt? Isn't that what power *should* be used for?"

Dazzled by her, Rune could only stare for a long moment. Then he bent, kissed her and whispered, "That's exactly what power should be used for, Teresa. You make me proud to walk alongside you."

She took a deep breath, blew it out and said, "Thank you. Now, what do we do?"

He was about to offer a plan when from inside the apartment a short, sharp shriek of pain exploded, then died in the next instant. Time was up. Rune grabbed Teresa and flashed them both inside.

Moonlight slid through an open window and washed the narrow room with a silvered glow. Crocheted doilies dotted the surfaces of chairs and tables. Candles burned in scarlet glass votives, their flames creating dancing shadows on the walls. The scent of charred fabric scarred the air.

"Oh, God." Teresa pushed free of Rune's grasp and dropped beside the old woman lying crumpled on the floor.

"Tía Carmen?" she whispered.

Rune quickly swept through the small apartment, assuring himself that the intruder was gone. Magic lingered behind, though, a trace energy that felt as dark as it was powerful.

"Rune, she's alive!" Teresa's voice, strained with fear and what could only be tears choking her throat, reached him and he was at her side in an instant.

The old woman was the mirror image of Teresa's grandmother. The same wise eyes shone with patient stoicism, though the pain she felt had to be monstrous. Her left arm had been burned—in the same way Elena's body had been back in Sedona. Rune knew now that their enemy—whoever that might be—was in Barcelona.

"Teresa . . ." The soft, breathy voice came from her aunt and Teresa bent over her, talking quickly, quietly.

"Don't speak, Tía Carmen. Please. Be still. You'll be all right." She turned her gaze up to Rune, her eyes silently pleading and demanding that they save her aunt. "We have to help her. Please."

She needed him and he wouldn't fail her. "We will try. Together."

Taking Teresa's hand in his, he laid their joined hands gently atop Carmen's burns. The old woman winced and hissed in a breath, but otherwise lay still.

"Concentrate," he said. "Let your magic rise and focus it on your aunt."

Teresa closed her eyes instantly. A look of intensity came over her face as she breathed slowly, deeply, searching for the center of her power. Rune felt her strength join his and their combined magics swelled between them. He called on the fire and focused all he could on easing the pain and healing the flesh of the woman who meant so much to *his* woman.

Carmen jerked beneath their touch, moaned once, and an instant later lost consciousness. Pain and fear had claimed her and she slept through the last of the healing ritual. Rune kept watch on her while the magic and the fire combined to soothe the burns and heal her injuries. Moments later, he said, "It is done."

Teresa's eyes flew open and she looked first at him and then at her aunt, examining the now-unblemished skin on her arm. "She's all right? She'll be okay?"

"She will," he said. "We were lucky to get here in time."

"Lucky," she repeated, staring down at her aunt. She brushed aside a stray lock of graying black hair from Carmen's face, then let her fingertips trail along the old woman's papery cheek. "She was hurt because of me. Just like my grandmother died for us."

"Teresa—"

"You saved her, Rune." Her beautiful brown eyes filled with tears as she looked at him and Rune felt the slam of her emotions churning through him. "You saved her for me and a thank-you just isn't nearly enough."

"You owe me nothing," he told her.

"I owe you everything." She ran her thumb over the back of his hand. "You didn't just give me back my aunt. You showed me who I was. Supported me. Helped me. Trained me. You've been there. Always. I want you to know what that means to me."

Rune pulled her close, wrapped his arms around her and buried his face in the curve of her neck. He inhaled the scent of her and let it wash through him like a powerful blessing. This witch, this woman, had become everything to him.

Her voice came soft against his ear as she said fiercely, "I'm tired of death, Rune. I want this finished."

"And so it will be," he swore, pulling back so that he could look into her beautiful brown eyes. "We find the Artifact and this is finished."

She nodded and looked down at her aunt again. "Can we leave her?"

"She will sleep and be better for it. Whoever did this won't be back—they've gotten what they could already." Cupping her cheek, he turned her face up to him. "The only way to ensure her safety is to finish this. Finally."

"Yes," she said, reaching up to cover his hand with her own. "I'm ready, Rune. With you, I'm ready."

Rune carried Carmen to her bed and Teresa covered her with a quilt that had been neatly folded at the foot of the mattress. After looking around once more to make sure there was no danger, they left the apartment and slowly went back down the stairs the way they had come. Teresa's gaze swept the stairwell and he saw her noting the crosses and the garlic. She rubbed at her chest again, as if her heart were aching, and he thought, *Of course it is.*

But he couldn't help wondering if there was more to it than grief for all she had lost. Was she feeling the presence of the black silver? Was her pain more than regret? Was sense memory rising up inside her?

She stepped into the shadows of the narrow street and Rune came up behind her, laying both hands on her shoulders. He felt her tension and shared it.

Moonlight poured from the sky. The moon itself was nearly full. Their thirty days nearly done.

Teresa tipped her face up to the moon and let its light shimmer over her, through her. He watched as she gathered her strength, filling herself with the moon's magic. When finally she turned her head to look at him, her eyes were clear, but worried.

"There's something happening here, Rune. Beyond what happened to my aunt. There's something . . . dark."

A shout, scuffling feet and then a scream jolted the quiet atmosphere and they both whirled around to stare down the street. A police car, lights flashing in the night, was parked outside an apartment. As they watched, a woman was dragged kicking and screaming from her home. Even from a distance, Rune spotted the white-gold chain around her neck as two burly policemen strong-armed her into the backseat of their marked car. An old woman walking by spat at the trapped woman, and Teresa hissed in a breath.

"So," she murmured, "the Spanish version of MPs?"

"Close enough," Rune told her and steered her in the opposite direction of the police. They didn't need more trouble. They had more than enough already. "Come on. Keep walking."

"To where?"

"That's up to you," he said, keeping one arm around her shoulders and her body pressed along his side. "Open your mind. Your senses. Call on the moon again. Whisper a chant. Just . . . trust your instincts, Teresa. Open yourself to the past and let it lead you."

"It already is," she said softly. "I can feel the black silver. It's like a dark hum of energy burning through my mind. Can you feel it?"

"I sense its presence. But no, I can't feel it yet."

"Others are sensing it, too, Rune." She glanced around the street as they passed, noting for the first time the tight features of the people. Shops were closing, windows were shut against the night, curtains drawn, sealing people inside their homes as if they were hiding.

"It's like the black silver is waking up." She shivered a little in the damp cold seeping in off the ocean. "The Artifact is connected to the Awakening witches, Rune, and it knows that we're coming."

He pulled her to a stop, unmindful of the cursing people who were forced to go around them. An icy wind shot down the narrow passageway directly off the ocean and wrapped them both in a chilled embrace. Looking down into her eyes, he asked, "Are you saying that the Artifact is alive?"

"Not breathing, but, yeah. In a way, I think it is." She swallowed hard and gazed off into the distance. "I think the magical energy we infused it with has somehow become . . . more than it was eight hundred years ago. I think it's waiting for us to use it again. And that darkness that's inside it? It's spreading." She glanced at the shadow-filled street, at the scurrying people. "Look around, Rune. The black silver is affecting everyone here."

"If that's true, then we have less time than we thought."

"I know." She took his hand and started moving. "The closer the witches come to containing the Artifact, the more it will fight to survive. We have to go, Rune. Now."

She sped up, her footsteps clicking against the cobblestones. Rune kept pace, refusing to let go of her.

There was danger all around them. Her aunt had nearly been killed, cops were on the prowl and there was an unknown enemy waiting for his chance. And if Teresa was right about the black silver . . . then the danger the other witches and their Eternals would face would only grow.

The fire that made him roared within, flames churning. His power was stronger since they had mated and he knew he was going to need every advantage when he finally faced their enemy. But Rune would do whatever was necessary to see this task to completion.

His gaze sharp, he continuously searched the streets, the alleys, the people passing by. A baby wailed in an upstairs apartment. From somewhere nearby came the sound of a solo violinist, creating haunting, sighing sounds that drifted through the night like tears.

And Teresa was hurrying now, following her own instincts.

"There—"

They stopped in a square, another plaza situated between Barri Gotic and the Via Laietana. A section of the old Roman wall faced them, with three massive towers still standing.

Teresa looked up at it and pointed at the tallest of the spires. More than a hundred feet high, it was slender, with curved arches cut into the stone. Rune opened his senses to what Teresa was feeling and experienced it himself. The black silver created a smear in the air, like a spill of darkness through a sunlit meadow. No wonder the people of Barcelona were beginning to react to such a menace in their midst.

Even humans would be sensitive to the malevolence building in the black silver.

"It's there." Teresa pointed again at a section of the old Roman wall with an excited, if wary smile.

The wall itself was impressive as hell. Tall, sturdy, looking much as it had when the Romans had first constructed it so many centuries ago. Rune had seen it being built and he felt a flicker of admiration for those long-dead Romans. They were gone, but their legacy, their stamp on history, remained.

Now . . . .

"The Royal Chapel of Saint Agatha," Teresa said on a sigh. "It's in that bell tower."

"And the Artifact is there? In a church?"

"No," she said, with a shake of her head and a rueful smile. "Even I wasn't nervy enough to plant such evil inside a chapel. It's just outside. Close enough that I hoped something of the sanctity of the chapel would help control it. I remember it all now. Everything."

Her gaze lifted to his and he read resignation as well as regret and fear shining in her brown eyes. "What is it, Teresa?"

"I just wanted you to know, before we go in there—" She paused for a look at the ancient wall and the stone steps that led to the chapel. Then she blew out a breath and said, "Where do I even start. Remember when I told you I wouldn't let myself love you?"

"Yes," he said, threading his fingers through her thick hair with a gentle touch. "I remember."

"Well," she said, reaching up to grab fistfuls of his black shirt and pull him down until their mouths were just a breath apart, "forget that. I didn't mean to. But you've been there. Every moment. You taught me to fight. Stood beside me. You make me feel strong even when I know I'm not. So, before we go in there and face . . . whatever, I want you to know that I do. Love you, I mean. I really do, Rune."

His unbeating heart fisted as he looked into her eyes and saw more truth, more love than he had ever found anywhere before. The eternal cold that had been his only companion for more centuries than he cared to count began to thaw and his soul drank in the woman before him.

Rune knew what that admission had cost her. She had loved before and had her love used as a weapon against her. Now, in the midst of the trials and danger they faced, she found the courage to love again.

"In all our time together," he said softly, "all those centuries, all those lives, you have never said this to me."

She dipped her head briefly, then lifted her eyes to his again. "I was an idiot. But I'm not anymore. I do trust you, Rune. And I love you with every beat of my heart. I just wanted you to know that before we finish this."

"I'm glad you told me," he said, bending to kiss her hard and fast and deep. When he came up for air, he held her face in his hands. "I love you, Teresa Santiago. I am in awe of your strength, your courage, your resilience. You humble me and make me proud."

A fresh sheen of tears swamped her eyes, but the tears were obliterated by her brilliant, if a little shaky, smile. "Okay, then," she said, turning her face toward the Roman wall and the past that would lead to their future. "Are we ready?"

"*We* are," he told her and took her hand again for their walk into the past.

Chapter 60

Teresa entered the chapel, despite the twinge of trepidation curdling inside her. She knew what she had to do, but damned if she was enjoying it. This mystical scavenger hunt had taken too much from her already and she couldn't help fearing that she had yet more to lose.

The stillness was oppressive.

Her own footsteps on the stone floor sounded disrespectfully loud and almost eerie in the quiet. Like a ragged heartbeat. Like there was someone or something *else* in here besides her and Rune.

She felt his presence, of course. As linked as they were, emotionally and physically, Teresa knew that she would always be aware of him whenever he was close. And she was desperately grateful to have him close at the moment.

Her gaze swept the chapel as she walked down the nave. The center aisle of the church was slender, as if it had been designed for the fragile, wealthy ladies of a court long gone to dust. Arched stained glass windows ringed the interior of the chapel, but the moonlight outside muted the brilliant colors that would have filled this place in sunlight like the spun wheel of a kaleido-scope. Directly in front of her towered an amazing al-tarpiece, with different sections, each telling the tale of the Epiphany.

"Teresa?"

She glanced back at Rune, just a step or two behind her, and nodded. "I'm okay. We go through that door-way on the left."

He followed as she led, and with every step she took, she walked deeper into the past. Memories rose up in her mind, nearly choking her with their intensity. She had been here so long ago. Scared. Desperate. Ashamed.

She still carried the echoes of her sisters' screams in her heart and mind. She could still smell the sulfur that had wafted through hell's gate with the swarm of de-mons. She could feel Rune's fury, his disappointment, and she wanted nothing more than to hide away until her death when she could begin the reincarnations that would lead to her atonement.

So she had come here. To Barcelona. To the wall built by the Romans, because she had recalled Rune telling her of his days here. She'd remembered his reluctant ad-miration of the strength of the Romans and she had thought to borrow some of that legendary strength to protect what she herself hadn't been able to.

Teresa stepped through an arched stone doorway into the blackness of what had once been a storage area. Now it was simply a small unused stone room, its walls echoing with the voices of the past.

"Teresa?"

"God, I remember this," she whispered, her soft voice rippling in the tiny room like the tide rushing to shore.

She took a breath, let it out and whispered, "It's here. In the wall."

"*In* it?"

She turned her head to look up at him and gave him a small smile. "Yeah. I thought that the Roman wall would somehow be strong enough to conceal it, to shield it."

Turning back, she walked to the far wall, dropped to her knees and touched a dark stone, skimming her fingers across its surface. Instantly, the stone rippled, its surface trembling with a barely leashed power.

Rune went down on one knee beside her. He felt her hesitation, her doubt, as he would have his own— and how could he blame her for it? Eight hundred years had come and gone and she was once again having to face who she had been. What she had done. As if the black silver sensed his presence, it began to hum and vibrate with the magic rising inside it. Teresa swallowed hard, glanced at Rune and then reached for the stone.

It fell into her hand, instantly morphing into the black-silver Celtic knot it had been centuries before. Power emanated from the thing in thick, inky waves that seemed to reach for them with greedy fingers.

Hissing in a breath to steel himself against the draw of the dark magic, Rune looked to Teresa and saw her gaze fixed on the now-gleaming black metal. She stroked it with a single fingertip and seemed to enjoy the current of power that washed through the black silver at her touch. "Teresa?"

She stroked it again, but looked up at him. "I was right, Rune. It's almost alive. I can feel it. It's calling to me."

"It has been waiting." A deep, unfamiliar voice spoke from the right.

Teresa and Rune turned as one to face the tall blond man with swirling gray eyes who entered the anteroom.

"The Artifact has been waiting for your return and its chance to reenter the world," he said with a courtly bow. "Just as I have."

Chapter 61

Rune pushed Teresa behind him and drew his knife. Looking into the man's Eternal gray eyes gave him a jolt of shock. But Rune didn't recognize him.

He held the wicked blade out in front of him and crouched in a stance of readiness. Whoever the hell this was, he wouldn't be getting anywhere near Teresa. "Who are you?"

The blond laughed and the sharp sound echoed weirdly in the chapel. "Your question tells you exactly who I am."

"You talk in circles and you don't belong here. Get out now."

Instead, the man walked lazily toward Rune, giving the impression of a predator slinking up on its prey. Well, Rune was no man's prey and he damn sure would make certain Teresa wasn't, either.

As the man passed them, Rune began to edge Teresa toward the doorway and the chapel. He didn't want a confrontation here in this small antechamber. There was no room for movement, and in close quarters like this Teresa stood a chance of being injured. She moved with him. Though he couldn't look at her, he heard her footsteps on the stone and knew that she understood what he was trying to do.

He had another worry as well. He had heard from Torin how the Artifact had affected Shea when they had gone to retrieve her shard. How the dark magic had come close to overpowering her and how they had had to battle their own dark desires to keep from surrendering to the call of the black silver.

Now, with this . . . man interrupting them, Rune couldn't give Teresa his support as she held the Artifact. Instead, he was forced to keep his entire focus on the immediate threat.

Straightening up to his full, formidable height, Rune continued to back out of the room, though he held up one hand with the palm facing the man and called on the fire in the same instant. Living flames engulfed his raised hand, swimming and burning over his flesh in brilliant colors. Shadows leaped on the historic stone walls and danced in his opponent's eyes. "Get out now before this goes too far."

Rather than being put off by Rune's display, the blond man lifted his own hand and within a moment's time he, too, displayed the living flame that danced across his flesh. "You have nothing to show me that I don't already know, Eternal."

"What the fuck—" Rune broke off, stunned and shocked.

From behind him, he heard Teresa gasp, but he focused on the surprising man opposite him. "What are you?"

"I'm *you*," he said tightly, disgust clear in his tone. "Or I should have been. You Eternals. Belen's chosen." He laughed shortly, a harsh sound that scratched at the air. "Did you think that you and your brothers were the first time the god decided to play at being the father of a race?"

Rune studied the blond immortal, looked into gray eyes that were so much like his own and then reached back into the eons of time for a slip of a memory. When he found it, he shook his head. "Impossible. You can't be. You're all dead."

"Not dead," the being countered, flicking a glance at Teresa that was filled with both desire and determination. "We are the Forgotten. I am Parnell, one of many. We are the true Eternals. The first race created by Belen. The better race."

"Rune?"

He heard the question in her voice and couldn't blame her for it. Hell, Rune could hardly think straight himself. This shouldn't be happening, but it made sense—in a twisted, truly fucked-up way. At least this explained how Elena had died and how Teresa's aunt had been burned. At the hands of one who should have been an Eternal. A guardian.

He didn't remember much. He'd had no cause to retain the details over the long centuries of his immortal life. The Forgotten were a part of the distant past. No more than a legend among the Eternals.

Speaking to Teresa, Rune kept his gaze on his enemy. "I told you that Belen created us from the heart of the sun."

"Yes, but—"

"What I didn't tell you was that Belen created others before us. They were meant to be your mates. To be your guardians. But they were flawed."

"Flawed?" Parnell's outraged shout rang through the rafters of the chapel. A rustle of wings sounded in the distance as the doves roosting in the towers took flight

at the noise. "We were better than Belen wanted. We were powerful. Too powerful." Parnell lifted his chin and his gray eyes, color swirling, stared into Rune's with hatred flashing so brightly it was as if the emotion itself was alive. "Belen looked at us and trembled. So he thought to destroy us and create instead a lesser race. One that wouldn't challenge him."

"One that wasn't homicidal, apeshit crazy, you mean?" Rune scoffed at him, and he saw that Parnell didn't take kindly to criticism. *Good. Keep him off balance*, he told himself.

Danger simmered all around him. Teresa's life hung in the balance of whatever was going to happen in the next few minutes. Parnell was a formidable foe and he was also nuts, which put a whole new spin on the fight. You couldn't figure what a crazy man would do. Couldn't count on him making rational choices.

"Trust the Eternal, beware the immortal," Teresa whispered behind him and Rune remembered the warning Elena had delivered from beyond her grave.

"Now we know," Teresa murmured.

Yes, he thought, now they knew.

He took another step backward, into the chapel, knowing that Teresa was moving, too. *Keep her away from Parnell*. His only thought rang out loud in his mind and everything he was centered on keeping her safe.

"Come to me, Teresa," Parnell said, reaching out one hand to her even as he kept the flames alive on the other. "I will be your other half. Your mate. I will protect you as I have been doing all along."

"Protect me? What does that mean?"

"Don't talk to him, Teresa," Rune ordered as they cleared the doorway and backed into Saint Agatha's chapel. "Just take the Artifact and get out of here."

He didn't look at her. He couldn't afford to take his gaze off the man in front of him. Parnell might be wearing civilized slacks and a silk shirt, but he had the presence of a warrior and it wouldn't pay to discount him. Especially now, Rune thought, knowing the man to be one of the Forgotten. They were immortal, dangerously unpredictable and until this very moment, believed to be dead.

"How did you survive?" he asked, keeping Parnell busy as he hoped Teresa turned to leave.

"We were able to mask our presence from Belen," Parnell said with a shrug. "He doesn't pay much attention after all, does he? Too wrapped up with his witch goddess to notice whether he actually killed his children or not."

The only light in the chapel came from the flickering flames dancing on the skin of the two immortals facing each other. Shadows spun and danced on the stone walls and shone on their faces.

"Rune . . ." Teresa's voice, breathy, soft, uncertain.

It twisted a knife in his guts. He wanted nothing more than to be there for his woman. To help her through this greatest of challenges. To share his strength with her so that she could withstand the pull of the dark magic enveloped within the black silver.

"Teresa, you have to go. Go now," he ordered.

But she didn't.

He sensed her, still right behind him in the chapel, and he hoped to hell the black silver wasn't working its darkness on her.

"What do you want?" Rune asked, keeping his knife blade up and aimed, the flames on his free hand burning brightly.

"What's rightfully ours, of course," Parnell told him. "It's the Awakening. We want our witches." His gaze slipped past Rune to Teresa. "We want what should have been ours for the taking."

"The Artifact," Rune said.

"Yes," Parnell told him with a smile. "The Artifact and the witch who charms it. We will be the power in this world. We will bring Belen out of his dimension screaming. We will become what we always should have been. Eternal."

"You are out of your fucking mind," Rune told him with a shake of his head. "Nothing is yours. Not the witches. Not the Artifact. Go back where you came from. Hide from our god, because once he knows you're not dead, you soon will be."

From behind him, Rune heard Teresa's deep sigh. "Rune, it's getting warm. The Artifact. It's heating up."

"It's the call of the dark, Teresa," Parnell whispered in a coaxing tone. "It recognizes your soul. As it would know mine. It urges you to be what you once were."

"Don't listen, Teresa," Rune told her firmly. "Just go. Now."

"Now it's . . . humming," she said softly. "The power is—"

"Indescribable?" Parnell offered. He smiled at her and his eyes briefly flashed black.

Demon energy. The immortal had demon power charging through his system. He—and maybe all of the Forgotten—had made a deal with the demons. Who knew what kind of power that merging would create?

Rune's instincts roared. He had to get Teresa away from both Parnell and the Artifact before the black silver could do damage to her will and spirit.

"Put it down, Teresa. Drop it."

"Don't," Parnell said, taking a half step, only to stop again as Rune shifted position to cover him. "Hold it, Teresa. Feel the pull. Feel the power." His voice was seduction. Dark, hypnotic. "Open yourself to it."

"Rune . . ."

"Can't you feel it?" Parnell continued. "All you ever wanted is within your grasp. The past doesn't matter. Only the future and what it can bring."

Rune felt her hesitation. He feared for her in the face of the strong pull of the dark magic. For what might happen if she forgot who she was in the rush of what she was feeling now. He couldn't risk looking at her, but he could give her something. He could tell her what he should have said in the street outside. Before they ever came into this place to find the piece of their missing past.

"Teresa . . . I trust you." The words were soft but implacable. And long overdue. He had finally learned to let go of old betrayals and ancient pains. He had come to discover that Teresa was a woman of honor. Loyalty. She deserved his very best and he would not doubt her again. Ever.

He heard her soft intake of breath and knew she was surprised at his words.

"We are mates," he continued, his voice only for her as his gaze remained fixed on his enemy. "We are one. Together we are unstoppable. I *trust* you, Teresa."

"Teresa, come to me now," Parnell said again, his tone commanding, brooking no argument.

"You said you were protecting me before, Parnell," she whispered. "What did you mean?"

"That doesn't matter," he snapped, inching closer to Rune, Teresa and the black silver.

"Did you kill Elena?" she asked.

Rune gritted his teeth, knowing the answer but wishing she hadn't asked the question. He would spare her pain if he could.

"She was nothing," Parnell argued. "As the old woman was. As the one you saved tonight is. Humans to get in the way of your future. *Our* future."

"They were my *family*," Teresa said, every word stained with the power of her raw agony.

"You don't need them. You only need me," Parnell said, keeping one eye on Rune as he inched ever closer.

"You bastard!"

A wave of power sucked all the air out of the room and then rushed back in—like the buildup to a tsunami—as a lightning bolt slammed into the stone floor in front of Parnell.

The flash of lightning was just the distraction Rune had been hoping for. He launched himself at Parnell, taking the big man down in a thundering crash that shook the glass in the windows high above them. Rune called on the flames, covering his body with fire, heat roiling off him in waves. His powers were intensified, the pulsing rage overtaking him. His strength was immense, thanks to the Mating ritual. He was more powerful than ever before and he used every ounce of it in the blistering fight with his enemy.

Parnell's flames erupted as well, blinding heat surrounding the two combatants as they rolled across the stone floor. Each of them was armed and knife blades flashed and gleamed in the fiery light.

Parnell's strength was formidable, fed as it was by the demon trace energies inside him. His eyes went from black to gray and back again countless times as the immortal and the demon within seemed to battle for dominance.

Rune brought his blade down in a wide arc and made contact—he heard the other immortal's hiss of pain. But it wasn't enough. There was only one way to kill an immortal, he knew. He had to take Parnell's head.

He couldn't see Teresa, but he heard her voice, calling to the moon, chanting, working a spell, and he hoped whatever she was trying would work. He did trust her. Always would. His only job now was to rid them of Parnell. Forever.

Parnell flashed out of the fight and reappeared a few feet away. Roaring his frustration and outrage, he charged and Rune met the challenge. Two massive bodies collided in a flurry of flames and darkness. Deep shadows flickered in the fire drenching Parnell's body and Rune knew that his enemy had a well of power to draw on. The dark ones had claimed him and Parnell had surrendered to them, in a futile effort to claim what was never his.

"Bastard!" Parnell shouted as his own knife swept across Rune's broad chest. Blood welled and then stopped as the wound sealed itself in the eternal flames wrapped around his body.

"You sold yourself to a demon," Rune shouted, pummeling his enemy with his huge fist even as his knife hand arced for a deep blow.

"We found power!" Parnell pushed away, breath heaving, flames darkening as demon energy pumped anew inside him. "The power your god denied us." He threw his head back and shouted, "Belen! See what you did! Look at us and tremble!"

Madness ruled him. Through the flames swallowing Parnell's body, Rune saw the glint of insanity in the immortal's eyes and wondered if it had always been there. Or had the demon energy pushed him over the edge?

Parnell charged again, his hamlike fists swinging. The blade of his knife winked in the light. Rune rolled with a punch thrown by his opponent and gained his feet instantly. Teresa continued to chant as Rune charged at Parnell again, his knife leading the way. Rune stabbed and slashed at the man trying to take Teresa from him.

Outside, lightning boomed and pummeled the earth in a series of electrical blasts as the very sky came alive to Teresa's power. Each bolt seemed to shudder through the ancient stone walls, shaking them to their foundations.

His head snapped back with the slam of Parnell's fist into his jaw, but Rune wouldn't be stopped. Again and again, the two immortals battled for supremacy as the witch they both wanted called on the moon and the sky-fire she wielded so well.

Parnell, fighting wildly now, dealt a blow aimed at Rune's neck and missed. Rune came up fast and swung out with his own knife, its edge razor sharp. In the last flickering moment before his blade made contact with Parnell's neck, he saw the immortal's eyes widen in the knowledge of what was to come.

Then it was over.

Parnell's body and severed head hit the stone floor and a moment later the lightning suddenly ceased. A curtain of silence descended on the ancient, sacred place. Rune let his own fire fade away and drew in heavy, fast breaths before turning from the fallen immortal to Teresa.

She stood near the altar, wrapped in a cloak of moonlight pouring through one of the stained glass windows above. The Artifact lay in her cupped palms, secure in a glowing sphere of silvery light. Within that sphere, miniature lightning bolts crackled and spat at the black silver as if daring it to challenge Teresa's power.

"Teresa?"

Her gaze met his and she smiled. "I called on the moon, Rune. I used her magic to capture the Artifact. With the strength of the Mating and the influx of raw energy from Palenque, I'm strong enough to hold it. Its lure can't tempt me. Or you."

Humbled, awed, he walked to her and carefully placed a gentle kiss on her forehead. "You are the witch you were always meant to be. You are the woman who holds my heart. You are the air I breathe and the light to my darkness. You are . . . *everything.*"

Tears shone in her eyes, but a beautiful smile curved her mouth as she looked up at him. "I love you, too. And thank you."

"For what?"

"For the gift of your trust," she said, lifting one hand to stroke her fingers along the line of his jaw. "You gave me the strength I needed, Rune. Knowing you believed I would do the right thing made all the difference to me."

"I have loved you throughout time," he said, "and Belen willing, I will love you until eternity itself ends. And then beyond."

She went up on her toes and kissed him. Then she said, "Let's get this thing back to Haven. Then I want a weekend in bed with you. No interruptions."

In spite of everything, Rune's body tightened and an ache of desire erupted inside him. "One weekend? I think we can do better than that."

Sighing in anticipation, Teresa unwillingly looked past Rune to the fallen immortal. Quickly, she looked away. "What about . . . ? We can't leave him here."

Drawing on the fire, Rune allowed the flames to cover both of his hands. "I'll take care of it."

He walked toward the body. Teresa didn't watch.

Chapter 62

In a series of jumps, Rune took them across Spain, through France and then over the English Channel. From there, they made their way to Wales. And Haven.

On the evening of the thirtieth day, Teresa stood in the circle of Rune's arms and looked up at the still-majestic walls of Manorbier castle. Holding the moonsphere in her cupped hands, Teresa felt the steadying presence of Rune beside her as her gaze touched on the familiar scene stretched out in front of her.

Clouds scudded across a sweep of blue sky. October winds soughed in off the sea. Bracken and ivy climbed the stones and the neatly tended grass was an otherworldly green in the soft light of dawn.

Memories poured through her as she listened to echoes of the past ring in her mind. Laughter. The clash of swords. Babies crying. And the chanting of her sisters. It was all there. Like a song fondly remembered.

"Are you all right?" Rune whispered, dipping his head to hers.

"I am," she said, still cradling the moon-wrought sphere of power that encapsulated the black silver. "It's just . . . weird. Feeling so at home in a place I've never been before."

"Your soul recognizes this place, Teresa," he told her in the quiet. "It is where you belong. Where we both belong."

She looked up at him, into those gray eyes that softened with love and understanding, and she knew that no matter what Rune said, *he* was where she belonged. Wherever he was, that was her home.

Glancing toward the cloud-filled, lightening sky, with the sweep of coral and crimson staining the horizon, Teresa took a breath and said only, "Haven's waiting for us."

He draped one arm across her shoulders and walked beside her as she headed for the stone steps leading up to the castle proper.

She led them unerringly. Her mind and heart and soul remembered the way as they crossed what had once been the great hall and walked through into the chapel.

"The coven made its home in the chapel?" Rune asked, clearly surprised.

She looked up at him, confused. "You didn't know?"

"No. You and your sisters guarded Haven even from the Eternals."

Teresa stopped, looked around her at the stone walls sweeping up to highly arched ceilings. The stones themselves seemed to pulse with power, with magic, and she felt the rise of it inside her. As she turned to smile up at her mate, she could only say, "I'm sorry. For who I was then. For what I cheated us out of."

"No," Rune told her, cupping her face in his palms. "There is no need for apologies, Teresa. The past is dust. And the future is ours. At last."

She smiled as a wash of love, deep and rich and pure,

rose up inside her. How had she lived her life without him? How had she ever given him up so long ago? That was a mystery she might never resolve, Teresa thought. But he was right. The past was gone, dust in the pages of history. What mattered was *now*. Who they were, what they did.

Shifting the moonsphere into the palm of one hand, she linked her free hand with his and threaded their fingers together in a sign of solidarity. Then she continued to the far end of the chapel where a solid stone wall stood. She didn't glance at the faded glories of the paintings still hanging in place. Instead, she released his hand, laid her palm flat on the cold gray stones and whispered, *"Haven."*

An opening appeared in the wall and Teresa smiled, took Rune's hand again and together, they stepped into the dimly lit darkness. Instantly, the wall behind them sealed and they were left standing in a cavernous room.

Flaming torches set into silver brackets mounted on the surrounding walls threw dancing shadows and light across the interior. The walls themselves shone and glittered as the firelight touched the veins of silver embedded in the stone.

Teresa sighed and felt the soft push of power slide into her system. Silver enhanced an earth witch's power and these veins that sparkled and shone were incredibly rich. Her gaze tracked over the symbols carved into the stone and outlined in silver. She knew them all. Her memory was clear at last and the sight of this chamber filled her with a sense of peace she had never known. All around her were carved symbols of power, of magic, of the coven that had once called this Haven home.

There were pentagrams and the sacred circle that signified unity and female power. The Bindu, circles with a single dot in the center—the circle as woman, the dot as man, joined as they were meant to be joined. She also spotted an ancient Medicine Wheel and the carving of a snake devouring its own tail—the symbol of life, death and rebirth. And there was the spiral.

Teresa let go of Rune's hand and drew her fingers over the coiled symbol that represented the female and the birth, growth, death and rebirth of the soul. Power shimmered inside her at the contact and she smiled, letting this place and all that it had once meant to her welcome her home.

"Welcome."

Teresa and Rune spun around to face the woman who had spoken. But there were two women standing there. Two witches, flanked by their Eternals. The women were tall, each of them had waist-length red hair and each of them was dressed in a white togalike garment that was cinched at the waist and fell in a column to their bare feet.

The togas they wore were one-shouldered, baring their left breasts to the room, displaying their mating brands proudly. One woman boasted a circlet of red roses, while the other's skin was marked with dark red flames. Their mates stood behind them, matching tattoos on their bare chests.

Teresa blew out a breath, stunned, a little shocked and yet proud that she belonged with these women. She, too, wanted to show the world that she and Rune were matched. That they were a single unit, bonded by love and trust and magic.

The women came closer.

"Teresa," the older one said with a smile, "we've been waiting for you. I'm Mairi and this is my niece, Shea. Welcome to Haven. Welcome home."

"Thank you," she said as Rune stepped past her to greet the other Eternals. "It's good to be here. At last."

"You've brought your shard of the Artifact," Mairi said, with a glance at the moonsphere, still glittering with power and caged lightning.

"We have," Rune said, returning to Teresa's side to drape one arm around her shoulders.

"Then the ceremony will begin as soon as you're ready," Mairi told them. "Shea and Torin will show you to your quarters."

Chapter 63

An hour later, Teresa and Rune reentered the main chamber. Teresa wore the traditional toga, baring her tattooed breast in a show of respect and pride. The light of purest magic filled her, making her dark hair shine white and her eyes glow.

Rune watched her near-regal procession across the firelit main chamber. Shadows swam and the light danced across the silver-studded walls as Teresa, holding the black silver in her cupped palms, approached the far wall. There, three cages made of living flame snapped and hissed in the silence. The first cage held the Artifact returned to Haven by Shea and Torin.

Teresa walked to the center cage, deposited the black silver inside and then watched as the flames surrounded it. The living flame would hold it safely until the other pieces could be brought back and the Artifact reassembled. Then the coven would ritually destroy it for all time. Only then would the world be safe.

Teresa took a step back, bowed her head and crossed her arms over her chest. She chanted softly, as if the words were drawn from a memory as ancient as the room in which she stood.

The past is gone
Yet still lives
My test is won
This Artifact I give
I am home where I was meant to be
My debt is paid through eternity.

The light left her, returning her hair and eyes to the rich chocolate color that Rune knew and loved. Teresa turned to bow her head toward Mairi, the once and future high priestess of her coven. She exchanged a smile with Shea, then looked deliberately and solely at Rune.

Mairi, Shea and their Eternals slipped out of the chamber, leaving them alone for a moment, to celebrate their accomplishment. To share only with each other the moment when their world had, at last, righted itself.

He held her and felt the heat of her bare breast against his chest as the greatest gift he had ever known. They were one, as they had always been meant to be. "You were magnificent."

"*We* were great," she whispered, linking her arms around his waist.

As he held her, the mating brand burned brightly through each of them in one last fiery jolt of heat, completing the tattoo on their bodies that would join them for eternity.

Teresa sighed at the magic of the moment, then laid her head on his chest and smiled. "Your heart is beating."

Rune laughed shortly. "It feels . . . strange."

She reached up for a kiss. "You'll get used to it."

"As you will to being an immortal."

Teresa kissed him again then, as her love for him erupted. Her life had become rich. Full. She had lost a lot, but in finding who she was meant to be she had gained everything.

"An eternity in your arms? Sounds just about right."

As he kissed her, Teresa gave herself up to the *real* magic. The wonder and splendor of a love finally found and cherished as it should be.

ABOUT THE AUTHOR

Regan Hastings is the pseudonym of a *USA Today* best-selling author of more than a hundred romance novels. She lives with her family in California and is already hard at work on the next installment of the Awakening series.

Read on for a sneak peek at the next book in
Regan Hastings's Awakening series,

VISIONS OF CHAINS

Coming from Signet Eclipse in June 2012.

Deidre Sterling was used to being followed. Secret Service. Reporters. Paparazzi. But giant black dogs? That was new.

She peeled back the edge of the drapes and looked out the window of her friend's apartment. Her heart was hammering in her chest and her stomach was tumbling like an Olympic gymnast. If she had any sense, she'd leave before things got worse. But then, if she had any sense, she wouldn't have been there in the first place.

Three floors below, the street lay in complete darkness but for the puddles of light from the streetlamps gleaming on wet asphalt. Cars were parked along the curb. A newspaper hurtled down the street, tossed by the wind. Lamplight shone from a few other apartments facing her, and directly below her stood two men in black overcoats. Her Secret Service protection.

Hell of a thing to be a grown woman and not be able to take a walk without at least two armed guys following. But since her mother was the President of the United States, Deidre didn't really get to make that call.

Still, here she was, planning to ditch her guards, just to do what she had to do. Her gaze moved on, checking

every shadow, every slice of darkness that could hold—
there. The dog. It moved with a stealthy sort of grace that
gave Deidre cold chills. Its head was huge and its paws
were like saucers. What the hell was it? Great Dane?
Pony?

"What are you looking at?" Shauna Jackson walked
into the room and went to stand beside Deidre.

"A dog," she answered, feeling stupid. But she could
have sworn over the last few days that the damn thing
had been following her. Everywhere she went, she felt
its presence, even though she'd only caught a glimpse of
it once or twice.

Shauna took a quick look and shrugged. "Don't see
anything except your two human guard dogs in overcoats."

"It's there. At the mouth of the alley across the street."

Shauna looked again. "Nope."

Okay, why couldn't her friend see the dog? Deidre
wondered if maybe PTSD was becoming an issue for
her. Was she seeing things? And if she was, why wasn't
she imagining fluffy kittens? Why a dog that looked as
though it could—and wanted to—swallow her whole?

Deidre shivered as the huge animal tipped its wide
head up and fixed its dark eyes on her. Okay, she was
really freaking over this. The dog that couldn't be there
wasn't looking at her. How would it know what apartment she was in? At that thought, she almost laughed.
Crazy much? She let the drapes fall and told herself she
was getting way too paranoid.

"You're not trying to back out, are you?"

Deidre turned to face her friend. Shauna's hair was
clipped short, the tight, black curls trimmed close to her
head. Her chocolate brown eyes were narrowed. "Dee,
the execution is in the morning. You can't really walk

away, can you? You agreed that rescuing the witches was the right thing to do."

"I know." Five women were scheduled for the fires first thing in the morning. She didn't know if they were witches or not. And she didn't care. State-approved executions of witches and suspected witches were happening more and more frequently, despite her mother's attempts to rein them in. The general public was scared. And when scared people came together they usually became bloodthirsty.

Deidre ran her hands up and down her arms, trying to dispel the cold that had been with her since the night of the last raid she had gone on, two weeks before.

But the cold wouldn't lift any more than the memories would dissipate. She remembered everything. She saw it all over and over again whenever she closed her eyes. Her group, the RFW, or Rights for Witches, had infiltrated an internment camp to free the captive women inside. But something had gone wrong. Somehow the alarms had been sounded and guards had fired on them and men had been killed.

She hadn't pulled the trigger herself, but she might as well have. And that night, she had made the decision to step away from the RFW. Yet here she was, drawn back in. But how could she sit back and do nothing when the Bill of Rights was being crushed under the heel of angry mobs? How could she let innocent women be imprisoned or executed without trials?

"You're thinking again. You in? Or out?" The expression on Shauna's face was impatient and her eyes glinted with determination.

Deidre took a breath, then reached down for the black jacket on the couch beside her. "I'm in. I shouldn't be, but I'm in."

"Of course you should," Shauna told her, slipping into her own black jacket. She picked up a revolver, checked to make sure it was loaded, then tucked it into the waistband of her black jeans.

Deidre frowned, unable to stop thinking about the last rescue gone bad. "I thought we agreed no guns."

"We agreed *you* weren't going to carry one. But honey, if somebody shoots at me, I'm going to shoot back."

"This is nuts. The whole world is nuts," Deidre muttered.

"It's always been crazy," Shauna said quietly. "It's just now, the whole crazy ass world is on a mission."

A mission to kill witches and rid the world of magic. Which was why Deidre was here, ready to go on another raid. "There has to be a better way to end this."

"Well, if there is, we haven't found it," Shauna said flatly. "Besides, if anyone could do something about this, it's *you*."

Deidre laughed shortly, gathered up her blond hair and quickly braided the mass to keep it out of her way. "Right."

"Your *mother* is the President of the United States."

"Yeah and she won't be pleased to know I'm back in the RFW." Deidre didn't even want to think about her mother's reaction. She had been delighted to hear that Deidre was stepping back from the RFW. As president, Cora Sterling walked a fine line between the citizens who wanted magic stamped out—along with the witches who wielded the power—and protecting the witches, who—hello?—were also citizens and had rights.

But then, every major leader in the world was on that tightrope. Magic was out in the open now and those with power were being hunted down like rats by the very governments that should have been protecting them. At least her mom had shown some sympathy for the women being swept up and jailed. Or so Deidre had thought until she discovered that this execution was going ahead as planned *without* the intervention of the president.

Which was why, when Shauna called asking her to help, Deidre had immediately agreed. How could she not? She had seen firsthand the women who were tortured in prison. The women who were so broken by the time they were rescued that they would never recover. And that didn't even take into account the women who had *died*. No, as much as Deidre wanted to be able to turn her back, she couldn't.

"Anyway," she said, jerking her head toward the window and the two men standing in the street, "I still don't see how we're supposed to get past the Secret Service guys."

Shauna grinned. "They'll never know we're gone."

Twelve hours until the execution.

Finn leaned one shoulder against the doorjamb and watched his lieutenants prepare for battle. There was no conversation, only the occasional whispered comment. This group had been together only a couple of months and trust was still building. They worked on a first-name-only basis—that way if one of them were captured they wouldn't be able to give anyone else up. Danger was a constant companion, with death hovering around every corner, and still they came to fight.

He wondered if it was for love of freedom as they claimed—or if it was just that some people always needed something to rage against.

The lights were dim and seemed to soak into the dank rock walls rather than reflect off them. It smelled like old liquor and cats down here in the chamber below the apartment building's basement. High above ground, buildings sent spires skyward; down here, there was a labyrinth of tunnels and rooms long forgotten by those who lived on the surface.

Scowling, Finn looked at the people busily strapping weapons to their bodies, getting ready for the raid. Humans. Mortals. Willing to risk their already too-short lives in the hopes of saving innocents.

He had spent centuries avoiding contact with humans. He hated cities. The noise. The crush of humanity. The relentless reminders of just how alone he really was. Yet here he stood. In the heart of a city, surrounded by humans.

War made for strange alliances.

And they were definitely at war.

Finn pushed away from the wall and lifted one hand to his second in command, Joe. A former Navy SEAL, Joe was, like Finn, a born warrior.

"Everyone ready?"

Joe glanced at the others as they checked pistols, stuffed knives into scabbards. "As ready as they can be."

Finn nodded and reached for the curved bladed sword he had carried for eons. He slid it into the sheath that ran along his spine. "We'll leave as soon as she gets here."

"Whatever you say, boss."

Boss. How the hell had his existence come to this, with humans looking to him to lead them? Joe took orders from Finn because he agreed with the missions. He wouldn't blindly follow anyone for long, and Finn respected him for that. Trusted him. He didn't trust many, either. His brothers, of course, but humans? They were too fragile. Too easily broken or swayed by whatever opinion was in fashion. They lived foolishly and died too soon. What was the point of knowing them? To an immortal like Finn, a human's existence was equivalent to a fruit fly's.

He checked his knives, then tucked a few extra throwing stars into the pockets of his black leather jacket.

But one human was different.

At least, he hoped to hell she was different.

ALSO AVAILABLE

from

Regan Hastings

Visions of Magic
An Awakening Novel

In the ten years since magic has reemerged in the world,
witches have become feared and hunted. For weeks Shea
Jameson has been haunted by visions of fire. When she
unintentionally performs a spell in public, she becomes
one of the hunted. Her only hope is Torin, a dangerously
sensual man who claims to be her eternal mate.

**"Magic, passion, and immortal warriors—
this fabulous new series has it all."**
—*New York Times* bestselling author Christina Dodd

Available wherever books are sold or at
penguin.com

ALSO AVAILABLE

Lee Roland

Viper Moon
An Earth Witches Novel

Cassandra Archer is the Huntress. She has faithfully served the Earth Mother for years, rescuing kidnapped children from monsters—both human and supernatural—dwelling in the ruins of the Barrows District. But when two children are kidnapped under similar circumstances, all clues point to a cataclysmic event on the next dark moon. Now Cass must race against the clock and prevent a sacrifice that could destroy the entire town...

**Available wherever books are sold or at
penguin.com**